Acclaim fo...
The Eagle Elite...

Elite

"This is by far the best book I have read from this talented author."

—Book-Whisperer.blogspot.com

"4 enthusiastic stars! This is just so fresh and different and crazy and fun...I can't wait for the next book, *Elect*...Judging by [ELITE], this entire series is going to be fantastic."　　　—NewAdultAddiction.com

Elect

"Secrets, sacrifices, blood, angst, loyalties...This book has everything I love!...Rachel Van Dyken is a fabulous author!"　—GirlBookLove.com

"Takes you on a roller coaster of emotion...centers around the most amazing of love stories...Nixon has definitely made it to my best-book-boyfriend list."　　　　　　　　—SoManyReads.com

Praise for
The Bet Series

The Bet

"I haven't laughed this hard while reading a book in a while. *The Bet* [is] an experience—a heartwarming, sometimes hilarious, experience...I've actually read this book twice."　　　—RecommendedRomance.com

The Wager

"Rachel Van Dyken is quickly becoming one of my favorite authors and I cannot wait to see what she has in store for us in the future. *The Wager* is a must-read for those who love romance and humor. It will leave a lasting impression and a huge smile on your face." —LiteratiBookReviews.com

Other Forever titles by Rachel Van Dyken

Elect

The Bet Series

The Bet

The Wager

ELITE

RACHEL VAN DYKEN

FOREVER

NEW YORK   BOSTON

Forever
Hachette Book Group
1290 Avenue of the Americas
New York, NY 10104

www.HachetteBookGroup.com

Printed in the United States of America

RRD-C

Originally published as an ebook

First trade paperback edition: October 2014
10 9 8 7 6 5 4 3 2 1

Forever is an imprint of Grand Central Publishing.
The Forever name and logo are trademarks of Hachette Book Group, Inc.

The Hachette Speakers Bureau provides a wide range of authors for speaking events. To find out more, go to www.hachettespeakersbureau.com or call (866) 376-6591.

The publisher is not responsible for websites (or their content) that are not owned by the publisher.

Library of Congress Cataloging-in-Publication Data
Van Dyken, Rachel.
  Elite / Rachel Van Dyken.—First trade paperback edition.
    pages cm
  "Originally published as an ebook."
  ISBN 978-1-4555-5417-1 (trade pbk.)— ISBN 978-1-4789-5543-6 (audio download)   I. Title.
  PS3622.A5854845E66 2014
  813'.6—dc23
                                                                    2014002820

Acknowledgments

First I just have to thank God. Truly, he is the reason I am able to do what I love every single day!

Readers, I've said it once, I'll say it again. You guys rock my world! I feel like we're family. I can't even tell you all how much I appreciate your love and support. I'll keep writing as long as you keep reading.

I really wanted to write a book that was different. I'd been seeing a lot of New Adult novels coming out that dealt with people who had a lot of emotional baggage. Heck, I'd written a few of my own (Seaside Novels, anyone?), but I thought it was time to do something different.

Enter in...the mafia.

I mean, how cool would it be to be a part of a secret society? To grow up your whole life thinking one thing, only to find out you've been wrong the entire time? I am planning on doing seven books in this series. *Elect*, *Entice*, and *Elicit* are available now, and *Enforce* will be out December 2014.

As always, please feel free to leave reviews, good or bad, on Amazon / Barnes & Noble / Goodreads and anywhere else you can think of. If you want to connect with me to see what I'm working on, check out my website, www.rachelvandyken.com; Twitter, @RachVD; or Facebook.com/RachelVanDyken.

Media / review requests / blog requests can be directed to Angie: WhisperinAngel@gmail.com.

To contact me personally you can reach me at: rachelvandyken author@gmail.com.

Thanks again! Happy reading!

ELITE

Prologue

Whoever told me life was easy—lied. It's hard. It sucks. The crazy thing is—nobody has the guts to admit the truth. Everyone, and I mean *everyone*, has a secret. Everyone has a story that needs to be told. Hurt is everywhere; as humans we practically drown in its essence, yet we all pretend like it doesn't exist. We make believe that everything is fine, when really, everything within us screams in outrage. Our soul pleads for us to be honest at least once in our lives. It begs of us to tell one person. It forces us to become vulnerable to that one person, and the very second that we do, everything seems better.

For a moment, life isn't as hard as it seems. Effortless. It's effortless, and then the gauntlet falls.

When I met Nixon I had no idea what life had in store for me. In my wildest dreams, I could have never imagined this.

"Everything..." He swallowed and looked away for a brief second before grabbing my hand and kissing it. "Everything is about to change."

Chapter One

I can feel you breathing down my neck, Trace." Grandpa gripped the steering wheel and gave me a weak smile before he reached back and patted my hand.

Yup, patted my hand.

As if *that's* going to make me feel any less nervous.

I closed my eyes and took a few deep breaths, trying to concentrate on the excitement of my situation, not the fear. I refused to be scared just because it was new.

I mean, sure, I'd never ridden in an airplane before last night, but it wasn't as if I was freaking out... yet.

I missed my dogs and everything about our ranch in Wyoming. When my ailing grandma suggested I enter the contest, I obeyed to make her happy—anything to distract me from her illness. Besides, it's everyone's dream to go to Eagle Elite, but your chances of getting in are slim to none. One company did a study and said your chances were only slightly higher than that of your body morphing into the body of a whale.

Guess that made me a big, giant, fat whale, because I got in. I'm pretty sure the company did it as a joke, but still.

Out of millions of applicants, they drew my number, my name. So fear...it really wasn't an option at this point. Going to Eagle for my freshman year of college meant that I was basically set for life. I would be placed in a career, provided for in every way possible. Given opportunities people dreamt of.

Sadly, in this world, it's all about who you know, and my grandpa, bless his heart—all he knows is the ranch and being a good grandpa. So I'm doing this. I'm doing it for me and I'm doing it for him.

"Is that it?" Grandpa pointed, snapping me out of my internal pep talk. I rolled down my window and peered out.

"It...uh, it says E.E. on the gate," I mumbled, knowing full well that I was staring at a steel gate that would have made any prison proud. A man stepped out of the small booth near the entrance and waved us down. As he leaned over the car I noticed a gun hidden under his jacket. Why did they need guns?

"Name," he demanded.

Grandpa smiled. He *would* smile. I shook my head as he proceeded to give the guard the speech, the same one he'd been giving all our neighbors for the past few months. "You see my granddaughter, Trace." He pointed at me. I bit my lip to keep myself from smiling. "She got into this fancy school, won the annual Elite lottery! Can you believe it? So I'm here to drop her off." How did Grandpa always stay so completely at ease all the time? Maybe it was because he was always packing a gun, too, but still. He and Grandma were the coolest grandparents a girl could ask for.

I swallowed the tears burning at the back of my throat. It should have been him and Grandma here with me, but she died of cancer about six months ago, a week after I found out about the school.

They were my world, Grandpa and Grandma. Being raised by your grandparents isn't all that bad, not when you have or had grandparents like mine. Grandpa taught me how to ride horses and milk cows, and Grandma could bake the best apple pie in the state. She won at every state fair using the exact same recipe.

My parents died in a car crash when I was really young. I don't remember much except that the night they died was also the night I met my grandparents for the first time. I was six. Grandpa was dressed in a suit. He knelt down and said something in Italian, and he and Grandma took me away in their black Mercedes. They moved their whole lives for me, saying it wasn't good for a little girl to live in the city. Chicago hadn't seemed that bad to me, at least from what I remember. Which wasn't much.

I gave Grandpa a watery smile as he reached across the console and grasped my hand within his large worn one. He'd sacrificed everything for me, so I was going to do this for him, for Grandma. It may sound silly, but as an only child I felt this immense need to take care of him now that Grandma was gone, and the only way I could see myself doing that was getting a good job and making him proud. I wasn't sure about his retirement, or about anything, and I wanted to be. I wanted to take care of him, like he took care of me. He was my rock, and now it was my turn to be his.

Grandpa winked and squeezed my hand again. He was always so perceptive. I could tell he knew I was thinking about Grandma because he nodded his head and pointed at his own heart, and then pointed at mine as if to say, *She's in your heart. She's in mine. We'll be okay.*

"You aren't from around here, are you?" The man interrupted our exchange and directed the question at me.

"No, sir."

He laughed. " 'Sir'? Hmm...I have to say I like the sound of that. All right, you check out. Drive straight down the road for one-point-five miles. Parking is on the right and the dorms will be directly in front of the parking lot. You can drop her off there."

He slapped the top of the car and the gate suddenly opened in front of us.

My heart was in my throat. Large trees lined the driveway as Grandpa drove the rental toward the dorms.

Nothing in my life had prepared me for what I was seeing. The buildings were huge. Everything was built in old stone and brick. I mean, I'd seen pictures, but they did not even come close to reality. The dorms looked like ritzy hotels.

Another security guard approached the car and motioned for Grandpa to turn it off. My mouth gaped open as I stepped out of the car and leaned my head way back so I could look up at the twelve-story building.

"New girl's here," came a voice from behind me. I flipped around and my mouth dropped open again.

"So squeaky clean and innocent. Like a little lamb. Right, Chase?" The guy tilted his head. Dark wavy hair fell across his forehead; he had a lip piercing and he was dressed in ripped jeans and a tight t-shirt.

I backed away, like the little lamb/whale that I was.

My grandpa stepped forward protectively, reaching inside his jacket, probably for the gun that was usually present. I'm sure he was just trying to freak the guys out. "A welcoming committee? This place sure is nice." Anyone could see the guys standing in front of us were not here to welcome us and certainly weren't part of any committee, but Grandpa was making a point, marking me as his to protect. I stepped behind him and swallowed at the dryness in my throat.

"Is there a problem?" Grandpa asked, rolling back his sleeves. Whoa. Was my seventy-two-year-old grandpa going to get in a rumble or something?

The guy with the lip ring stepped forward and then squinted his eyes in Grandpa's direction. "Do I know you?"

Grandpa laughed. "Know many farmers out in Wyoming?"

The guy scratched his head, causing his shirt to rise just above his hips, revealing a lovely view of his golden tanned abs. I swallowed and grabbed my grandpa's arm.

The guy named Chase smirked and hit the other guy on the back. He glared in my direction and then stepped right up to me, reaching out to lift my chin, closing my gaping mouth.

"Much better," he whispered. "We'd hate for our charity case to choke on an insect on her first day." His eyes flicked to Grandpa's and then back to mine before he walked away.

His friend joined him and they disappeared behind the dorm. I could feel my face was heated with embarrassment. I didn't have much experience with guys. Okay, it was safe to say my first and only kiss had been with Chad Thomson and it had been awful. But still: Something about those guys warned me they weren't good news.

"I don't like those boys. They remind me of . . . Well, that doesn't matter." Grandpa scratched his head then went to the trunk of the car to pull out my few things. I was still trying to get over the fact that I had embarrassed myself when someone walked up to us with a clipboard.

"No parents allowed in the dorms. Sorry. Rules." She popped her gum and winked at my grandpa. Was she flirting with him? What the hell kind of school was this? The guys had piercings and treated people like dirt, and the girls flirted with old men?

My grandpa shot me a concerned look and sighed, placing his hands against the rental car as if trying to brace himself for the emotional turmoil of the day. "You sure you'll be okay here?"

I sighed heavily and looked up at the intimidating building. I needed to do this for him, for us. It was why I had applied.

Taking a deep breath, I stepped away from him and gave them both my most confident smile. "I'll be fine, Grandpa, but I'll miss you so much." Warm tears streamed rapidly down my face as I stepped into his embrace.

"I have some things for you. I know..." Grandpa coughed and wiped at a few of his own stray tears. "I know she would have liked you to have them, Trace."

Wordlessly, he walked away from me and pulled a small box from the back of the car, then returned and handed it to me. "Don't open it until you're in your dorm. Oh, sweetheart, I'm going to miss you so much."

I hugged him again and closed my eyes, memorizing the way his spicy scent filled my nostrils with all the comforts of home. "I'll miss you more."

"Not possible," he said with a hoarse voice. "Not possible, sweetheart."

He released me and folded some cash into my hand. I looked down into my clenched fist, where several hundred dollar bills were rolled with a rubber band. "I can't take this." I tried to give it back, but he put his hands up and chuckled.

"Nope, your grandma would roll over in her grave if she knew I was dropping you off at some fancy school without an emergency fund. You keep it. You hide it in your pillow or something, okay?"

"Grandpa, we don't live in the Depression anymore. I don't need to go hiding money under my mattress or in my pillowcase."

He narrowed his eyes and laughed. "Just keep it safe."

I hugged Grandpa one last time. He sighed heavily into my shoulder. "Be safe, Grandpa. Don't let the cows out and keep milking the goats. I really will miss you."

"And I you...Just, do me a favor." He pulled away and looked into my eyes as I nodded. "Be careful. There are people out there who..." He cursed. Grandpa rarely cursed.

"What is it?" Okay, he was starting to scare me.

He looked behind me and pressed his lips together in frustration. "Nothing. Never mind. Just be careful, okay, sweetheart?"

"Okay." I kissed his cheek.

Grandpa grinned and got into the car. I waved as he drove off, then turned back toward the girl with the clipboard.

"Okay." I took a soothing breath and faced my future. "So where to?"

"Name?" she asked, sounding bored.

"Trace Rooks."

The girl smirked and shook her head as if my name was the most amusing thing she'd heard all day. Was everyone rude here?

"It's your lucky day," she announced, motioning toward the building. "You are in the United States."

I looked around just to make sure I wasn't getting punked. "Um, yeah, I know. I'm American."

"Gee." She put the pen in her mouth and sighed heavily. "I didn't know that. You seemed foreign to me. Where did you say you were from? Wyoming? Do they even have electricity there?"

I opened my mouth to defend myself, but she interrupted me... again.

"I know where we are, New Girl. Rooms are themed based on countries. Don't ask me why; it's just how it's done. Your room is the United States Room. Go make yourself at home. Oh, and welcome to Elite." She eyed me from head to toe twice before finally spinning around and returning to the building.

How was I supposed to get all my stuff in the building? Wasn't there some sort of welcome packet or directions or something?

I vaguely remembered some information that had come in the mail the week before. It had my student ID card, amongst other things. I rummaged through my purse and found the packet and quickly began scanning it for the schedule.

"Are you lost?" a deep voice asked from behind me. I turned around and quickly came face to face with the same guy I'd seen before. Only this time he had three friends with him, not one. Lucky me.

"Nope. Apparently I live in the United States." I gave him my best smile and tried to lift my heavy suitcase with my free hand. It didn't budge and I almost fell over. Awesome.

"I'm Nixon." He moved to stand in front of me. His icy stare did weird things to my body. I'm pretty sure what I was experiencing was called a panic attack. Every part of my body felt hot and then cold, as if I was going to explode any minute.

"Tracey, but everyone calls me Trace." I held out my hand.

He stared at it like I was diseased.

I quickly pulled it back and wiped it on my jeans.

"Rules."

"What?" I took a step back.

The guy from before named Chase left the waiting group and approached us. "He's right. As cute as you are, Farm Girl, someone needs to tell you the rules."

"Can it be fast?" I asked with an overwhelming sense of irritation. I was tired, jet-lagged, and about five seconds away from crying again. I'd never done public school, let alone a private Elite school where the guys were tattooed, pierced, and better looking than Abercrombie models.

"You hear that, Chase?" Nixon laughed. "She likes it fast."

"Pity." Chase winked. "I'd love to give it to her slow."

I gulped. The two guys behind them laughed hysterically and high-fived each other.

"The rules." Chase began circling me slowly, making me feel like one of those carcasses vultures feed on. Fantastic.

"No speaking to the Elect, unless you've been asked to speak to them."

"Who are the—"

"Nope. You've already broken a rule. I'm speaking, New Girl." Chase smirked. "Geez, Nixon, this one's going to be hard to break in."

"They always are," Nixon replied, lifting my chin with his hand. "But I think I'll enjoy this one."

Okay. It was clear someone had just dropped me into a horror movie where I was going to be offed at any minute.

"If an Elect talks to you, never make eye contact. Because,

technically, you don't exist. You're just a pathetic excuse for a human being, and at this school, you're a real tragedy. You see, while one of the Elect is out running for president and basically ruling the free world, you'll be lucky to be working for one of our companies. You follow the rules, and maybe we'll throw you a bone."

Furious, I glared at him, ignoring their second rule. "Is that all?"

"No," Nixon answered for Chase. This time his touch was smooth as he caressed my arm. I tried to jerk away. His face lit up with a smile, and honestly, it was like staring at a fallen angel. Nixon was gorgeous. He was an ass, but he was a gorgeous ass. "You feel this?" His hand continued moving up my arm until he reached my shoulder, and then his hand moved to my neck and his thumb grazed my trembling lips. "Memorize it now, because as of this moment, you can't touch us. We are untouchable. If you as much as sneeze in our direction, if you as much as breathe the same air in my atmosphere, I will make your life hell. This touch, what you feel against your skin, will be the only time you feel another human being as powerful as me near you. So like I said, feel it, remember it, and maybe one day, your brain will do you the supreme favor of forgetting what it felt like to have someone like me touching you. Then, and only then, will you be able to be happy with some mediocre boyfriend and pathetic life."

A few tears slipped down my cheek before I could stop them. I knew I needed to appear strong in front of Nixon and Chase. I just... I didn't have it in me, not when he would say such cruel things. I choked back a sob and stared them down, willing the rest of the tears to stay in. I didn't care who these guys were. They had no right to treat me like this, though it still stung. I so desperately wanted to fit in.

He jerked his hand away from my face. "Pathetic. Are you going to cry? Really?" Nixon scowled and held out his hand to Chase. Chase handed him some Purell.

"Don't want to get farm on my hands, you understand." Nixon smiled such a mean smile that I literally had to clench my hands at my sides to keep from punching him in the face and getting expelled.

"Don't even think about it, New Girl. You touch me, I tell the dean, who just so happens to be Phoenix's dad. We control the teachers because, guess what? My dad pays for everything. Now, if you have any questions about what we talked about here, please direct them to Tex and Phoenix, 'kay?"

The two guys who had been standing back from us waved and then flipped me off.

"That's how they say hello," Nixon explained. "All right, Chase, it seems our job here is done. Oh, and Farm Girl, don't forget. Classes start tomorrow. Welcome to Hell."

Chapter Two

Four tears. I counted them. I only let four escape, which was pretty good considering the circumstances.

I left my suitcase outside and prayed it wouldn't get stolen or run over or anything, and took the box from my grandma into the building with me.

My purse kept banging against the box, making the contents shift inside. I tried to put everything in one hand in order to use my finger to follow the map of the place. The United States room was on the third floor in the right wing.

Great. Stairs.

I looked around for an elevator but didn't see a sign or even a place to put one. Blowing the hair out of my face, I jimmied the door to the stairs open and made my very slow ascent to the third floor.

By the time I reached the third floor door I knew three things. One, I was horribly out of shape. Two, I should have eaten something this morning, and three, apparently I was the only one checking in right now. I didn't see anyone else, which was weird. Maybe they were already in their rooms.

I jerked the door at the top of the stairs open, again balancing everything in one hand, and walked down the hall to the right wing.

The door to the stairs slammed behind me, and slowly people began trickling out of their rooms. Girls who looked more like my Barbie dolls than real people openly stared at me. Some cursed in my direction, and others just smirked, as if they knew a giant secret that I didn't.

I kept my eyes focused ahead of me even though I knew I looked a mess. I was sweating, my hair was falling all over my dripping face, and my hands kept slipping on the box.

Finally, I saw the end of the hall and a sign that said THE UNITED STATES.

"Thank God," I whispered under my breath.

I placed the box on the floor and dropped my purse next to it.

The girls had yet to say one word to me unless it was something derogatory, and now they were watching me as if something terrible was about to happen.

Dear God, please don't let there be some scary clown hiding in my closet. I'd probably jump out the window and kill myself in the process.

I reached for the door and turned the handle. Nothing happened.

I pushed against it.

Again, nothing happened.

Finally, I used all the strength I had left in me and slammed my body against the door. It flew open before my body made full contact, sending me sailing onto the floor.

My head landed smack onto a pair of shiny expensive boots. Boy boots, to be exact. I hated those boots instantly, because for some reason I knew that they had to belong to a boy. And if any boy was waiting in my room, I guessed it had to be one of the Elect, trying to make my life hell.

Speaking of, how in the heck did they make it up here so fast?

Girls giggled as I slowly pushed myself to my knees and looked up…into Nixon's perfect face.

Of course it was Nixon.

He offered his hand, but right before I took it he put on a glove.

"Germs, you understand." He winked.

Maybe it was because I was tired. Maybe it was because I was going insane with stress, but instead of taking his hand, I slapped it away and got to my feet on my own.

People gasped behind me.

Muscles twitched in Nixon's jaw. "Leave us," he barked.

The sound of doors slamming down the hall may as well have been nails in my social coffin. One, two, three, six…I closed my eyes and waited.

My door was the final one to close, but I hadn't done the deed. No, it was Nixon, and now he was behind me.

"You don't like rules, do you, New Girl?" he whispered in my ear. He wasn't touching me, but my body shivered involuntarily anyway. Treacherous hormones.

"There is one, final, rule." Nixon moved from behind me and was now standing a foot away from me.

"What?" My voice sounded braver than I was feeling.

He closed the distance between us. I backed up; he pursued.

The cool metal door met my back, making me shiver. My sweat had run cold and now I was completely terrified.

"You earn the right to use what we have. The elevators are locked. The Elect have copies of the key card. The pools, the weight rooms—everything you have access to, even your food—needs a key card."

He reached into his pocket, pulled out a blue key card, and dangled it in front of me. "Say thank you."

"For what?" I would not cry. I would not cry!

"Allowing you to eat, of course."

"What?"

"I'm not finished talking," he said smoothly. "This key card gains you access into the elevator only once a week. It also gains you access into the cafeteria, twice a day. Not three times. We don't want you gaining weight. Use it wisely and if you impress me with your ability to follow directions, I may just up your freedom. Until then…" He shrugged and cleared his throat. "Move aside."

I couldn't move. This felt like a nightmare. Who the hell was this guy, and seriously, who'd made him the president of the school? I was afraid to talk to anyone. Afraid to do anything except stand there and stare at the card in my hand. It said *E. E.*, but it may as well have said *Nixon's*.

"Move aside," Nixon repeated, and this time his teeth were clenched together. I jerked up my head and looked at him. I mean, really looked at him. His eyes were a crystal blue, like the fires of hell had frozen over and the ice staring back at me was the result of orange flames dying slowly. His entire face was symmetrically perfect. As if some famous supermodel and actor had decided they should create a love child and programmed perfection in a computer. His hair fell over his forehead haphazardly.

Nixon slammed his hand on the door above my head.

Okay, that was it.

I could take someone talking down to me. I could take someone making fun of me...I mean, hello? I knew I wasn't anyone important, but for someone to threaten me with violence? To my face? Especially some guy who was probably souped up on steroids? Hell. No.

Something snapped. I pushed against his chest. He stumbled backward, and the look on his face changed from complete anger to disbelief.

"Did you just touch me?"

"You threatened me."

"I threaten everyone."

"Then you're a bully."

He opened his mouth and then snapped it shut again. A wicked smile played across his lips. "So you wanted to touch me?"

"No, I want you to leave me the hell alone."

"Say please."

"Please?" I begged, looking directly into the depths of his soulless eyes.

"Hell. No," he whispered and then moved past me and jerked open the door. A girl was waiting outside. He backed into my room and slammed the door again.

"I thought you were leaving."

"Change of plans," he muttered and then went over to the window and flung it open.

"What, you're going to shimmy down the drain pipe?" I joked nervously. If this guy stayed any longer in here I was going to kill him myself.

"Nixon, open the damn door!" The girl screamed from the other side.

He laughed and stepped out of the window onto the ledge.

"Are you insane?" I yelled at him and grabbed his shirt. I would not be witness to his death, even as deserving of it as he might be.

"Hands off," he barked, and then he was flying through the air. *Holy hell, I've made him commit suicide.*

"Nixon!" I yelled and looked over the ledge. On the grass was a giant blown-up tarp. Nixon landed on his back and then jumped off of it. He blew me a kiss and jogged off. For the first time, I noticed several tents and tarps were set up outside the dorm. It almost looked like a carnival.

The girl was still banging on my door. I rushed over to open it. She breezed past me. "That son of a bitch!" she yelled out the window. "Nixon, I swear I'm going to kill you when I see you!"

"I like you," I said out loud.

"Did he hurt you?" The girl swallowed nervously and examined me from head to toe, looking at my neck and my arms.

"Um, no?"

"He's Satan," she grumbled.

"And you are?"

She grinned and held out her hand. "Monroe. I'm Satan's sister."

Chapter Three

Monroe could be a supermodel. No, I take that back. She should be the girl who tells supermodels how to be supermodels. She was ridiculously beautiful, making my mind immediately transport to every single book I'd read in the past year that warned me against girls who looked like her.

This girl was like a walking advertisement to horny guys. For one thing, the dress she was wearing was so short I found myself gaping and then blushing when she leaned over to pick up a box to take to my room. Wasn't there a dress code at this school?

"So, that's all you have?"

She flipped her jet black hair back and pulled some lip gloss out of her bra. Her black dress inched higher again. Oh gosh, I was so completely out of my element.

"I...have a suitcase downstairs, but Nixon said—"

"Screw Nixon. Last time I checked, he wasn't God, nor would he be wanted by Him. Now, let's go grab your suitcase and I'll show you where the elevator is."

She linked her arm with mine and skipped down the hall. I had trouble keeping up with her even though she was the one in six-inch heels. We walked into the main corridor and then through a door facing a brick wall. As soon as we went through the door, I saw a row of elevators.

"Any reason they keep these hidden?" I asked.

Monroe nodded and then pointed up toward the ceiling, where several security screens showed the interior of each elevator. "Added security, since last year someone tried to bomb the school. Thus all the access cards and secrecy about the elevator. Last year someone was able to make it to the top floor before security caught wind of it."

"So it really is like prison?" I gulped.

Monroe laughed. "No, it's not that bad. But I mean, when you have the type of students that Elite has, you can't be too cautious."

I didn't ask what she meant, because everyone knew what type of people went here. Children of diplomats, of celebrities—even some of the presidents' kids had attended.

Once we reached the bottom floor, the elevator door dinged open and she walked me outside.

"Uh, is that yours?" She pointed to my suitcase. Correction: She pointed to my open suitcase. Clothes were strewn everywhere on the pavement.

I screamed and ran toward my clothes before they blew away. All of my possessions were in the process of making a sweep of the campus.

Monroe, to her credit, ran after and helped me gather up as much as possible.

Pretty sure I lost some of my underwear.

"He's a jerk." Monroe helped me off my knees once I'd zipped up the suitcase. "Look." She glanced behind her and hurried me inside.

"He's the favorite because he's a suckass and my dad believes women are beneath him."

That apple sure didn't make it far from the tree.

"Anyway, if I throw a fit, my dad will probably just turn the other way and say his hands are tied. I can help you with the other kids, but with Nixon, you're kind of on your own. Did he give you a key card?"

"Yup." I pulled it out of my pocket and flashed it to her. "Two meals a day and one elevator ride a week. I'm truly living the high life."

Monroe threw her head back and laughed. "Stick with me, and you very well may be right. Come on. There's a kickoff party tonight, and we have work to do."

"Wait…" I dug in my heels. "Why are you being so nice to me?" I hated being suspicious, but then again I'd never met people like those who went to school here.

"Oh, I'm sorry. I thought I told you. I'm your roommate."

That made sense. We walked in silence to the elevator. "Are you this nice to all your roommates?"

"No. I killed two of them, but my dad covered it up…"

Speechless, my mouth dropped open.

"Wow, I'm totally kidding. I've never had a roommate before this year. My dad thought he was punishing me by cramping my space. Instead, I'm relieved. I can't stand those bitches on the third floor."

"So, does that make you and Nixon a year apart?"

"No." Monroe flashed me a smile. "That makes us twins."

"I'm sorry."

"Oh, me too." We had reached the top floor again. Monroe took my bag. "Let's go, New Girl. People to see and boys to flirt with."

* * *

She wasn't kidding about not having much time. Three hours later I was a new woman. She'd used this weird rod thingy to curl my long brown hair into beach waves and then proceeded to pluck my eyebrows into oblivion. I'd always liked my eyebrows. Sure they were thick, but they framed my face quite nicely. I hoped by the time she was done I would still have some hair.

I wasn't allowed to look at myself until she was done with my makeup.

"Okay, almost done. Now, what did you bring to wear?"

I jumped from the chair and reached into my suitcase, pulling out the tea length dress I'd worn to Grandma's funeral. It was the nicest thing I owned and I'd even ordered it online from Forever 21. So it had to be trendy.

"That's cute." Monroe wrinkled her nose. "But it's kinda young for you."

"Young?" I repeated, looking at the yellow-and-white striped spaghetti strap dress.

"Yeah. I mean, it's cute and it would probably be killer for a picnic or something fun. But this is the first party where everyone's going to meet you. You need to look serious, you need to look hot, and you need to look untouchable."

"Okay." I chewed my lip.

"Don't worry. I think I've got the perfect outfit."

My stomach launched into nervous somersaults. If it was anything like the dress she was wearing now, then I was going to be put in prison for prostituting myself out.

"Here." She threw me a short black leather skirt, an oversized sweater with holes, and some tights that were completely black until they reached mid-thigh and then went sheer.

I quickly threw everything on. She kept handing me things and I kept dressing. Two bracelets and one freakishly long necklace later she declared me ready.

I was finally allowed to look in the mirror.

I smiled at my reflection. I looked perfect. Not like her and not like a supermodel, but like me. The makeup made my brown eyes pop, and my outfit looked classy but still fun.

"Shoes!" Monroe yelled. "Crap, what shoe size do you wear?"

"Eight?"

"Crap." She began to pace. "I wear a ten."

Of course.

"Um, I may have something." I tore open my suitcase and pulled out Grandma's old vintage heels, the ones I'd used to play dress-up in when I was little.

"Nice! Where'd you get those?"

"My grandma." I shrugged.

"Remind me to tell her what a kickass dresser she is next time she visits."

"She's dead," I said it quietly, quickly.

The room fell silent. My eyes shifted to the floor. I hated this part. The part where people don't know what to say but all you really want is for them to say nothing.

"That sucks." She exhaled heavily and then placed the shoes on the floor. "I think she'd want you to rock 'em. What do you think?"

I swallowed the knot in my throat and nodded with watery eyes. "I think she would, too."

"Great. Now let's go party and show my brother what a complete loser he is."

We linked arms and made our way to the party. It was the first time in six months I'd had another female to talk to. The first time in my life I'd had a friend who was a girl. I really liked it.

Chapter Four

The night air crackled with excitement. People talked excitedly down the main sidewalk as everyone made their way toward a huge building with a sign that said WELCOME BACK!

"Damn, Monroe. How do you walk in those things?" Tex fell into step with us and winked. What? Did he suddenly find me acceptable now that I was walking with Monroe? I glared back, remembering our first meeting where he flipped me off because his idiot group leader told him to. Minion.

"Tex, I take it you've probably met Trace already?"

"I waved."

"So you flipped her off?" Monroe stopped walking.

"Nixon said—"

"I swear if you finish that sentence I'm castrating you in your sleep." Monroe poked his chest. "Now apologize to Trace."

His red hair was spiked all over his head, and his teeth were gleaming white in the dusk air as he walked around her and stood in front of me. "I'm sorry I flipped you off. I'm also sorry I didn't get to see you this close up. You're pretty. Care to ditch the party tonight? I'm sure we could find a way to entertain—"

"I said apologize, not hit on her." Monroe pushed him away. He laughed and then pulled her into a hug. "Excuse him, Trace. He's almost as big of an ass as Nixon."

"She said *almost*." Tex laughed and walked between us, putting an arm around each of us as we made our way into the main lobby of the building.

"Speaking of the devil..." Monroe said under her breath as Nixon held court in the middle of the room.

I felt like I was walking in slow motion. Like I wasn't actually living this life but watching someone else live it. Or at least watching it on TV.

Nixon stood in the middle of the room. He was wearing black slacks and a tight baby blue shirt with a skinny tie and vest. He looked like he was modeling for Gucci or something. He even had aviators on. *Oh gosh, I have officially died and gone to magazine model hell.*

Chase was next to him, in tight black jeans and a sweater vest that could have done Tommy Hilfiger proud. Tex moved past us to knock fists with them. And then I saw Phoenix make his way through the crowd and embrace Tex, thumping him twice on the back.

Nixon took off his sunglasses and examined me slowly. His eyes narrowed until I could barely see the icy blue. He snapped his head to Monroe and nodded just once. "Nice work, Monroe. She looks like she actually belongs here."

"She does belong here, you idiot." Monroe moved past me and air kissed her brother on either side of his face before returning to me.

"The way I see it..." Nixon grinned. "She won a silly contest. The same contest we put on every year so that the poor underprivileged people of the world are able to join the high society. She"—he pointed at me and smirked—"is just a number."

"At least I'm not an ass," I spat. To my utter horror and complete humiliation it fell silent all around us.

Nixon slowly approached me. Rage was evident in his eyes but I couldn't back down. I refused to be bullied by some privileged rich kid who thought he ruled the known universe just because he was good-looking and had money.

"Is this on?" A guy spoke into a microphone. "Attention, everyone."

Nixon shook his head and backed off, making his way toward the stage.

"Your student body president would like to welcome you all back to school!"

Okay, so maybe he was a type of president. I clenched my teeth and waited. Monroe patted me on the arm as Nixon made his way to the stage.

People chanted his name over and over again. Funny how his name was Nixon. I smirked to myself but noticed that Nixon's eyes never left my face.

"I'd like to introduce someone . . . ." *Oh no, oh hell no.*

"She's new here"—he stared at me coldly—"and I want everyone to give her a warm, Eagle Elite welcome! Please clap your hands for . . . Dr. Tessa Stevens, our new history professor."

I blew out the breath I'd been holding and struggled to keep my hands at my sides. The only way I could smile was by imagining my hands around Nixon's throat.

A pretty middle-aged woman waved from the side of the stage. Nixon clapped in her direction and flashed a devastating smile.

Suck up.

"Now, I know all of you are eager to start the welcome party." He winked in my direction. The bastard.

Monroe wrapped her arm around me and whispered for me to calm down. Did I look that angry? I got my answer the minute I felt another hand on my back.

I flipped around and saw Chase smile and touch me briefly on the shoulder, inclining his head in my direction. I seriously almost punched him in the nose. I felt manipulated when they were mean and I felt manipulated when they were nice. It was like I always had to watch my back.

"I'm sure you've all noticed we have a new student. The winner of the annual Eagle Elite lottery registered this morning." Nixon's dimples widened right along with his smile. "Trace, why don't you come up here and say a few words?"

No. I shook my head and dug my heels into the ground. But Chase had hold of my arm and tugged me toward the stage. I looked back at Monroe, but she was currently fighting her own battle with Tex. He held both of her arms firmly behind her back in a tight grip. At least he mouthed *sorry* to me.

Phoenix was nowhere to be seen, but I'm sure he was around for backup just in case I decided to attempt to break Chase's nose.

Each step clanged in the large room. I could feel my own heart-beat as I made my way toward the stage.

Nixon held his hand out to me, but I was afraid to take it, afraid that if I did he would jerk back or embarrass me. I couldn't trust him, and he knew it. Yet if I didn't grab it, I would be insulting him, which was apparently an unforgivable sin.

I prayed he'd take my hand.

Shaking, I reached out to grasp his.

Shock at his warm touch overwhelmed me. His eyes hooded as

he looked down at our joined hands. Briefly, his face relaxed and I saw a different person. One who wasn't in league with the devil.

As quickly as it had happened, his face tightened and he dropped my hand. I watched as he rubbed his palm on his slacks and then flexed his fingers as if I had somehow held on too tight.

He cleared his throat. "Trace Rooks, everyone."

People clapped because he was clapping. They weren't actually excited to see me up there, nor did they even care. Most of them had bored expressions on their faces. I nervously scanned the crowd for Monroe; she was beaming. Her expression gave me strength. I immediately got choked up thinking of Grandma, how she'd told me I could do this. That nobody could tell me I wasn't worthwhile.

"Trace Rooks. If that isn't a backcountry name, I don't know what is," I joked into the microphone. "I come from a place where cows outnumber people and the local bartender knows everyone by name." I took a deep breath. "I guess you could say I'm completely out of my element, but I'm thankful nonetheless. I'm thankful for the opportunity to expand my education and even more so, I'm thankful that while I've been standing here Nixon hasn't attempted to trip me or knock me off the stage. Guess there's hope for me yet. Moo."

Did I just moo?

I cracked a smile.

And then I noticed more smiling faces around me.

And one clap, followed by more, and then shouting.

I backed away and walked slowly down the stairs. This time, Chase escorted me like a normal human being. When we reached the crowd of students, he whispered in my ear. "I knew you would be different."

"Different?"

"It's a compliment, Farm Girl. Get used to it. Because you've just earned half the student body's respect."

"And the other half?" I asked slowly, making my way back to Monroe.

"...follow the Elect and will stop at nothing to destroy you." He stopped me with his hand and turned me to face him.

"And whose side are you on, Chase?"

His eyes examined mine for a brief second before he tucked a piece of my hair behind my ear. "I always side with the pretty girls."

I waited for him to say, "And that's not you." But instead he held up my hand and kissed it, then walked off.

People around me began whispering. My mouth must have dropped open because suddenly my throat felt dry.

Monroe found me within seconds. "Hell, I think my brother almost choked on his tongue. Nice work, Boots."

"Boots?"

"Yeah, it's your new nickname."

"Why?"

"Because you *moo*'d in front of the entire student body and I can't very well call you a cow. But when I think of farms I think of cowboy boots. So Boots. Yup, Boots."

Nice logic. "All right then, Boots it is." I shrugged.

"He's going to shit himself." Monroe looked all too pleased as Nixon finished making his speech. Applause erupted when he finished, and we were dismissed to the party.

"What now?" I asked Monroe.

"Now"—she grabbed my hand—"we dance."

Chapter Five

I should have known that Elite wouldn't do anything half assed and that a college dance and welcome party would be anything but that in their eyes. It may as well have been prom, or a coronation ball, or the Oscars. Seriously.

The auditorium had holograms playing across the ceiling and dancing along the walls. The music played to the shapes on the walls and a music video of some band was playing toward the far wall where the dance floor was located.

Everything was in black light and I half-expected someone famous to pop out on stage and start a concert.

"Cool, huh?" Monroe nudged me. "Let's get something to drink."

I followed her to the food and couldn't close my mouth even if I'd wanted to. Everything was on ice. And I mean everything. Tons of desserts I'd never seen before were placed on and around ice sculptures. Toward the end of the table there was a type of blue waterfall with glasses lined around it.

"Elixir of the gods," Monroe yelled above the music. She had two plates in hand and had piled on pieces of chocolate-covered fruit and desserts in no time. We made our way toward the blue stuff. She picked up two champagne glasses and filled them full.

Maybe it was some sort of punch?

We found a table and sat.

"Try it." She pointed to the punch and grinned.

It looked harmless. I took a big swig and began coughing wildly.

"What? They don't have alcohol in Wyoming?" an irritating voice said from behind me.

The four Elect were standing right next to our table, each of them smiling at my misfortune.

"Yes, but when you drink underage you get arrested, smart ass." I put the glass down and grabbed a chocolate-covered strawberry. At least I knew that was safe.

"There is no law here," Nixon said, pulling out the chair on my other side. "And if there was a law, I'd be the sheriff, judge, and jury."

"Good for you."

I knew the rules. I patted him on the arm anyway.

Much to Monroe's amusement. She chuckled next to me.

Tex held out his hand. "May I have this dance?"

Monroe blushed and took his hand. "Don't kill my brother, Trace."

"I will try to control my urges." I saluted.

"Oh, I wish you wouldn't." Chase plopped down next to me and smirked.

"Leave!" Nixon yelled. Both Phoenix and Chase left the table.

"Why'd you do that?" I gave him a pointed look.

"Because he shouldn't be flirting with you." Nixon shrugged and plucked a strawberry off my plate.

I felt myself blush. "He wasn't flirting."

"Yes, he was." Nixon stole another strawberry.

"No." I smacked his hand, sending the strawberry to the floor. "He wasn't. He was just being nice. You should try it."

"Sweetheart, I can be nice to you. Believe me. I can be so nice you won't know what hit you. But is that what you really want? For me to be nice?" His breath smelled like strawberries as it trickled across my face. I licked my lips and forced myself to look away from his piercing gaze.

"Here." He held out a strawberry.

I reached for it, but he pulled back. "*Tsk, tsk.* Allow me."

He held it out again. I groaned and leaned forward.

"Open."

"No." I gritted my teeth.

"Then no strawberry."

"I think I'll survive." I jerked away from him and stood. His hand shot out and grabbed my wrist.

"Sit."

I did.

"I don't want to make your life hell. You know that, right? I don't want you to cry to sleep every night or curse me every morning. Know that you make your own choices. You create your own destiny. And baby, I have the keys. So either play by my rules, or don't. The choice is yours."

"Why does it matter, anyway? Either way I could never trust you."

His eyes flickered before he broke his gaze with mine. "Trust is like love. It doesn't exist. It's a fairy tale society feeds us in order to get us to conform. I don't expect you to trust me. I expect you to follow the rules. Rules keep you safe."

"And if I don't?"

He stood and dropped the strawberry on the plate. "Then you will be forcing my hand, and the last thing I want is to hear stories from my sister about how you cry yourself to sleep every damn night just because you couldn't follow a few simple guidelines."

I swallowed. "Fine."

He smirked and straightened his tie. "I knew we'd understand each other...eventually."

"I'm not agreeing with you. I just knew that would be the quickest way to get you to leave."

Nixon was deathly silent and then he reached up and touched my cheek. I fought against every instinct to slap him. My treacherous body was starved for touch, for attention. I missed my grandma. I missed my grandpa. I wanted someone to hug me and tell me what to do. But I was alone.

I shuddered.

"Dance with me," he commanded.

I opened my mouth to deny him, but he was already leading me toward the dance floor.

People gaped as a slow song came on and Nixon pulled me into his arms. He didn't say much. Neither did I. Instead, I began to shake because I knew. I knew it had already begun. I'd challenged him and he was going to make me pay. He was going to make my life hell. I didn't know how or when, but I knew he would strike, and it would be where it hurt most.

Right when I began to relax, just as the song was coming to an end, Nixon pushed me away. I stumbled but otherwise stayed on my feet.

The music stopped.

Great.

"What?" Nixon yelled and then laughed. "Are you insane?"

Clueless, I looked around me, then back at him.

"You think I would actually sleep with someone like you? What type of girl are you, anyway? Do they do things different out on the farm?"

I felt my face turn bright red.

"Oh, they must, huh?" Nixon folded his arms across his chest. "Trust me, Farm Girl. I don't care how much makeup you put on, or how expensive your clothes may be. I don't even give a rat's ass that half the student body likes you right now. You are charity. I wouldn't even screw you if you paid me. So, the answer is no. And next time you feel like showing up to one of my school's parties, at least have the decency to wear some new shoes."

I broke. I lunged for him, but strong arms held me back. I didn't want them to see me cry. I didn't know what else to do. I was shaking so hard that I thought I would pass out.

"Shhh..." Monroe said in my hair. "Tex, let's get her back to the room."

He nodded and soon Chase fell into step with us.

"Get away from me!" I screamed at them, but instead of leaving, Tex and Chase walked on either side of me. And then I realized why.

People were attempting to throw food at my head. But the minute the guys offered their support, people stopped and watched us leave the party.

Nixon was going to be pissed. But I didn't care. I was so incredibly ashamed of myself. Ashamed that I would fall for anything that guy said. And most of all, angry that he would make fun of my grandma's shoes. The very same shoes that had given me confidence today.

It was silent until Monroe started cursing under her breath. The only sound was of her grumblings and my footsteps echoing across the cement as we walked back to the dorm.

The guys didn't say anything. They didn't joke around. And Monroe had yet to stop cursing her brother.

Finally, they made it to the elevators. I panicked. I didn't want to use my one elevator pass just because I was embarrassed and ashamed and a little bit pissed.

Chase pulled out a shiny black card and swiped it across the elevators. I'm sure his card had all kinds of unlimited access on it. We all walked in. Even the boys.

I had thought everyone worthwhile was at the welcome party.

I'd thought wrong.

A few doors on my floor opened. It was as if the minute they opened and the occupants saw who was escorting me, a surge of estrogen hit the fan, causing giggling to break out around the entire right wing.

Girls whispered, "That's Chase and Tex! What are they doing here? So hot! So damn sexy! Chase, Chase!" One girl started chanting his name and I fought the urge to yell at her. Clearly I was dealing with a lot of emotions right now.

Monroe opened the door to my room. The guys shuffled in. I sat on my bed and waited for the yelling to start.

Monroe moved to my feet and slid off my grandma's shoes. "He's an ass. I know I shouldn't defend him, but if he'd known they were your grandma's shoes..."

Chase looked at the shoes then at me. "I don't get it. What's so important about—"

"She's dead, you asshole! And they're vintage, and she left them with Trace, okay? They're the nicest shoes she owns!"

Chase was silent. His concerned green gaze held mine for a while before he cursed and left the room. Tex threw his hands into the air and followed him out. Monroe locked the door behind them.

"Guess this means war, huh?" I tried to smile.

"I'll talk to him." Monroe didn't look so sure about that idea. She paced in front of me. "I never thought he'd take it this far. He's never taken it this far. People are too afraid of the Elect to do anything, or say anything."

"They aren't gods." Though to be fair, I had absolutely no idea what they were, other than a little club for guys with expensive clothes and way too much time on their hands.

Monroe laughed bitterly. "No, they're much worse. At least Greek gods stayed up on Olympus where they belonged. Ours haunt us here at school, as if college isn't bad enough, right?"

"He'll tire of me."

"That's the thing." Monroe started stripping. I would've killed for that woman's body. She grabbed a shirt that said SEXY and slipped it on, along with some pajama bottoms. "He usually threatens the people who don't conform and then that's that. If they challenge him, they usually get kicked out of school. Only one other kid challenged him and was bullied out of here, but everyone hated him anyway. I mean, Nixon's an ass, but he protects everyone. He's like the Godfather around these parts."

"And that makes me . . . what?"

Monroe chewed her lip. "I don't know." She nodded to my suitcase. "Got any pajamas in there?"

"Fingers crossed they weren't stolen," I joked.

Monroe walked over and started helping me sort through my suitcase. "It's okay to cry, you know. I won't tell anyone. For the record, I think you're really brave."

I felt the tears then. The choking feeling you get when you try super hard to hold back all the emotion and the headache that almost always surely follows. I nodded and broke eye contact.

"Hey, why don't I loan you some pajamas? Then you can just go to bed right away, okay? We'll put away your clothes tomorrow after class."

I groaned. "Ugh, class."

"Look on the bright side." Monroe threw me some shorts and a tank. "At least you won't have to endure Nixon. He shouldn't be in all of your classes—maybe two. If you're lucky, one."

"I'll wish on a shooting star," I muttered.

"'Night, Boots." Monroe laughed and turned off the light to her side of the room.

I threw on the shorts and tank top. My eyes landed on the box from Grandma. I sat cross-legged on the bed and opened it.

Monroe was right. It was okay to cry. Grandma's happy smile stared back at me from a picture we had taken last summer. I touched the glass and allowed myself a few selfish tears. What would her advice be? What would she tell me?

"Keep your head high. Ain't nothing to look at on the ground," I mumbled her favorite phrase and laughed through my tears. Tomorrow would be hard, but I had been chosen, I was here, and I was going to earn it. Nixon better watch his back because I, Tracey Rooks, was here to stay.

Chapter Six

The sound of music catapulted me out of my bed at lightning speed. Monroe was standing in front of the mirror dancing and singing while eating Cheerios. Now why hadn't I thought to bring my own food?

"Want some?" she asked as a Cheerio dropped out of her mouth. Well, beggars can't be choosers.

I nodded.

"My stash is under the bed. Take what you want; you'll need your strength today. Oh, and this came for you." She went to the door and picked up a large box.

"Huh? Who from?"

Monroe took another bite of Cheerios and shrugged. "I don't know. One of the resident directors dropped it off at like six a.m. I almost punched her in the face."

I laughed. Yes. I could totally see that happening. At least she wasn't a total morning person. Though I wasn't sure I would ever get used to her off-pitch singing in the mornings.

"Open it, whore!"

"Whoa, okay, fine." I pulled apart the box. A note fluttered to the floor. Picking it up, I read the scribble and gasped.

*They aren't your grandma's shoes. So I know they don't have the same
meaning. But I wanted you to have something to make you smile on
your first day of classes. Sorry about last night.*

Chase

"Oh my hell, Chase Winter just sent you a present!" Monroe
clapped her hands together. "I can't believe this! He never does things
without Nixon's consent."

I shrugged. "Maybe he asked permission from Nixon?"

"No, this has Chase written all over it." She beamed and pointed
to the box. "Do you have any idea how much all of this stuff costs?"

"No." I looked at the school uniform in the box, the knee-highs
and Italian leather boots. I'd briefly forgotten that the brochure had
boasted about E.E. making students wear uniforms to keep everyone,
well, uniform.

"At least ten grand, I'd say..." Monroe looked inside the boots.
"Yup, they are original Win."

"Huh?"

"W-i-n," she said slowly. "As in the beginning of Chase's last
name. His parents dabble in fashion design. They make high-end
accessories, boots, and scarves. Lucky you. Last time I got a pair of
these I was twelve, and it was only because I promised Chase I'd get
my friend to French kiss him."

"I can't accept these." I pushed the box away.

"Sure you can, and when you see Chase you give him a giant hug
in front of everyone. I'm proud of him. He's finally grown a pair."

"A pair of... what?"

"Balls." Monroe threw me a wicked smile and pointed to the

outfit. "Put it on and get ready, Boots." She clapped her hands together. "Perfect, now I really can call you Boots. You know, because he got you over the knee, one-of-a-kind leather Win boots that will make every girl on this floor want to murder you where you stand."

"Great, more fans." I pumped my fist lamely into the air.

"Just wear them, whore, before I help them kill you and steal them off your cold lifeless corpse."

"Fine," I grumbled. "But first food and then coffee."

She threw the Cheerios box at my head. "The breakfast of champions. Eat up."

"Right." I snorted. "Especially considering I only have two meal passes."

Monroe froze. "What did you say?"

"Your idiot brother gave me an access card with two meal passes. Remember? I told you that yesterday."

She squinted as if trying to remember and then asked. "What lunch are you in?"

I shrugged. How was I supposed to know?

She rolled her eyes and held out her hand. I snagged the card from my desk and put it in her hand. She flipped it over and typed the bar code into the school's website on her computer.

"I can't believe it." She shook her head.

"What? What's wrong? Don't tell me he lied! I'm going to starve!" I yelled toward the ceiling and stomped my foot. I was from Wyoming. I liked my food.

"He, um…" Monroe scratched her head. "He put you with us."

"What do you mean?"

"Nobody sits with us. It's a private lunch period, only for…"

Monroe snapped her mouth shut. "You know what? Never mind. Let's get you ready so we're not late."

*   *   *

Monroe wasn't in my first class, which was some sort of politics class. I wasn't really one for politics, but because most of the people who went to school here ended up being world leaders, it was considered core curriculum. I looked to my left where a kid had pulled out a flask.

On my right a girl texted someone and giggled behind her hand. The guy in front of me was reading a porno.

Safe to say the world of tomorrow was not in good hands.

Once the rest of the kids poured in, the lights flickered once, then twice. I learned quickly that meant that it was time to quiet down.

The door to the classroom opened. Nixon walked in.

You have got to be kidding me.

I looked around for an empty seat. There weren't any. Curious, I watched as he went and stood behind the desk at the front of the room.

"You all know me, and if you don't, well then, ask someone next to you because I'm not repeating my name. Professor Sanders had a death in the family, and because I'm doing a business internship for him, he asked me to fill in. Many of you are seniors who have put off this class until the last year here. Welcome to Freshman Politics. This class is going to suck, it's hard as hell, and if you don't get a B, you basically flunk. But..." He stepped around the desk and leaned against it. "If you listen, do your homework, and keep your head out of your ass long enough to pay attention, you may just learn something."

Okay, so as a person he sucked. As a teacher, I kind of dug the honesty.

"Trace," Nixon called my name.

Just kidding. I wanted to feed him to a hundred piranhas.

"Yes?" I stood. Monroe had filled me in that every time a teacher called on you, you stood. At least I knew that much before being thrown into the lion's den.

"Name all the presidents of the United States. You have three minutes."

I smirked, mainly because I had known the answer to that question since I was in sixth grade, when Grandma made me memorize the presidents to the tune of a song.

I could bust them out without the stupid song. "Washington, Adams, Jefferson, Madison, Monroe, Adams..." I rambled off all the names within two minutes. When I was finished, I sat down.

Every student in the room was gaping at me as if I was an alien or something.

Nixon walked slowly and purposefully toward my desk.

Crap. I'd probably pissed him off because I was smart and not stupid. But what else was I going to do during home school? Watch TV?

His boots clicked against the smooth concrete floor. Finally, he stopped in front of my desk. I looked up and waited for his reprimand.

He smiled. A real smile. Not one that made me want to inflict harm on his person, but one that revealed to me how ridiculously handsome he was. Man, that lip ring was distracting against his white teeth and dimples.

"Nice boots." He looked down and then walked back up to the front of the class.

"First person who does exactly what New Girl just did earns an A for the day."

Hands shot up around the room. Apparently I wasn't Trace anymore. Well, that was short-lived.

For the next hour I watched while other students tried and failed to copy my performance.

Class was finally dismissed.

I grabbed my book bag. I'd ordered it online a few months back in hopes that it would help me fit in. It was leather and had cost way more than I knew Grandpa could afford. I shuffled out the door but Nixon's voice stopped me.

"Are those Wins?" he asked.

I paused in the doorway. I was the last student to leave. I turned on my heel and glared at him. "Yes."

"Are they from my sister?"

"No." I felt my nostrils flaring.

"Did you buy them?"

"No."

"Who are they from?"

I shrugged.

"Mature." He snorted and threw his hands in the air. "Can't we have a simple conversation? Who bought you the boots, Trace?"

"The boot fairy," I replied and stomped off, glad Chase had given me something so awesome that even Nixon would take notice.

The next two classes were easy. I'm happy to announce that Nixon made no appearances. I looked down at my watch. It was already time for lunch. Monroe had instructed me to walk to the cafeteria and hang a left immediately before I came to the main two doors. I did as she said and noticed a small door on the side. I waved my card across it and the door opened.

To a restaurant.

And not just any restaurant. This was no McDonalds. No. There was a chandelier over my head as I walked through the curtain. Leather wallpaper lined the walls. Beautiful wood panels went halfway up each wall. The lighting was dim. I seriously felt like I'd just stepped into a different country. Candles were lit, and I nearly pinched myself when I saw a violinist playing in the corner. This was a joke; it had to be.

Phoenix, Nixon, Monroe, Tex, and Chase were sitting at a large table in the middle. Chase waved me over. I gulped and followed him.

Nixon kept his eyes down.

Monroe nudged him in the side but he still wouldn't look up.

"Holy shit!" Phoenix slapped his hand on the table. "Don't tell me those are from the 2014 collection! What the hell, man! You been holding out on us?" He threw his fork at Chase.

Chase's eyes warmed as they met mine, and then he pushed away from the table. I looked at Monroe for support. She nodded her head.

I bit my lip and stepped right into Chase's arms. Crap. I was breaking another rule, but maybe those were more Nixon's rules than Chase's. Shaking, I pulled back and, finally gaining courage, kissed him on the cheek. "Thanks for the boots."

"Sweet. Imagine what she'd do if you bought her a car." This from Phoenix. I heard the clattering of more silverware.

Chase smiled and licked his lips. "I'm sorry about—"

I waved him off. "I've got boots. We're even."

He inclined his head and led me to my seat.

"So, a restaurant? At a school? Really?" I directed my question to Monroe. She blushed and looked at her lap.

"Nobody really knows about it."

"We like our privacy." Nixon interrupted our conversation and snapped his fingers. A waiter appeared to take our order.

Nixon ordered in French. Of course he would.

But then everyone else followed suit. When it was my turn, I opened my mouth, but all that came out was a cross between a grunt and a whimper. Great.

Chase said something to Monroe in French. She laughed and then rapidly fired off orders to the waiter, who gave me a warm smile and disappeared.

"French?" I squeaked. "How many languages do you guys speak?"

"Three." Tex held his water in the air as if saluting me.

"Two." Phoenix shrugged.

"Five," Chase said.

Nixon cleared his throat.

"Tell her, man." Chase nudged him.

Nixon cursed and refused to make eye contact as he mumbled, "Ten."

"Ten?" I exclaimed. "I can barely speak English."

"We know." Phoenix laughed. I thought it appropriate to throw my fork this time.

He ducked and then hit Nixon on the hand. "I like her."

"Yeah, well, I like kids. Doesn't mean I run around screwing everything I see in order to have one," Nixon spat.

The table fell silent. How did they deal with his crappy attitude all the time? Monroe shrugged at me and began asking questions about my classes. Before I knew it hot food was in front of me.

"I'm afraid to ask what this is." I poked the hot meal with my fork. It smelled delicious.

"Heaven. It's heaven. It melts in your mouth and makes you scream with ecstasy. Girl, if you don't have an orgasm after experiencing that particular meal, then you're a hopeless case." Phoenix bit hungrily into his food and winked.

I felt my face heat severely.

Monroe nudged me. "Don't worry, Trace, Phoenix always talks like that. I think it's because he's never really had—"

Phoenix pointed his fork at Monroe and glared. "Don't even finish that sentence."

Tex and Chase laughed.

And again Nixon was silent.

I ate the meal. Correction: I inhaled the meal, and I promised myself I would start running so that I wouldn't gain ten pounds my first day here.

"So." I looked at my cell and back at the rest of the table. "Who eats here next lunch hour?"

Everyone looked to Nixon. He sucked in his lip ring and put his hands behind his head, leaning back on the legs of his chair. We were all in uniforms, but he had taken off his jacket, so I could see the outline of his dark tattoos underneath his crisp white button up. The shirt stretched over his muscles in such a way that I couldn't stop staring. I mean, the other guys were attractive, but Nixon was a step above the rest. He was chaotic perfection.

"Nobody."

"Huh?" I was still staring at his bulky arms.

"Eats here," Nixon said pointedly. "It's just us. Just this lunch hour."

"But..." Confused, I looked around. "Then why am I here?"

"We like to slum it sometimes." Nixon grinned smugly. "Now run off before you're late."

I didn't move.

Chase put his head in his hands and groaned. "I hate it when Mom and Dad fight."

Phoenix burst out laughing. I had to admit to finding it quite funny myself. Nixon, however, was not amused.

He pushed his chair back and stormed out of the room. The door slammed behind him.

"Is he always like that?"

"Actually..." Tex leaned forward. "No. I think you bring out the worst in him."

"Yay me," I said sarcastically.

"You're the first outsider who has ever eaten in here," Monroe said to my right. "He hands out key cards to control the cliques. To make sure fights don't break out between the kids from different countries at war and stuff. I just assumed he put you in one of the normal lunches."

"What do you mean?"

Chase shrugged. "He's not just in charge of the key cards, he's student body president. He makes sure that access is limited for each student. Take, for example, a kid from North Korea going to school here. You think they're going to get along with a South Korean? Or better yet, some ritzy American kid?"

"Um...no?"

Everyone laughed.

Phoenix shook his head. "That's a *hell no*, New Girl."

Chase crossed his arms. My mouth went dry at the sight. His dark hair wasn't as unruly as Nixon's, but he still had that dangerous look about him. "What if some sheik's kid goes to school here but he's from a different sect than some other kid? What if those same kids eat in the same lunchroom that serves pork?"

"Oh." I huffed. "I guess that makes sense, but then doesn't that segregate everyone?"

Monroe laughed. "Boots, it's college. We're segregated regardless, whether it be by major or class. This is just the way things are here. It keeps everyone safe. Keeps the fights down."

The table fell silent again.

I looked up at Chase. "But if he hates me so much why would he want me here?"

A clock chimed in the restaurant causing everyone to push away from the table and stand.

My question remained unanswered as we all shuffled to the door.

I made my way out down the hall, but Chase caught up to me and whispered in my ear as we walked. "Protection."

"What?"

"See ya!" He waved and walked down the hall, leaving me to wonder what in the heck I needed to be protected from. Or whom.

Chapter Seven

So tired…" I mumbled, swiping my card across the elevator door. Okay, so I knew it was lazy for me to use my one pass on the first day of school. But my brain was fried. I was chosen to speak during my last three classes. My final class had been a kinesiology elective which was basically like PE. I had no idea colleges enforced exercise!

Lucky for me, I had it all wrong.

They don't do PE at Elite.

No, they did defensive arts. Seriously. That's what they called it. Not as in the dark arts from Harry Potter, but as in defensive arts. It could have easily been the same thing with how my body felt.

For the past hour, I swear, my soul had left my body and I'd served as victim to some guy named Spike, who'd taken it upon himself to teach me how to fight by continuously and brutally attacking me.

At least now I knew how to gouge someone's eyes out, which I knew was going to come in handy if I had to sit and eat with Nixon every day.

I chewed my lip. The elevator doors opened. I stepped in and leaned against the wall. Why would he be so mean to me and then make sure I was always around him?

The elevator stopped. Great. I hit my floor number again. It still didn't budge and now a shrieking noise began coming from above me.

I hated small spaces. Panic set in. I was just about to use the little red phone to call the fire department, or SWAT, or something, when the elevator moved again.

"Thank God," I mumbled as the elevator opened to my floor.

I shuffled to my door and stopped in front of it.

Where there was a picture taped to it of my face on a cow's body.

Should have known that was going to happen sooner or later.

Clever. Bet they nearly killed off all their brain cells to come up with that one. I decided to join in the fun and drew a heart around my head with a little bubble that said *MOO*.

Take that.

I pushed open the door and immediately threw off my jacket, followed by my shirt. Then I addressed my skirt. I heard chuckling.

My hands froze on my skirt's zipper. I looked up.

Nixon lay across my bed. "Please, don't let me interrupt. Continue."

I flipped him off.

He laughed harder.

I quickly pulled on the tank top I'd worn to bed and thrown across the chair. "What do you want?"

"Not sex, but thanks for the offer."

"I was not..." I took three deep breaths. Arguing got me nowhere with Satan. "Why are you here?"

"Waiting for my sister. What else?"

I exhaled in relief.

"What, you disappointed I didn't want an afternoon screw?"

"Not at all." I sat far far away on Monroe's bed. "Besides, if you needed one, all you'd have to do is knock on any door on this floor. Just be sure to use protection. I know how you are about germs."

"Only yours," he sang.

I threw a pillow in his direction, hoping to smack him in the face. He caught it mid-air and scowled. "Can you at least wait for her outside?"

"Nope."

"Why?" I ground my teeth together. At the rate I was going I would have nothing left to grind.

"Because, I like your bed. It's comfortable."

"It has my germs and I swear to you I drooled all over my pillow last night."

He shrugged. "I only hate germs on people, not objects."

Nixon looked at his watch then put his hands behind his head and closed his eyes.

"Why?"

"Why what, Farm Girl?"

"Why don't you like people touching you? Is that *your* rule or an Elite thing?"

"You ask a lot of questions for someone so stupid."

That stung, but I was too tired to let it sink too far into my consciousness. "It is the only way to find out how to survive in this place."

"You'll survive, if you follow the rules. I thought I told you that." He propped up on his elbow. "The system works, Trace. I know you think I'm an asshole, but if I was nice, they would eat you alive. Wouldn't you rather I do the tasting?" He smirked.

Damn, I was literally itching to punch him in the jaw.

"Why can't everyone just be nice and get along?"

He groaned into his hands and stood. "Maybe I will wait outside."

"You do that."

He walked to the door and then stopped. "Has anyone made fun of you today?"

"Is this a trick question?" I asked, jumping off Monroe's bed. "You make fun of me all the time!"

"Other than me." He shoved his hands into the pockets of his slacks. "Tell me the truth."

"N-no," I stuttered. "No one made fun of me today." At least not out loud; there was still that stupid cow poster.

"I guess my point is made."

"The hell it is." I bent down and picked up another pillow to throw at his face. "You think you have that much power? To protect me from them? You think you're that much better? That what you do is better than what typical college kids could do to me?"

His eyebrows rose. "Care to make a wager?"

"Fine!" I poked him in the chest.

Nixon closed his eyes as if in pain. "Please don't touch me."

I backed off but only because he'd said please.

"I'll stop bothering you...but when I win—when you can't take it anymore—when you are living in hell every single day, I want to hear it from your lips. Not Monroe's, not Chase's. I want you to approach me. I want you to tell me..."

"Tell you what?" I whispered.

"That you need me."

"When hell freezes over!" I snapped.

"Bring a parka, because life's a bitch and you just bought a first class ticket, sweetheart."

I was still in a crappy mood when Monroe finally arrived. True to his word, Nixon sat outside, at the door, waiting for her. Why he didn't text her or call her I have no idea.

I couldn't really hear what they were saying. But Monroe was yelling, and Nixon was yelling, and I was pretty sure one of them was going to throw a punch.

So I was really surprised when Monroe bounced into the room with a wide smile on her face. "Guess what!"

"You killed your brother?"

She rolled her eyes. "I'm not that lucky, no." With a huff she sat on her bed. "The Elect are throwing a party tonight and I get to bring you!"

Excuse me while I pull out my pom-poms. "Swell."

"Boots, don't go raining on my parade. Besides, Tex will be there and…"

I raised an eyebrow.

She flushed. "Fine. I like Tex. Happy?"

"Does Satan know?"

"He sees all," she grumbled.

"Is that why you guys were fighting?"

"What should I wear?" Monroe clapped her hands. "I don't want to look too easy, but I still want to look hot, you know? Hmm, maybe a red dress? You think? With Louboutin heels?"

"Uh…Loub—who?" I laughed. "You're beautiful in pajamas. Just wear something you feel confident in." I didn't miss that she'd changed the subject, but I decided maybe it was best if I didn't know all of the happenings of their family.

Monroe began pulling clothes from her closet and tossing them onto the floor. Finally, she chose a purple dress with a plunging front and back. Only it was covered with some sheer material so technically it could not be defined as slutty.

I did say *technically*.

"Your turn."

"Um, I have a lot of homework and—"

"Nope, you're going. Nixon said you could."

"Oh, well, if the great and powerful Oz said I could go...."

Monroe threw her head back and laughed. "Can we please call him Oz from now on?"

"Sure, he'd love that." I smirked. "He'd probably threaten me again."

"Whatever." Monroe rummaged on the floor and grabbed a tight t-shirt and short jean skirt. "Here." She tossed them at my face.

I caught them. Both pieces of clothing were smaller than the tank top I wore to bed. How was that supposed to work?

"Um, Monroe, this outfit is kind of—"

She rolled her eyes. "Wear flip-flops so you don't look as tall, and we'll give you a leather jacket. It will look awesome. Trust me."

I wasn't sure I could trust anything coming from her mouth, considering she was the one wearing a purple getup that would make people at the Jersey Shore blush.

"Are you sure I should go? I don't know, Nixon and I got in a fight and—"

"I need you!" She stood to her full height and stomped her foot. "I need a wing person."

"For Tex? You're kidding, right?"

"Please?" She jutted out her bottom lip.

I glared, but she kept giving me that pitiful stare of hers. "Fine, I'll go." But I had a really bad feeling about this party.

Chapter Eight

Note to self: If you have a bad feeling about something…if your gut is twisting at the idea of following through with a bad choice… just say no. Do not be a *yes* person. I closed my eyes and opened them again. Maybe if I closed my eyes I'd become invisible. I tried it again. Nope. No such luck. Crap.

"Monroe, I should go," I yelled above the music.

"No! Stay!" She was dancing with Tex. I mean, I guess you could call it dancing. His hands were everywhere, and honestly I was waiting in anticipation for Nixon to punch him in the nose for holding his sister that close.

But Nixon was nowhere to be found.

Not that I was looking for him.

And even if I was looking for him, it was only out of self-preservation and survival. Like on the Discovery Channel, when the antelope see a lion. They don't just hang out and give the lion a chance. No, they run like hell.

"Okay, five more minutes," I chanted to Monroe, but she was too busy making out with Tex. Hmm, I'd never really found redheads attractive, but he was kinda cute. When his tongue was in his mouth and he wasn't completely drunk and humping my roommate.

So basically he'd been cute this afternoon. Tonight? Not so much.

"Hey, New Girl," a male voice said from behind me.

I turned.

Phoenix stood there, two drinks in hand. His Harvard good looks would get him far. His sandy blond hair was slicked to the side, but it totally worked for him because it made his thick black eyelashes stand out against his chocolate eyes.

"Drink?" He held out the red plastic cup.

"Did you put a roofie in it?" I asked nicely.

"If I did I wouldn't tell you," he said with a deadpan expression.

And there went that sick feeling again in my stomach.

He smiled warmly and tilted his head. "Take the drink, Trace. I promise I didn't drug it..." I grasped the cup and took a tentative sip. "This time," he finished.

"Good to know."

He put his free arm around me and guided me to the outside. I hadn't realized how stuffy it was in that tiny room until now. We were at some sort of party house located on campus. One that security literally guarded so that kids could get wasted without having to worry about driving or doing something stupid.

Were there really no rules here?

"Rule number six." Phoenix folded his arms across the banister of the balcony and sighed. "Never accept drinks from a stranger."

"Do you qualify as a stranger?" I asked, taking another sip.

"No. We're..." He seemed to think about it for a few seconds. "Friends."

"Wow, that must have been hard to say out loud."

"You should be more careful." He sighed into his hands. "Look, I don't even know why I'm telling you this. If Nixon finds out, he'll kick my ass, but he's just trying to protect you. You don't know what the people are like here. I mean, you're from a farm, for crying out loud."

"You sound just like him." I played with the plastic cup in my hands and then set it on the balcony. "Everyone here is under the age of twenty-one, right?"

He shrugged. "Some are, some aren't."

"And they're so bad that you guys have your own mafia to keep everyone in check? I don't believe it. Sorry, but what about the security, what about the adults, the teachers?"

Phoenix looked down at the ground. "They look the other way."

He started to look like he had two heads. I licked my lips. My throat suddenly felt really dry. I drank some more of the liquid from the cup. I felt parched. Finishing the drink, I put it back on the banister and looked at Phoenix.

"I . . . I'm so thirsty."

He smirked. "Really? Do you want some of mine?"

I reached out to grab his cup and it tipped over the edge, efficiently landing on someone's head. They flipped me off. Or at least I think they did. I saw like twenty fingers.

Something was wrong. My mouth felt like cotton. "Y-you said no drugs..." Why did my words sound so funny?

Phoenix laughed loudly. "I also told the new history teacher that I was a virgin in need of an older woman's expertise..." He pulled me close to him and tilted my chin up. "Now you'll see why you need us. Don't worry; I won't let anyone else hurt you. I'm doing this for Nixon, so he can see. He needs to see. Nobody can control us, especially not some farm girl who moos in front of the entire student body."

I was being carried or pushed. I wasn't really sure which. But suddenly we were back inside, and he was carrying me down the stairs and out to the front of the house. I tried to fight him, but I had no strength in my body. This was bad. So very bad.

"H-help." I gave a weak, pitiful yell. Actually, it sounded loud to my ears, but then everything sounded loud.

"Phoenix...pleashhh."

"Sorry, Trace. I really am. But this is for your own good."

How is drugging me for my own good? This was what I wanted to yell to him, but when I opened my mouth nothing came out.

"What the hell, Phoenix!" I heard another male voice. *Please let it be a teacher or someone. Tex, even!*

"She's drunk. I'm taking her back to her dorm."

"Like hell you are! And her dorm isn't in that direction. What are you doing?"

I saw Chase's face. Well, I saw three of him. At least I think it was Chase.

"I'm doing her a favor, doing us a favor. Back off; you're already on Nixon's shit list. I'm making everything better; you'll see."

I lifted my hand up to grasp Chase. He looked concerned but not enough to do anything. I wanted to cry, but then again, I wanted to keep my tears in. I felt so dehydrated.

"I'll take her," Chase mumbled.

"You're going to do it? Really?"

"Just let me do it." Chase held out his arms. I was being transferred. That was a good thing, right? I mean, Chase had given me boots!

Chase mumbled something under his breath as he carried me to a waiting car. He gently placed me in the front seat and drove off. I tried not to nod off, but it was hard. And Chase kept mumbling something like, "...can't believe she's pushed him this far. What is Nixon thinking?"

That was the last thing I remembered. Everything went black.

*   *   *

A loud bell ringing woke me up. Apparently I had been run over by a truck the night before. I remembered the party, and then I remembered drinking something from Phoenix. He'd looked hot last night...and then...Chase? Had Chase been there?

The bell rang again. I shook my head and rubbed my eyes. Where was I? I felt comfortable, like I was in my bed, but it wasn't my bed.

Oh no.

I jolted upright and noticed the room was masculine. Definitely not my room. I hadn't done anything, though, right? I had all my clothes on, and my body felt fine. Well, other than the pounding of my head. I quickly grabbed my jacket and bolted out of the room.

The guys' dorm. Of course. The only way I even knew it was their dorm was because Mo had let it drop that while the girls' dorms were arranged by country, the boys' dorms were arranged by animal. The eagle on the wall hinted that not only was this the boys' dorm but that it was the upper-class dorm. Awesome. At least nobody was around to witness my shame.

But then one by one doors to the hall opened, and guys poked their heads out, almost as if they'd all been sent some simultaneous signal to check the hallway for escaped New Girls being framed for sluthood.

"Ah! He bagged another one! Go Tim!" someone shouted, and

then a giant wall of muscles greeted me as an Asian guy with killer golden eyes and an even greater smile came out of the bathroom. I gulped.

"Tim bagged the new girl!" someone else shouted.

I tried to get by, but he kept blocking me.

"What is your problem?"

He smirked and leaned in so close I could smell his toothpaste. "What, baby? No good morning kiss from the sex god you spent the night with?"

Anger and shame washed over me simultaneously. I didn't do that. I would never do that! My eyes darted to all the guys around me. They were high-fiving and texting, and of course taking pictures of me. Great.

"Get the hell away from me!" I pushed against his muscled chest. But he only pulled me closer. I struggled out of his grasp, mainly because he let me get free, and jogged down the hall only to find the door to the main lobby already open. And there stood Phoenix, waiting. Chase was by his side.

As well as about one hundred other males from the dorm.

I launched myself at Phoenix, but Chase blocked my way. "Let it go, Trace."

"You son of a bitch! Why would you do that to me?"

Phoenix smirked. "Maybe you shouldn't drink so much next time."

Chase released me. His eyes were sad, but I didn't care. I charged out of the lobby. All around me voices were screaming and calling me a whore.

By the time I reached my dorm, tears were streaming down my face. I checked my pocket for my key card.

It was gone.

I'd already used my one elevator ride anyway. I jogged up the stairs, sweating by the time I reached the third floor.

To my utter horror and humiliation, I was welcomed by several girls clapping. "Way to go, New Girl, bagging the quarterback of the football team. Well done!"

"What a slut!" another girl yelled. "Tim has a girlfriend! Who does that?"

I choked back sobs as I reached my door and pushed it open. Thank God it wasn't locked.

Monroe was still sleeping.

I didn't know if I wanted to wake her. I didn't know if I wanted to tell her. I paced the room five times before finally making the decision.

"Monroe." I sobbed. "Please wake up! Please!"

She jolted awake and then cursed. "Where the hell have you been?"

"Oh you know, getting my brains screwed out by the quarterback of the football team." I didn't even try to hold the tears in as I collapsed on her bed and told her the whole story, or at least what I remembered of it.

"Are you sure?" she asked when I was finished.

"What do you mean?"

"Are you sure you didn't just drink too much and leave with Tim?"

"Yes!" I shouted. "Why don't you believe me? Why doesn't anyone believe me!"

"Whoa, calm down." Monroe stood and yawned. "I'll talk to Nixon. He'll fix it."

"He won't." Dread filled my stomach until I thought I was going to puke. "He told me he was done protecting me."

"Come again?"

"We kind of made a wager…"

Monroe threw something against the wall. "Why the hell would you make a deal with the devil?"

"He provoked me!" I yelled.

"Wow…" Monroe paced in front of me. "Well, at least you don't have to face any of them during lunch time. That would be… catastrophic."

Crap. Crap. Crap. "I kind of lost my access card."

Monroe slumped to the floor. "Girl, I hate to be the one to say this, but you are totally and completely screwed."

I nodded. I knew it was true. And I hated that I had to face all those people today.

"How do I eat?"

"I'll think of something, okay?" She bit her lip. "It's just the only one who has passes is Nixon. I'll bring it up to Tex and see what he says."

Great. Who the hell had given him the keys to the world?

"Look, just get ready for school, and we'll sort it out this afternoon, okay?" Monroe threw me a granola bar and started getting dressed. I could do this. I could face a whole bunch of my peers. What could they do? Stab me?

Chapter Nine

It was official. I hated college. It was bad enough walking into the classroom to everyone snickering in my direction. I slumped as low in my seat as I could without falling off my chair and flashing everyone my underwear, which would have just solidified my reputation as a hussy.

Nixon walked in. For the first time in two days I wanted him to pay attention to me. I wanted him to walk over to my desk and say our wager was stupid. I wanted that damn access card. In fact, I would kill for the one elevator ride a week, and I'd only been in class for five minutes.

"Today we're going to work in teams." He began handing out sheets of paper. "I know many of you are familiar with Settlers of Catan. It's a board game where you are in charge of your own country and you sell and trade with other countries. It's more complicated than that, but today I want you to form your own countries. Each of you has something someone else needs, whether it be oil, wheat, or even land. You will barter with team members in order to build your own country. Come up with a flag and a team motto. You have the rest of the class period to do so."

Sounded easy enough. He handed me the paper. I noticed there weren't any names assigned on it.

I raised my hand.

"Yes, Farm Girl?"

Rolling my eyes, I asked as nicely as possible, "Aren't the teams assigned?"

People snickered as if I had just asked the dumbest question in the world.

Nixon didn't snicker, nor did he smile. "Nope, you work with groups. So pick a group and work with them."

"Any group?"

"Any group," he snapped.

Okay, I grabbed my sheet of paper and approached the three people to my right. "Hey, can I work with—"

"We don't work with whores." The blond girl flipped her hair and then gave me the bird. Lovely.

I walked toward the back of the classroom where the guy who was drinking during class sat with his group. "Do you guys possibly have room for one more?"

The guy opened his flask, took a big swig, and then wiped his mouth with his jacket. "Yeah, we're totally into threesomes, aren't we?" He looked at the other girl in his group and high-fived her.

Tears threatened again.

I hated this school.

I hated stupid Phoenix and Nixon and Chase and everyone!

With a steadying breath I marched to the front of the room and politely waited for Nixon to notice me. He was reading some crazy long book in a different language. Boring.

"What can I do for you, Trace?" His eyes didn't leave the book.

"The groups won't take me."

"Then I guess you fail."

I gasped. "It's not my fault..."

"Ah, there's the excuse I was looking for." This time his eyes met mine. "This is the real world, Trace. You can't just tattle on the mean kids in class. Nobody wants you to be in their group? Be in the group anyway. Make them notice you, make them pay attention. Now, run along."

Part of me was shocked at the truth of his statement, while the other part wanted to smack him on the head with that super large book and then burst into tears.

I fisted the paper in my hand and marched toward the back of the room again. "The third part of the threesome is here. Let's get started."

The students around me looked shocked and then, surprisingly, we began working on our project. I looked back at Nixon. He was watching me intently, but then he nodded just once and went back to his book.

By the time class was finished some of my embarrassment had left me. I walked down the hall with a purpose, despite the mean stares and snickers around me. Monroe waved me over from near one of the windows. I still had five minutes before history class so I went over to her.

"So, how was class?" Monroe took a long sip of coffee.

"Bad. Then worse, then...surprisingly better."

She exhaled in relief. "Good. I was worried about you."

"Thanks."

"Sister," Nixon said from behind us.

"Lucifer," she greeted coldly.

I didn't want to turn around, but my body made me. It was like I couldn't help but ask for trouble.

"Please tell Farm Girl to stop looking at us," Nixon said coldly.

Why was he pissed? I was the one who'd been taken advantage of! And all because he'd wanted to prove how important he was!

I quickly averted my eyes and bit my tongue to keep from saying something offensive.

My eyes fell on all the students around us. They were watching and waiting. I was getting sicker and sicker by the minute.

"Thanks for . . . this," Monroe said.

"I'm doing it for you. Not for her," came Nixon's reply. "Wouldn't want anyone uncomfortable."

I flinched.

Monroe grabbed my hand and placed an access card in it. Somehow it didn't feel right that she would be afraid of her own brother. But then again maybe this was just how things worked in her family.

Within seconds the shiny boots left my line of vision and marched down the hall. I gulped and looked at the access card.

It was red.

I flipped it over, but there was no bar code.

"What is this?" I asked Monroe. She was putting on lip gloss and practically ignored me, but then again she did seem to have a short attention span.

"It's all I could do, Boots. I'm sorry. I didn't want to tell him you lost yours, so I came up with another story to tell Tex and Phoenix. Nixon doesn't like irresponsibility. He's a control freak like that. At any rate, at least you can eat." She patted my shoulder and walked off.

I knew by then that in order to see what lunch period you were in, you had to type in the code on back into the school web program, but when I checked there was no code!

Ugh. I decided to worry about it at lunch.

By the time lunch came, I was so hungry I was ready to throw the card at Nixon's head.

I walked toward the lunchroom, hoping my card would work. I swiped it at the door to the cafeteria. Nothing.

I swiped it again.

And again, nothing.

I kept swiping until finally a little red alarm went off. Oh great.

"Need help?" I looked up to see Chase's blue eyes piercing into mine. I still wasn't sure if I liked him or hated him.

"You could say that."

"Here." He held out his hand. I slapped the card into it and waited for him to swipe it. Instead he put it in his pocket and grabbed my arm, leading me down the opposite hallway.

A small sign on a door said THE RED ROOM.

"Is this Hell?" I asked in a small voice. Because on the opposite end was that super fancy restaurant. I didn't even want to know what was in here.

"Not exactly." Chase gave me a sad smile. "But it's best to be seen and not heard in here; you get it?"

Terrified, I could only nod as he swiped my card. The red light went off and the door clicked open. "Good luck, Trace. And for the record. It will get better."

"Right." My chin trembled as I gathered my card and walked into the dark room.

It didn't look so bad. Until my eyes adjusted and I noticed something was very wrong about where I was.

"Fresh meat," a girl purred beside me. I jerked away and kept walking toward an empty table. I smelled food, but I didn't see any food anywhere.

People whispered in low voices but for the most part nobody paid attention to me. I sat at the table and looked at the menu.

All the options were for vegans. Great. No meat. *Damn you, Nixon.*

When the waiter came and took my order I nearly cried. Something about having to eat a tofu burger was just so wrong after being brought up around cows.

I checked my cell for messages. Nothing. Not even from Monroe.

Lunch officially sucked. People were talking about me. I had no friends, and I couldn't eat meat. To make matters worse the only free table was smack dab in the middle of the cafeteria, meaning I was on display for all to see.

I waited for my meal.

And waited.

And waited.

Finally the bell rang.

The waiter arrived with a large platter and took the top off of the plate.

No food. Only a note that said, *Moo. Maybe if you ate less, Tim wouldn't complain about how terrible you were in bed.*

The tears came then. Full force. I was already the type of girl who got really moody when I couldn't eat. The waiter had already disappeared.

I was going to be late for class.

The rest of the day slipped by. My only companion was the growling in my stomach. And yes, I was aware of how pathetic I was. I was actually quite thrilled to be invisible, considering how the morning had begun.

Then Lucifer decided to make an appearance. It was as if he appeared out of thin air. I mean, I guess I was looking at the ground. But still, the minute my eyes snapped up, there he was—icy stare full of beautiful sin.

I sighed and put my hand out on my jutted hip.

"There were rumors you didn't get lunch."

My eyebrow arched. "Rumors, huh? Well, alert the authorities. Oh, wait, I forgot. You're what? The judge, jury, and—"

"Stop." He said it so low I almost didn't hear the word. Nixon walked toward me. I had nowhere to go but backward down the hall, and really that just seemed like a waste of time, so I tried to sidestep him.

His muscular arm popped out of nowhere, nearly bruising my windpipe in the process. He placed it against the wall, directly in my line of vision. "I'm speaking to you."

"And I'm leaving."

"Just…" He scratched his head and then did something totally out of character.

Nixon smiled.

My heart skipped a beat, or maybe seven. I lost track when I stopped breathing like a normal human being.

Without me even realizing it, he had pulled me to the side of the hall and pinned me against the tiny alcove in the wall. *Great, nobody to witness my death.*

"Eat," he urged.

My mouth snapped open to say something snotty, but the minute it did, he held up his hand as if silencing me, then slowly unwrapped a granola bar and pressed it against my lips. My mouth watering, I took a bite.

My stomach growled with joy and my embarrassment skyrocketed as he looked down and smirked. "See? I knew you were hungry."

I took a bite and pulled the granola bar out of my mouth. "Of course I was hungry, you ass! I was in the Red Cafeteria! I half-expected to be eaten myself in that place, and they don't serve meat. No meat, Nixon! Some cow has to live another day because the people in there eat tofu! Do you even know what that stuff is made out of?"

His eyes widened. He opened his mouth but I poked him in the chest. He flushed and then jolted away.

"And let me tell you something else. I did not sleep with Tim! Well, I may have slept, but I definitely didn't touch his—and, and...I..."

His eyebrows rose as I lost my train of thought. He licked his lips and leaned forward. "Oh, do continue. I love getting reprimanded. You gonna spank me later, too?"

I felt my nostrils flare, but of course my stomach hadn't forgotten it was starving, which of course made Nixon laugh harder. "Good Lord, woman! Just eat the damn granola bar and say thank you!"

Thank you? Did he want me to thank him for what had transpired over the past twenty-four hours?

And suddenly I remembered. I hadn't seen him last night. That was all Phoenix and a bit of Chase. Bastard.

"Where were you last night?"

Nixon's smile froze on his face. "I gotta run."

"Wait." I grabbed his arm. His muscles flexed beneath my fingers.

I noticed a light tremble in his arm as he jerked away. "Please." His eyes closed briefly. "Don't touch me."

And then he was gone.

Chapter Ten

I wish I could say my days got easier. That after the granola bar incident everything was peachy. The Red Cafeteria still served nothing but tofu and vegetarian options. By Friday, I'd made a mental note to go grocery shopping for snacks that weekend the minute classes were over.

Luckily, the notes had stopped.

Well, actually it wasn't necessarily lucky, because that meant I had to eat whatever was in front of me. But I decided that tofu burgers weren't so bad if you bathed them in ketchup, which I did every day. I even closed my eyes in hopes that God would sense my plight and turn my tofu into a giant cooked cow.

I was just finishing my burger on Friday when someone approached my table. Yes, I was still sitting alone.

"Can I help you?" I asked sweetly.

The girl leaned forward until her boobs almost spilled out of her white button-up shirt. "Yes. I was told to give you this." She thrust a note into my face and waited for me to take it.

My fingers gripped the small white paper. Carefully I opened the note. It said, *Meet me outside.*

Outside? As in outside by all the grass and trees or outside the cafeteria?

The bell rang, signaling I had to leave anyway. Tossing the note onto the tray, I picked up my bag and rushed out of the room.

Kids were lining the halls. Weird.

I kept my head down and gripped my backpack as I kept walking.

"Slut, Slut, Slut," they chanted as I made my way through the hall. Great. Trying to ignore your peers is about as easy as trying to ignore your own face in the mirror. You don't want the words to affect you, but it's impossible. Weight descended upon my chest, making it hard to breathe.

And then someone threw something at my head.

I staggered and reached up to touch the liquid running down my face.

Egg.

Another one hit my messenger bag, which upset me more than when the first egg hit my hair. The bag was the most expensive thing I owned, next to the boots Chase had gotten me. I didn't count grand-ma's vintage shoes, because those were passed down.

I kept my gaze focused on the end of the hallway and kept walking.

Eggs flew by my head. I had to close my eyes a few times in order to wipe the slime away from my line of vision. Once I reached the end of the hall, I turned to the left, and ran right into three strong boys. Each of them had a bucket.

"Better get you clean. Elite doesn't like dirty whores." They lifted their buckets and dropped ice cold water all over my body.

In theory I knew what they were doing was assault, bullying in its worst form, but from everything I'd seen, the teachers didn't control what the students did. They looked the other way. So telling a teacher seemed like it would just make things worse. And telling Mo? Well, she'd just tell Nixon, who would in turn finally realize that maybe, just maybe, I did need him more than I realized. Which was stupid. Wasn't he the guy pulling the strings anyway?

Water droplets fell down my face in rapid succession. I was completely drenched and more than a little horrified.

Ruined. Everything was ruined. My one and only uniform was ruined. My messenger bag, possibly my cell phone, and all the textbooks I was carrying with me that I knew I would have to replace.

I choked on a sob and pushed through them. Passing my classroom, I began walking faster and faster, until finally, I broke into a run. I turned back to make sure they weren't chasing me.

They were.

And everyone was laughing.

The minute I turned forward I tripped and fell, scraping my knee like a little first grader.

People circled me, still chanting *whore* and *slut* as if I had done anything to deserve it.

"You don't belong here, Farm Girl!" one guy shouted.

"Spend so much time on your back you're gonna get sores!" a girl spat and then dropped a condom on top of me.

It was at that point that I wasn't sure if I wanted to close my eyes and wait for everyone to leave or just cry and embarrass myself. Hell, I was already beyond embarrassment. I wasn't *that* girl. I was a virgin, for crying out loud! I'd kissed one boy in my entire life! Ruthless; they were ruthless. More condoms followed until I was literally covered in them, and then one of the girls from the Red Cafeteria walked up to me and pulled my hair toward her, nearly dragging my body along with her.

"You are nothing. Do you understand?" she said in even cold tones. "You don't belong here. Say it."

I refused to say it.

She pulled harder. I shrieked and tried to fight her. Damn, she was strong, but I managed to sit up on my knees. "Say it!"

"I—"

Tears burned my vision again. How had this happened to me?

I swallowed bravely and stared her down as I rose to my full height, even though I knew it was stupid and pointless. "I belong here."

People laughed behind her. Some gasped, and yes, I did see some people averting their eyes. So not everyone was heartless, but it didn't matter. I had no protection, nothing.

"Leave her alone," a low voice said from behind the crowd.

I didn't realize I was trembling until I tried to rub my eyes to see better.

"And who do you think—" The girl's words died off. She jerked away from me as if I was diseased and then she was scrambling for words. "I did it for you, Nixon, for you! She can't dismiss you like that. She can't—"

"Stop speaking." Nixon pushed her into a waiting Chase's arms. "Take care of this, will you?"

Chase smirked and grabbed the girl and somehow the rest of the crowd as he made his way down the opposite end of the hall.

"Are you hurt?" Nixon leaned down and touched my face. I slapped his hand away and then started bawling like a little kid.

He cursed and tried to pick me up.

I shied away.

"Shit." He pulled out a hankie from his back pocket. Did guys still carry hankies? "This wasn't supposed to happen. I didn't…" He bit his lip until it turned white, then he held out his hand.

My brain was on overdrive. I didn't want the devil's protection, but then again, maybe I did. Because there was no way I could last another day of this. I couldn't take it. What normal girl could? I'd thought he was kidding. I'd thought wrong.

Reluctantly, I put my hand in his, but the minute I did, he used all his strength, pulled me into his arms, and carried me down the hall.

Wasn't this touching? Why was it different when it was him doing the touching and not me? I didn't have time to think of such things as people slowly trickled out of the classrooms. I saw two professors then. They nodded at Nixon and one even took a sip of his coffee as if this was a normal thing to face every day.

I closed my eyes and leaned my wet head against his chest.

He smelled so good.

I raised my free hand and rested it against his muscled chest. He tensed, sucking air into his mouth as if I had just caused him great pain. And then he relaxed as we walked into another building.

It was smaller than the three large classroom buildings and was nestled between the science hall and the gym.

He tapped his card against the first steel door we came to. The door slid—yes, slid—open, *Star Trek* style.

Nixon walked in but didn't put me down. I struggled in his arms, but damn, that boy was strong. My eyes caught a glimpse of the room. A pool table stood in one corner. A flat screen TV took up an entire wall, and there were several leather couches and a bar. Wow, it looked like the president's suite.

I glanced up at his face. It was impossible to read. He bit his lip, causing the lip ring on the side to disappear, and then I saw it. I almost blurted out loud that he could seriously be Channing Tatum's twin. That is, if Channing Tatum had dark curly hair and a lip ring, but still. It was almost uncanny. I told myself to stop staring, but I couldn't help it.

His gaze fell to mine, then lowered to my lips. He spoke in low tones. "You need to clean up."

"Because I'm a whore?" I choked back the tears.

He laughed, the bastard. "No, I think we both know you're not a whore. You need to clean up because you smell like egg and sugar water."

Was that why I felt itchy? Ugh, I hated college kids. He led me further into the suite.

"Get in." He opened the door to a small room, a bathroom, and began pulling my clothes off so fast I couldn't stop him.

"What the hell, Nixon! You can't just strip me—"

"I can and I will. Now step out of your skirt like a good girl."

Too tired to argue, I stepped out. The sound of running water filled my ears. When had he done that? I lifted my arms as Nixon tugged my button-up shirt, then my tank top, off, leaving me in my bra, underwear, and knee highs.

Nixon's face froze.

Embarrassed, I tried to cover myself up. It was all too much. Being called a whore, having eggs thrown at me. No meat!

I crumpled into his chest and sobbed. "I miss cows!"

Nixon burst out laughing. Good Lord, but that boy's laugh was musical. I wanted to bottle it up and keep it all for myself. "Sweetheart, I'm sure they miss you, too. Now do you think you can manage the rest?"

"The rest?" I repeated, pulling slightly away from his chest, the same muscled chest I had just ruined by sobbing all over.

He raised his hands and cupped my face. His touch felt so good. I closed my eyes. "Open your eyes, Trace."

I opened them. And they were staring directly at his perfect lips.

"Do you need me to help you take off the rest of your clothes, or can you make it from here to the tub without killing yourself?"

My legs did feel shaky, but it was embarrassing enough standing there in nothing but my underwear. "No, um, I can do it."

He breathed into my neck. Was he smelling me? Didn't I smell like egg still? "You sure? I wouldn't want anything to happen to—"

I slugged him. Laughing, he stepped back. "Towels are in the cupboard under the sink. We have everything you need next to the tub. Just...don't drown, okay?"

"Why would I drown?"

He sighed heavily. "Just..." He slammed his fist against the counter. Holy crap, what did I do now? "Just don't make me worry, okay? I hate worrying."

Didn't everyone? "Fine." I nodded. "I'll try really hard to keep myself from mermaid-ing it. Deal?"

Without looking at me, he nodded his head and walked out of the bathroom, slamming the door behind him.

Geez, that boy had more mood swings than Grandma'd had when she went through menopause.

I quickly stripped off the rest of my clothes and leaned over to feel the water. It scalded my hands. Perfect.

It was tricky lowering myself into the Jacuzzi tub. Finally I was immersed, except for my knee. The scrape was still bleeding, and I knew it would hurt like hell the minute it went underwater.

I just didn't know how bad.

"Ow, ow, ow! Crap!" I blew on my knee and waved my hands in the air.

The door to the bathroom burst open. "What happened?"

I looked at Nixon. A shirtless Nixon. Was he planning to join me too?

Then his gaze locked with mine and went lower. I didn't cover up this time. I think I was in shock or something. Warmth spread through my body, and it had nothing to do with the bath water. His eyes darkened.

He took a step toward me and then another.

"Nixon! Are you in here? Is she okay?" Chase called.

With a curse Nixon backed out of the bathroom and slammed the door. My heart beat wildly in my chest. What had just happened?

Confused and exhausted, I decided to be quick about the bath. I ducked my head under the water. Peace and quiet. It was so nice. My stomach grumbled underwater. Of course it did. I was losing weight on this whole vegan kick, mainly because I was eating Cheerios and granola bars like they were going out of style.

After fifteen minutes, my hair was washed and I was squeaky clean. But I didn't have any clothes to change into. I paced the bathroom for a few minutes and tried to even my breathing. I didn't want to barge out of the bathroom in all my naked glory asking for clothes. What if other people were out there?

"You can do this, Trace. Just ask for some clothes." I gave myself a pep talk, nodded my head once, and reached for the door. The minute my fingers touched the knob it jerked open and I fell directly into Nixon's shirtless, muscled, and tattooed arms.

We both froze. His fingers dug into my shoulders. My face smooshed against his chest. He was breathing heavily, and I was trying to remember not to faint.

"You need something?" he whispered into my ear. Lord, how did even his whisper sound sexy? Shouldn't there be laws against guys crazy as sin being sexy?

"I need..." My voice cracked. Great. "Um, I need something to wear."

"Hmm..." He gently pushed me away and looked down at my towel. "Are you sure about that?"

My knees seriously began knocking together. Why did he have to be so beautiful? And why did his touch make me want to sell my soul?

I licked my lips and broke eye contact.

Nixon released me and immediately I felt so cold I shivered. "I'll find you something. Give me a few minutes."

He jogged off, giving me a beautiful view of a tattoo on his back. It was huge, almost taking up his entire torso—a cross with the word *Famiglia* under it, and a few other things.

My eyes scanned the rest of the large room. It basically looked like a bachelor pad. Or a hangout. There were chairs with individual game consoles hooked up to them, each labeled with a name. On the far side of the room opposite the TV little closets with uniforms in them had names above each uniform.

Holy hell, I was in the Bat Cave. This must be the Elect headquarters. I'd just taken a bath in the Elect bathroom.

All I needed was to be seen leaving this place and the entire campus would be even more relentless in calling me a whore. Then again, maybe they would see me as being under Nixon's protection and leave me the hell alone; one could only hope. But luck hadn't exactly been on my side, so I wasn't going to hold my breath.

I slumped against the wall.

Nixon appeared a few minutes later with some clothing. Every piece had a tag on it. "So..." He scratched his head. "I, um, I guessed on the sizes, and I honestly didn't want to offend you by guessing too big or guessing too small, which is why it took me five years to pick something out. So don't get pissed if I was wrong, okay?"

A laugh escaped my lips. "Okay, I promise I won't get mad." I took the clothes from his hands and went back into the bathroom.

The jeans were designer. The only reason I knew was because the tag said three hundred and ninety dollars. I swallowed and pulled a sweater from the pile. It was cashmere and soft, exactly the type of thing I'd want to wear after a crappy day.

A small pink box near the bottom said VICTORIA's SECRET. What? Was there a freaking mall in this place? Well, it was the Bat Cave, and it was Eagle Elite. I shrugged and opened the box.

My eyebrow lifted. A thong? Really? The matching bra wasn't so bad, and wonder of all wonders, it was a 34C, which actually was my size. Then again he had just seen me topless and...oh crap. I leaned against the counter and took a few deep breaths.

It only took me a few minutes to get dressed. I tried to comb the tangles out of my hair with my fingers and grabbed my dirty clothes off the floor.

Nixon was waiting in the large room drinking something and watching TV. "Better?" He took another sip from his cup and never took his eyes from the TV.

"Squeaky clean, and I'm happy to announce that no drowning took place in your bathroom."

He smirked and nodded his head.

Okay, so was this the part where I was supposed to say thank you and bolt like a scared deer?

I cleared my throat. He still didn't move.

Right. "Well, thanks for...everything. I'll just go back to—"

"You aren't going anywhere until classes are dismissed. You have two hours to burn, so make yourself at home."

"But..." I held the damp egg-smelling clothes in my hands. "I need to get these cleaned and..."

Nixon swore and launched himself from the couch, stalking his way toward me. He grabbed my uniform along with my underwear and tossed them into the trash. "Done."

"What, you have a magical trash can that cleans clothes?"

"Nope. You can't wear those again. They're ruined and there are rules here. You can't just wear a ruined uniform."

"I hate the stupid rules!" I stomped over to the trash can and tried to free my clothes. "This uniform is all I have!"

Nixon pried away the death grip I had on my clothes and dragged me over to the couch. "Sit."

"But—"

"Sit." It wasn't a question, it was a command. I stuck out my tongue. He licked his lips and smiled. "You thirsty?"

Deep breaths. "No."

"Hungry?"

My stomach growled. *Damn traitor!*

"That's what I thought."

I refused to turn around even when I heard him messing around in what was probably the kitchen. A few curses and slamming of pots and pans, and then he returned.

With a cow.

Okay, not a live cow. A dead one, in the shape of a hamburger and fries. My mouth watered and sadly I felt tears prick in my eyes. "Thank you."

I was now officially the lame homeless lady who had no money, no food, and cried when people offered her meat. Sigh.

"You need to eat more." He cursed.

Just then the doors opened. Chase strolled in with a garment bag, followed by Monroe, Tex, and Phoenix. *Welcome all to the room of humiliation!*

"Are you okay?" Monroe ran to my side and hugged me.

My mouth was full so I just nodded.

"I made her half a cow." Nixon laughed. "I'm sure she's in meat lover's heaven right now."

"Aww, you killed a cow for her?" Monroe sighed happily.

"Good God, people, he put frozen meat in the microwave and pressed defrost," Chase muttered. "Is this all you needed, fearless leader?" He held out the garment bag.

Nixon nodded. "Right sizes?"

"Yup."

"Good," Nixon said in a clipped voice. "Just put the bag over there, and we'll take it over once classes are out."

Chase's face was stern but he did what Nixon said. His jaw flexed as if he wanted to say more but was held back.

Phoenix kept looking at me funny, as if I might launch myself at him and beat the living daylights out of him. I kind of wanted to, all things considered, but I felt kind of powerless against him.

Tex sat between me and Monroe and put his arm around her. "So, what are we doing this weekend?"

"We"—Monroe ducked under his arm and placed it back on his knee—"are doing nothing. *I'm* going to be a good friend and hang out with my roommate, who was brutally assaulted by stupid assholes who go to our school."

Tex pouted. "Nixon, can't you just order a hit on the ones who started it so I can have some alone time with your sister?"

I laughed. "Order a hit? You guys talk like he's mafia or something."

The room fell silent and then everyone burst out laughing.

But it was the kind of nervous laughter that happens when nobody knows what else to do.

Freaky.

I finished the burger while Monroe and Tex argued over what to do with me where I wouldn't get into trouble or cause myself physical harm. Finally I couldn't take it anymore.

"Guys! Just go hang out. I was going to go to the store anyway."

"No!" everyone said in unison.

"Is the store dangerous or something?"

Monroe shrugged. "No, it's just not smart. I mean you shouldn't leave campus by yourself. Besides, you need a car. You don't have a car."

No, but I had a bit of money stashed away. "I'll take a cab."

Monroe looked horrified. "A cab?"

Tex burst out laughing. "Do those still exist?"

Nixon turned off the TV, which got everyone's attention.

"So…" Chase began, thrusting his hands in his pockets. "What will it be, Nixon?"

He eyed me briefly before answering. "I guess we're all going shopping."

"But—" Monroe started and Nixon gave her a warning glare.

"We'll take security." He shrugged.

"But last time—"

"I said"—Nixon's nostrils flared—"we'll take security."

Chapter Eleven

After the last class ended for the afternoon, Monroe walked me back to the dorm. It was safe to say my messenger bag was completely destroyed. Grumpy, I threw it on the floor and grabbed the box that Grandpa had given me. I hadn't looked past the framed picture since that night, but I had stuffed that wad of cash underneath a whole bunch of stuff in the box in order to keep it safe.

I hoped Grandpa wouldn't be too upset that I was using the emergency fund for food and a new bag.

At least Nixon had gotten me a new uniform. Correction, he had bought me three. Each outfit had a different sweater underneath—one was red, the next gray, and the final one was blue. Typical Eagle Elite colors.

I guess that was the errand he'd had Chase run, and honestly I was super thankful. The last thing I wanted to do was buy a new uniform that would cost more than my book bag.

"Ready?" Monroe asked from her side of the room. She'd been eerily quiet since the whole "We'll bring security this time" talk. Maybe she didn't get out much? Or maybe Chicago really was as scary as I thought it was.

"Yup, just let me get my cash." I opened the box and dug for the cash. My fingers hit something cold. Curious, I dumped the box onto my bed.

A few things came out: the small picture of Grandma and me and a picture of my parents. Weird. I hadn't seen one of those since I was really little. We didn't display many family photos around the house. Grandpa said they just made him sad.

My eyes focused on the wad of cash and then on something totally unexpected. A necklace; a giant silver cross with diamonds in the middle lay across my bed. I picked it up, expecting it to be costume jewelry and therefore really light. It wasn't. In fact, if I wore this thing around my neck and went swimming I'd probably drown.

I examined it in my hands and then flipped it over. "Alfero."

That word sounded crazy familiar when I repeated it out loud.

"What did you just say?" Monroe asked, suddenly right behind me. I tucked the necklace into my jeans pocket and shrugged. For some reason, repeating the word out loud made me panic, like I wasn't supposed to be saying it. So I lied. I lied to the only friend I had.

"Alfredo," I said. "I could go for some Alfredo."

Monroe's pale face sagged with relief. "Oh, oh sorry, I just thought…" Her eyes narrowed. "Never mind. No biggie. You ready?"

I nodded and grabbed the stash of cash, then carefully put all the contents back in the box. "Let's shop!"

We walked arm in arm down the three flights of stairs, deciding we didn't want to talk to anyone if they were in the elevators.

The minute we reached the first floor, I felt a freedom I hadn't felt since I'd arrived five days ago.

Monroe began chatting about Tex, so I wasn't paying attention to the commotion outside until Monroe stopped talking and let out a heavy sigh. "Looks like everyone is ready."

I gawked. Four black Escalades were lined up against the driveway with a black Range Rover in front. So five cars. "Are we taking the whole school?" I asked breathlessly.

Monroe laughed. "No, silly. Just us and the guys."

"Right." I watched in amazement as the guys, aka the Elect, got out of the Range Rover and motioned for us to get our butts in gear.

"Are all those cars coming?" I pointed behind me.

Monroe shrugged and said nothing.

A guy with aviators and an earpiece ran to the front door and opened it for me. He looked like he belonged on Air Force One, not here at the school.

I mumbled a thanks and got into the car. "Um, does someone want to tell me why we need so much security?"

Nixon started the ignition. "We're important."

"Right."

Monroe was in the backseat with Tex. I assumed Phoenix and Chase were in one of the other cars. My tension increased as we drove down the long tree-lined driveway and finally reached the gate.

The armed guard there waved then spoke into his walkie-talkie and motioned for us to go on through.

Had I thought my little grocery excursion would be this ridiculously guarded, I would have snuck out. I mean, four cars?

I groaned into my hands.

Nixon stopped at the first light and nudged me. "What's wrong? Are you sick or something?"

"No, I just…Is it really that unsafe for you guys out here?"

"You could say that."

He leaned forward to turn on the heat. Great. Now I was going to sweat to death. The guy was already killing me with his good looks. Heat? Heat I did not need right now.

We drove in silence, and for some reason each time I moved, the necklace in my pocket kept poking me in the thigh. Stupid tight jeans. Exasperated I pulled it out and clasped it around my neck.

"Are we almost there?" I asked, adjusting my cashmere sweater so that the necklace dropped over it prettily.

"Yup, in like ten— Holy shit." Nixon slammed on the brakes. "What the hell, Trace?"

"What? What's wrong?" I looked around for the obvious danger, but Nixon wasn't staring out the window. He was staring at my chest.

"Where the hell did you get that?" He reached for my necklace but I smacked his hand away.

"Stop." He shook his head, hit his hand against the steering wheel, then started cursing in some sort of language that sounded vaguely familiar.

"It's not worth cursing over," I snapped. "It's just a necklace."

"You understand me?" he asked in whatever language he was speaking. I could only nod because honestly I had no idea how I understood what he was saying.

A vague flicker of a memory entered into my brain. A man with dark hair pushing me on the swing and telling me in that special language how beautiful I was. That I looked just like my mother. And then some strange men came and began cursing, just like Nixon had cursed.

Suddenly I couldn't breathe.

"Crap," Monroe muttered. "I think she's having a panic attack."

I nodded and tried to unbuckle my seat belt. Nixon's hand came flying down across mine. "We're in the middle of traffic. You're staying here. I don't care if you think your freaking heart is going to explode. We can't be vulnerable, and right now, we are."

I nodded through the swell of tears that began pouring down my face. What was wrong with me? And why was I suddenly having flashbacks? Was that man my dad? Who were those other men?

Nixon continued to curse until we made it to the grocery store. Finally, once we'd parked, he turned to Monroe and Tex. "Leave, both of you. I'll deal with this."

They scrambled out of the car. Geez, it wasn't like he was going to shoot them or something.

I waited, my chest still heaving with frustration and a little bit of confusion and fear.

"What's your last name?" Nixon asked, quietly popping his knuckles.

"Rooks," I answered dumbly. "Why, what's yours?"

"I'm asking questions. You're giving answers. You understand?" His eyes blazed hot. I tried to back away, but my seat belt pinned me in place. "Now, I can ask nicely or I can use force. What is your last name?"

"Rooks!" I all but screamed. "It's all I know!"

He raised his hand and leaned in. I flinched, afraid he was going to hit me. Instead he reached for the necklace and turned it over. "Damn it!"

"What?" My lips trembled. "Look, Nixon, this was a bad idea. Just take me back to the dorms. I don't need the security detail like you guys do. I'll just come back in a cab or something. Plus, you're freaking me out. I'll just find my own way home."

"The hell you will!" He reached across and grabbed my hand. "Let's just...let's just get this over with, okay?"

Freaked out, I could only nod. My gaze left his face and that's when I noticed what was on his hip. "Why are you packing a gun?"

He closed his eyes and sighed. "Because it's part of the rules."

"Of the school?" I asked, incredulous.

"No." He smiled sadly. "My family. Now, let's go."

I guessed this part of the conversation was over.

Begrudgingly, I got out of the car and stomped into the grocery store. Grabbing the first cart I saw, I began mindlessly wandering the aisles. At least I tried to mindlessly wander. This was hard to do when every time I picked up a can or a package of something, one of the creepy men in black suits Nixon had brought along stared at me as if there might be a bomb hidden in the tomato soup.

Weird.

All I knew was that the Elect must be way more important than I could possibly imagine or even believe.

I finished in the dry goods section and made my way over to the candy aisle. I needed a little boost after all the crap that had gone down today. I settled on Twizzlers and sighed.

"Almost done?" Nixon asked out of nowhere.

I screamed.

And immediately ten men in suits were in my aisle, guns out.

Awesome.

Nixon laughed. "I scared her. Nothing's wrong."

The guys nodded and disbursed.

"Who are you?" I swallowed as Nixon's breath fanned my face. Oh gosh, I was going to faint if he kept getting this close to me.

"I could ask you the same thing." His eyes narrowed as he cupped my face and examined my eyes. "Brown. Interesting."

"Brown?"

"Your eyes."

"They're plain." I tried to pull my head free from his grip, but he tightened it.

"They are beautiful. Don't let anyone tell you any different, *bella*."

His eyes searched mine and then he leaned in more. Our lips were inches apart. My heart was going crazy. I leaned in.

"Hey, Nixon, the guys are getting antsy," came Monroe's voice. I wanted to tell her to leave.

Nixon jerked back immediately and shook his head, as if he had been the one under the spell, when he very well knew he was the bastard who'd cast it.

"You done?" He pointed to the cart.

"Um, yeah. I'll just go check out." I pushed my car to the checkout stand. Nixon stayed behind me, patiently waiting.

"Glad to see you're buying enough food so you don't starve in between classes." He smirked.

"It's your fault I have to buy food," I snapped, a bit irritated and still obsessing over the almost-kiss.

"What do you mean?"

"My key card, you asshole!"

He rolled his eyes. "Stop being difficult. You have two key cards."

"Huh? Are you high?" I threw a bag of potato chips at his head. "Phoenix stole my card the night you made him set me up! That same night you were off-campus doing who knows what! I only have the red card that you gave me the other day!"

The color drained from Nixon's face. "What the hell are you talking about?"

Okay, he was high. I mean, he was there! "In the hall when you said that was the best you could do, and you handed me the card to the Red Cafeteria!"

"Because Phoenix said you were uncomfortable eating with us. The Red Cafeteria is better than the Commons—"

He gripped the shopping cart, and I could tell a battle was waging in his mind. Finally, he shook his head. "Bastard. I'll deal with it. Do you still need this food then? If you're going to be eating with us now?"

"Yes." I swallowed, because who knew when I was going to make him or one of the other guys angry and lose my rights to eat meat again?

"That will be one hundred dollars and seventy-two cents," the checker announced, sounding bored out of his mind.

I pulled the roll of bills out of my hand and tugged off the rubber band. The wad of hundreds fell to the ground. This was what Nixon's stupid presence did to me. It made me nervous and a bit crazy.

I swiped the bills off the floor and froze.

Impossible.

"Something wrong?" Nixon asked in an irritated tone.

"Uh, no, yeah, umm…" I didn't really know what else to do, so I handed him the stack of bills. The same stack that was wrapped in a one hundred dollar bill, in order to cover the ten one-thousand dollar bills.

"Shit," he muttered, then pulled out his own wallet. He swiped his card in the ATM and punched in his code, then placed the card on the little table there while he pulled out his cell. "No, you ass. I didn't have cash on me. Yes, I know I can be traced. Who pays you, dipshit? Who? That's what I thought. Now deal with it."

"Abandonato," I whispered under my breath, reading the card while simultaneously trying not to eavesdrop. "Is that your last name?"

He didn't answer me. Instead he was firing off instructions to someone on the other end of the phone and grabbing the receipt.

Well, at least the checker didn't look bored anymore. Nope, he looked like he was about five seconds away from shitting his pants.

And then things got weird. As in, weirder than they already were.

Nixon's men in suits formed a circle around us as we walked back to the car, and that's when I saw something I'd only seen in movies: a group of expensive cars in the parking lot, and even more expensive-looking men and old men getting out of the cars.

Nixon said nothing as we got into our waiting SUV. Neither did I. I wasn't sure if I should be freaked out that so many men in suits were surrounding us or what.

"Are we, um... are we safe here?" I asked in a small voice.

Monroe was already sitting in the SUV and put her hand on my shoulder. "Of course. Why wouldn't we be?"

"Oh you know, because of that." I pointed as a man who looked as old as Grandpa pulled out a gun I'd only seen in action movies, and walked into the store.

"Um, are we witnessing a murder?"

Tex and Monroe laughed while Nixon shook his head and offered a smile. "No sweetheart, just business. That's all."

He handed me my wad of cash and looked back at Monroe and Tex. "You guys need to go. We have some more shopping to do, and it—"

Monroe rolled her eyes. "Yeah, I can imagine how it will be." She smiled in my direction. "See ya later!"

They hopped out of the car and walked to the other waiting
SUV in front of us.

"What was that about?" I asked, shoving the money back into
my purse.

"It's going to be a long afternoon." Nixon whistled.

"Why?"

"Because we are freaking living our own *Romeo and Juliet*." He
smirked and hit his steering wheel. "All right. New bag, right?"

"Yeah, oh, and I need to pay you for the groceries, too. I feel so
stupid. I had no idea I had big bills, or that they even existed, or that
Grandpa..." My voice trailed off. Why would Grandpa give me such
big bills? Was that why he wanted me to hide it?

"Those bills went out of circulation in the fifties. You know that,
right?" Nixon asked.

I shrugged and started playing with the radio. "Sorry, I'll figure
out a way to cash them out so I can pay you."

"You don't understand." He laughed without humor. "I would
never accept your money. Ever."

"What? Why?"

"It's no good to me!" He snapped. "Just drop it."

Was it because I was beneath him? Because I was from a farm
and, if not for the Grandpa's stash, poor? I crossed my arms over my
chest and looked out the window. We were silent the entire way to the
mall.

Chapter Twelve

Two of the SUVs followed us to the mall and two more were waiting for us when we got there. The minute I jumped out of the Range Rover, Nixon grabbed my hand and didn't let go.

I wish I could say that I didn't feel the warmth of his touch spreading all throughout my body. But I did. And it was amazing. He smiled as we made our way through the front doors, and I could almost imagine that this was normal. That we were just hanging out and shopping like two normal people.

Instead, we were being followed by a security detail that would irritate President Obama and stared at as if we were going to bomb the food court.

I hated to admit that I had no experience shopping. I wasn't really sure what to do, but I didn't want Nixon's charity or anything. "Do they have a secondhand store or something here?"

He looked horrified, as if I'd just asked if there were any puppies to kick.

"Hell, no. Secondhand store? Are you—" He cursed and shook his head. "Secondhand? A freaking used clothing store?"

"Okay, you can stop repeating it already," I snapped, trying to jerk my hand free from his viselike grip.

"Girls like you don't shop there."

And there it was again. Girls like me. Girls who didn't belong in Elite, who shouldn't be salivating over their student body president. I felt my face heat and dropped my gaze to the ground. "Um, what about a Ross? Or Walmart or something?" I was so embarrassed I couldn't even look at him.

He stopped walking, making me almost trip as he released my hand and cupped my chin. "Trace, did you not hear anything I just said?"

Tears blurred my vision. See, that was the problem. I heard everything, and I was so tired of being told I wasn't good enough! So exhausted pretending to be something I wasn't when I had only been at their damn school for a week.

I tried to pull free.

Of course Nixon wouldn't have any of that.

Instead, he wrapped his arms around my body and sighed into my hair, kissing my head. "You are...impossible."

I didn't really know what to say to that.

"Mason, don't follow so close, all right?" Nixon said over my head to one of the security guys.

"Of course, sir."

"Sir?" I repeated, although my words were muffled from my face being against his muscled chest. He pulled back and again grabbed my hand.

"It's a respect thing."

"You're like twenty," I pointed out, glad that we weren't focusing on me and my shortcomings anymore.

Nixon's face tensed, then flashed with humor. "Right, twenty." He looked away and mumbled, "Age doesn't really matter in my world."

"Your world?"

He didn't look at me. He seemed to be on a mission. And then we stopped walking. Well, he stopped walking. I would have kept going, because there was no way I was going into that store.

"Prada?" I said aloud. "Are you insane?"

He smirked and pulled me toward the store.

I dug my heels into the ground, or at least I tried to. But who I was kidding? Nixon was a god among men; he simply pulled my arm and I followed him into the beautifully lit store. My eyes couldn't absorb everything I was seeing around me. So many purses and bags and colors and... A girl could die happy this way.

"May I help you?" A skinny woman in a black suit smiled in our direction. Her gaze lingered longer on Nixon than should be proper, considering he was still in college. Although to be fair, he didn't look it. I stole another look out of the corner of my eye. Seriously, twenty? He looked so much older, more mature.

"Messenger bags. Do you carry messenger bags?" Nixon asked this as his eyes took in the walls of the brightly lit store.

The woman beamed. "Right this way."

Within a few minutes I had five different types of bags displayed in front of me. One was a men's leather bag, which was kind of cute. The others were nylon, which I guess was fine. I mean, they were Prada.

My fingers itched to check the price tags. Honestly, I didn't even want to touch them. I mean, what if the oil and germs from my hands somehow got onto the bag and—

"Trace, pick a bag." Nixon urged me forward, almost forcing me to touch the pretty objects. I reached down and then for some reason, probably my nervousness, I looked to the right. Near the counter on a display was a beautiful royal blue bag. I probably should have looked away, but I couldn't.

My eyes widened just slightly. I cleared my throat and looked back at the bags in front of me.

I felt rather than saw Nixon walk away. Shivers ran up and down my arms at his absence.

"This one." Nixon returned and handed the blue bag to the woman.

I didn't want to look at her, but I couldn't help it. Her face was impassive, but I could see a muscle twitch in her jaw. "This is a special edition—"

"For a special girl." Nixon put an arm around me. "Then it's perfect."

Shaking her head, the woman walked to the counter and rang up the purchase. "That will be one-thousand seventy-five dollars and eighty-nine cents."

I coughed. I swear it was involuntary. Was Nixon insane? That much? For a bag? I opened my mouth to say something, but he very purposefully elbowed me while he took out his wallet and flashed her a black credit card.

The minute he handed it over she checked the name. "May I see some ID, Mr.—"

The card dropped out of her hands. Shaking, she licked her lips and shook her head. "Never mind."

"What?" Nixon leaned forward. "You don't need my ID?"

"No, Mr. Abandonato. Th-this-this will be fine." With trembling fingers she handed over the receipt and the bag. "Is there anything else I can get for you?"

Nixon flashed a smile. "No, I think we've had enough. Thank you for your...help."

Good God, the woman was going to pass out. She nodded and pinched the bridge of her nose as we turned around and walked out.

"What the hell, Nixon? Are you like the Godfather or something?" I laughed nervously. He joined in but his laugh was hollow.

"So, frozen yogurt?"

"Why?"

He shrugged. "Because I'm hungry?"

I sighed. "Fine, but this isn't a date and this isn't babysitting detail. You know I can take care of myself, right? You can just take me back to the dorms. I've got a paper to write anyway and..." My voice trailed off the minute his hand touched mine. Confused, I looked down at our grasped hands. I didn't even realize we had stepped onto an escalator until we hit the top floor. He didn't release my hand. I was torn between wanting him to release it and wanting to smack him upside the head. He couldn't just toy with my emotions like this. Make me feel important for no reason other than his own entertainment. Growing angrier by the second, I tried to pry my hand free, but his grip tightened.

"It isn't safe, Trace," he said in hushed tones. "Just trust me, okay?"

"Then why are we getting frozen yogurt?"

At that he smiled, but still refused to answer. I called *false* to his whole "I'm hungry" statement. *Right, he's hungry. He wasn't the one on the no-cow diet for the past week.*

The food court was decent. Not many people were scattered around either, which I was thankful for. Our security detail basically circled us as we went into the small frozen yogurt shop and grabbed our cups.

"Okay, what do I do?" I held the cup in my hand and stared at him.

"Uh…" Nixon scratched his head. "You eat it?"

"The cup?"

"No, not the cup." Nixon barked out a laugh. "You're kidding right? You've never had self-serve?"

I swallowed and looked down feeling all kinds of stupid. "Look, just forget it." I tried to shove the cup back in his hand, but instead he grabbed my wrist and flipped me around to face a giant contraption on the wall.

I swear this guy's body heat could start a fire if he so desired. "Read the flavors…" he ordered.

"Out loud?" I snapped.

"Hmm, I think I may like that."

Okay, he was standing way too close to me. I could practically taste the minty gum he was chewing. *Focus, Trace. Focus.* I was just a plaything. Oh great, I was what rich boys resorted to when they were bored. Well, at least he hadn't called me Farm Girl for a while. "New York Cheesecake, Blueberry, Chocolate Chip, Vanilla, Chocolate, Cake Batter…"

"Why do they sound better coming from your lips, do you think?" Nixon whispered in my ear.

Holy hell, I couldn't feel my legs. The guy had me absolutely paralyzed.

"Want a sample?" He moved from behind me and grabbed a small pink spoon. Pink looked good on him, less scary, but not less hot. Unfortunately...

I briefly closed my eyes and imagined him in a Barbie minivan hoping to expel the way his masculinity made me want to strip down to nothing and throw caution to the wind.

"Open." I opened my eyes and my mouth, since I really didn't have a say in the matter. But then again, it was Nixon. I wasn't given a vote. Ever. The frozen yogurt was cold and creamy against my tongue. "You like?"

Oh, such an open-ended question. His eyes hooded as he dipped his head closer to mine. I couldn't tear my gaze away from his plump lips as they descended. His warm mouth was suddenly on mine and then like the little tease he was, it was gone.

"Sorry. I thought I saw some frozen yogurt. My mistake." He laughed and backed away.

Ass. "Liar," I said, breathlessly pushing past him. "So what—do I just pull on one of these thingies?"

"Well, I prefer the word 'stroke' but—"

My face erupted into flames. I jerked my head away and managed to shakily get some frozen yogurt into the cup. I didn't even look to see what flavor it was. I just knew I had to get the hell out of there before I allowed Nixon to get any closer.

The guy had already threatened to destroy me.

He'd proven he could do it.

So he was suffering from temporary insanity and being nice, all because of my necklace? Or was it because of what had happened at school?

Lost in thought, I started putting toppings on my frozen yogurt.

"Wow, didn't take you for a gummy worm type of girl."

"Huh?"

Nixon pointed to the cup in my hand, where I had stacked five gummy worms on my yogurt. "Uh, yeah, I love…worms." *Classic. Someone should record the gold that flows from my mouth.*

Nixon licked his lips. I could see the ghost of a smile dancing across them. This was the most I'd seen him smile…in forever. I both liked it and hated it. It nearly killed me every time he directed a smile in my direction, because I knew it wasn't just fleeting but fake. Nixon didn't seem to be the type who offered something without taking something in return, and I suspected my payback was coming up.

"Ready?" the bored teenager at the till asked.

"Yup." I handed him my cup. He placed it on a scale and then placed Nixon's on the scale. "Twelve dollars and nineteen cents."

For yogurt?

I kept my mouth shut while Nixon handed over his card.

The kid glanced at the card and then did a double take. His mouth dropped open and then he snapped it closed. At least he wasn't shaking like the last cashier had. With a quick swipe he handed back the card and the receipt.

We started to walk out, but he spoke up. "Um, I know this sounds really dumb, but can I have your autograph?"

Nixon froze. His nostrils flared as he looked at me and then handed me his frozen yogurt. I watched his right hand clench and unclench as he walked up to the kid. Holy crap, was he going to punch him in the face?

"Sure thing…" He bent over the counter and signed a napkin the kid had handed to him. "What's your name?"

"John." The guy looked like he just met Brad Pitt.

Nixon scribbled something and then handed the napkin back to John. "We have an understanding, John? Nobody knows we were here?"

John's eyes widened and then Nixon leaned over the counter. "I need to hear you say it, *John*."

"You weren't here." John stumbled over his words. "I swear."

"And where did you see us?"

"On the street. You, uh, you were going for a run."

"I do like running." Nixon lightly smacked the kid's shoulder and winked. "Thanks again, *John*."

"N-no problem, Mr. Abandonato."

I frowned the rest of the way to the car.

Chapter Thirteen

I wasn't really sure why I was so exhausted, other than the fact that I had just had both the most emotionally draining and the weirdest week of my life.

"One more stop." Nixon had been driving back toward the school but took a left before we came to the right road.

Boo. Was I never going to get a vote? Was it wrong to use my new Prada bag as a pillow?

"The bank?" I asked once we stopped.

"Yup."

"Why?"

Nixon laughed. "Asks the girl who's carrying around thousand-dollar bills. I take it you don't have an account?"

Embarrassed, I shook my head.

"Well, let's go then." He jumped out of the car. I had no choice but to follow him into the large glass building. It was four stories, but every angle and plane of the building was pointed as if it was some sort of angry porcupine.

Intimidated, I tried to stay close to him.

I noticed that we only had one security guard with us.

"Nixon, where'd the rest of the suits go?"

He turned and grabbed my hand but didn't answer my question.

Okay, the silent game. I could play.

We walked right past all the desks where people were answering phones and working and went into the elevator.

Expecting it to go up, I gasped when it shot down into the basement.

The basement? Really?

He grabbed my hand again as we walked through a long marble hallway. In front of us there was a giant wood desk, where a girl with long dark hair sat filing her nails.

"Hey, Priscilla, where's Anthony?" Nixon asked.

"Oh, you know, sharpening kn—" Her mouth shut as she stood and held out her hand. "I'm sorry, and you are?"

"Trace." I shook her hand. "Trace Rooks."

She nodded and then glanced down at my necklace. "Rooks, you say?"

"Yup."

"Doesn't sound like—"

"Pris, we need to open an account."

Her smile didn't reach her eyes. "Of course you do. I'll just let Anthony know you are here."

Nixon shook his head. "No need, I'll let myself in."

"Enter at your own risk, Nixon."

"Come on." Nixon tugged my hand. We took a left and walked down a shorter hallway lined with creepy old portraits of men in suits holding guns. Great. And we were in a basement.

Nixon pressed his thumb against the magnetic thingy and the glass door opened. "Anthony?"

"In here."

The office was beautiful. I thought we were in a basement, but there were still really wide windows beyond the desk that looked out onto a pond. Was that a plane? How was that even possible?

"We need to open an account," Nixon repeated.

" 'We'?" Anthony turned around.

Holy hell, the man looked like an older version of Nixon. Was this his dad? No, he looked too young. I waited to be introduced.

"Technically, she needs to open an account. I would have gone to one of the other branches, but lucky girl has thousand-dollar bills."

Anthony's eyes widened briefly before he turned to me. "What did you do, rob a bank?" He cracked a smile.

I grinned back. "I didn't know they were big bills. My grandpa gave me some money before I was dropped off at school and there was a fiasco with my uniform and bags and—"

"Fiasco?" Anthony's brows lifted. "This I have to hear."

"Anthony—" Nixon was cut off by the guy waving his hand in the air.

"Make yourself useful, Nixon, and grab yourself a drink."

Nixon muttered a curse and walked over to a bar in the corner.

"So, you were saying?" Anthony nodded his head.

My palms began to sweat. "I, uh . . . the people at school kind of drenched me in sugar water and raw eggs. My messenger bag suffered a very slow, sticky death."

"The worst kind, I'm sure." Anthony nodded.

"Absolutely," I agreed. "I guess technically it's my fault, since I rejected that one's rules on the first day." I pointed at Nixon, who narrowed his eyes. "But he did save me from social suicide. Not that I was already high on the popularity totem pole, anyway...but yeah. Long story short, we went shopping, I busted out my money. Nixon almost had a stroke. Men in suits entered the grocery store with guns. Pretty sure I'm going to see that on the evening news, and...now we're here."

Anthony's face remained impassive. "All right. Sounds like a normal day in the life of Nixon. Welcome to the family..." He held out his hand.

"Oh, no, no, no, no." I laughed nervously. "No, it's not like... that."

I waved both hands in the air like a crazy person.

Anthony's head tilted to the side. "I've known Nixon for a long time, and I can tell you one thing for sure. It is very much...like *that*."

I heard a groan from Nixon and something that sounded like another curse.

"Now, an account. Do you have your social security number?"

Embarrassed, I shook my head. "Grandpa said it was lost in the move."

"The move?" Anthony repeated, walking around his desk and hitting a few keys on his computer. "Where did you move from?"

"Chicago."

Nixon spewed the contents of his drink onto the floor and began coughing. "Sorry, Uncle Tony."

Ah, *uncle*. That made more sense.

Tony shook his head in annoyance but said nothing. "So, you're from Chicago. Why did you move? Your parents come with you?"

I shifted uncomfortably on my feet. What did this have to do with me opening an account? Soon I felt Nixon's hand grab mine. "My grandparents thought the city was too violent, I guess? I don't know. My parents were killed in an accident when I was six so…"

"An accident?" Anthony repeated. "My sincere apologies for your loss."

I shrugged. "I don't remember much."

"Probably for the best," Anthony said pointedly.

"Um, what does this have to do with opening a bank account? I'm sorry, I'm not trying to be rude; I'm just really exhausted."

"Shopping does that to you," Nixon said.

Anthony laughed. "I'd say Nixon does that as well…"

"Very funny." Nixon shook his head.

"All right. Miss Rooks, was it?"

I nodded, a bit alarmed that Nixon hadn't introduced me by name. Then again, he could have texted him, right? Or read his mind? Great, I really needed to put those vampire books down.

"I'll work some magic and open your account without your social security number. I'll add the address to the school. Do you have a phone number where I can reach you?"

I gave him my cell number while he typed. Thankfully it had not been destroyed as I'd feared.

"And the cash?" He held out his hand.

Nixon reached into his back pocket and handed him the wad that I'd pulled out of the box this morning.

If Anthony was surprised, he didn't say anything. Instead he counted the cash. It was around ten grand, which was what Nixon had guessed.

He put it through a little machine. I signed something and he gave me a temporary card. It was black, just like Nixon's.

"We good?" Nixon asked, folding some of the paperwork and stuffing it into his pocket.

Anthony nodded. "For now."

Huh? What was I missing?

"All right." Nixon grabbed my hand. "See you Sunday, Uncle Tony."

"You too, Boss. Don't forget the time, or your pops is gonna throw a fit."

"Yeah, yeah." Nixon waved him off and we left.

The ride back to school only took a few minutes. I was quiet, mainly because I was confused and tired.

Once we pulled up to my dorm I unbuckled my seat belt, but something was still bothering me about the whole situation.

"Why are people afraid of you?"

Nixon smiled. "Aren't you afraid of me?"

I gulped. "Sometimes."

His eyes got sad as he reached across the console and grabbed my hand. "You know I would never let anyone hurt you, right?"

"See?" I didn't mean to yell. "That's what I'm talking about! A few days ago you were telling me I was basically the cockroach beneath your shoe! Now you've taken me shopping? I'm sorry; it doesn't add up."

"Yeah, well, life rarely does." Nixon swore and then groaned. His face was tight, as if he was in severe pain. "Look, I was just warning you, that's all. And just because I'm being nice to you doesn't change the fact that you have to follow the rules if you want to survive here."

"Thanks. Got that memo loud and clear once I was drugged and drenched with sugar water." Not to mention condoms, but saying that out loud in front of a complete stranger who screamed money just didn't seem like the best conversation filler.

"Damn it, then why not just do what I say?"

I shrugged. "I don't like being bossed around."

"No shit." He smirked. "But sometimes it's for your own safety. Can't you see that? Maybe the world isn't as shiny and fun as you once thought. People are mean. Humanity is a cruel joke, Trace. I'm just trying to prevent them from getting the last laugh."

I sighed. "So, why do they listen to you? Why do you get to make the rules?" My mind couldn't connect the dots. If he was behind the egging, he wouldn't have saved me, and that's what he did. He rescued me.

He froze. A mask slipped from his face and then it was just a boy and a girl in a car, talking. The air felt electric as he reached out and touched my cheek. "I wish that wasn't the case. I wish I didn't have to make rules...or enforce them."

"Then don't." I reached out and placed my hand against his chest.

His eyes closed. "Sometimes we aren't given choices. We just are."

"What does that even mean?"

Nixon opened his eyes and slowly removed my hand from his chest. "It means that you should have listened to me on the first day of school." His head tilted to the side. "Don't touch the Elect. Don't breathe the same air as the Elect, and don't..." He cursed. "Just don't."

"Why?" My lower lip trembled.

"Because you are up to your eyeballs in shit, and you don't even know it. And once you know...what everything's about...the choice will be taken from you, too. Hell, what am I saying? The choice was gone the minute your gramps dropped you off."

"Choice?" I rolled my eyes. "You're pretty serious and cryptic to boot. You know that, right? What are you? Some kind of famous celebrity? A politician's son? The president's dirty little secret?"

At that he cracked a smile.

"…Hmm, that dirty little secret thing sure rings a bell. Don't worry your pretty little head over anything, all right? Go do your homework and relax."

Apparently I wasn't going to get any answers. I grabbed my new bag and my purse and hopped out of the car. "Thanks for… everything."

Nixon's full lips curved into a smile. "My pleasure. Now go get some work done. I'll send Chase over in a few."

"Chase? Why?" I put my hand on my hip. Was I still under baby-sitting protection?

Nixon shrugged. "So no one bothers you. Why else?"

"Why don't you check on me yourself? Why send a minion?"

He barked with laughter. "A minion, huh?" He bit his lip, making the ring tilt to the side. Damn, I hated how sexy he was without even trying. "If I came and checked on you, I'd definitely be bothering you."

"Annoying the hell out of me is more like it," I shot back.

"Bye, Farm Girl."

And there it was, the perfect ending to the weirdest day of my life.

"Thanks for that." I flipped him off.

His response was to moo. Classic.

Chapter Fourteen

Monroe was already in the room waiting for me.

"How was shopping?" She sat cross-legged on her bed, filing her nails.

"Oh swell. You know, other than seeing crazy guys in suits with guns and then having the devil buy me a Prada messenger bag to replace my old one."

Monroe grinned. "Come on. Everyone knows the devil wears Prada."

"Thank you, Monroe." I glared. "That was really helpful of you. Why'd you bail, anyway? Do you always do whatever Nixon says?"

She snorted. "Yes, most of the time. Even though he's the devil incarnate—and an ass—at least he keeps me safe."

"From what? Hormonal college students? Ice cream cones falling on your shoes? I don't get it. Who are you guys?"

"Wanna watch a movie?" She blew her hair out of her face and began searching through her collection of DVDs like a madwoman.

"Okay, I get it. Touchy subject. I'll just do an Internet search on your last name."

Her hand froze over a DVD, but she didn't say anything. Maybe it wasn't that big of a deal, but I quickly got on to the room computer and typed in *Abandonato*.

Holy crap. So not what I expected.

Their name was on everything. And when I say everything, I mean everything: Abandonato Enterprises, LLC. They owned the school. They owned the bank I'd just gone to, the grocery store, the actual mall, the gas stations. And my favorite—not car *dealerships*, no, because that would be too normal—they owned car brands. A few foreign brands. Crap.

"And I thought the Mormons owned everything..." I said under my breath.

Monroe choked on a laugh. "Heard that, Boots."

"What *don't* you own?"

"Disney World?" she offered.

Very funny.

"Is that why you guys take so much security everywhere?"

Monroe peered over my shoulder at the screen. "We're worth a lot of money. Our dad's kind of paranoid, you know? He's worth billions. Imagine if one of us was kidnapped for ransom?"

That made sense. Logically, I could tell myself that people would be afraid of power, but it still didn't explain why that one kid had asked for Nixon's autograph.

"Are you guys celebrities or something like that?"

Monroe laughed. "Around these parts? Let's just go with the *something like that.*"

A knock sounded at the door.

I clicked out of the screen and went to open it.

Chase stood there, hands in the pockets of his jeans. A tight sweater hugged his perfect body. I looked away.

"Hey, Chase," Monroe called.

"Hey, Mo…" His eyes turned to mine. "Hey, Trace."

"Nixon send you?"

"Yup."

"You staying?"

"Yup."

"You gonna say anything but 'yup'?"

He placed his hands on the door frame and leaned forward, his lips about an inch from mine. "I'm not much of a talker. I'm more of an action sort of guy."

"Bet you are." I nodded. "Please come in, make yourself at home in our lovely prison."

"It's not a prison." Monroe rolled her eyes. "Nixon just wants to make sure you're safe, and although I could probably kick a couple asses on our floor, we'd be screwed if the football team decided to pull a prank on us."

"And why would they pull a prank on us?" I asked.

"You're the shiny new thing. Who wouldn't want to play with you?" Chase shrugged. "I know if I had the chance to—"

"I think it's safe to say I know where that sentence was going to end."

"Oh yeah?" Chase plopped down onto my bed in the same manner Nixon had a few days ago. "And how's that?"

"With my shiny new boots up your ass." I smiled.

"Damn."

"What?" I pulled out my notebook and opened to English Comp.

"Nixon's a lucky bastard."

"Huh? Why?"

Chase grinned. "I've never been good at keeping my hands to myself, though."

Monroe groaned. "Chase, don't. It's like a death wish. Just…don't."

"You won't always be around, Mo."

"No, but if you touch what belongs to the devil he'll probably damn your soul. Just saying. And if you want a part of the businesses when you graduate, you need to be on your best behavior."

He cursed.

I had no idea what they were talking about. "Right, so that was a weird conversation. I'm just going to work on a paper."

Nobody said anything.

Three hours later, I was exhausted but finished. It was only eight at night. How pathetic. I was a freshman in college and I got my homework done early on a Friday night while being babysat by some boy who was part of the "Godfather"'s clique.

Gossip Girl had nothing on this school.

I purposefully plopped my book onto the bed, jolting Chase out of his sleep. "Shit! What did you do that for?"

"Fun. It was fun. And I'm finished; you can go. I have done all my homework in peace, because of you."

I got up and opened the door.

Chase laughed but didn't move from his spot.

"Chase! I mean it. You don't have to stay."

"He's just doing what I told him to," Nixon said from the doorway. "You done with your paper?"

I glared at him but then began frantically running around my room, throwing clothes into the air and checking my closet.

"Mo, your friend has officially lost it."

I heard her laugh, but I was on a mission. They had to have cameras or something. How had he known practically the second I finished my paper? Ridiculous! Maybe I was just being paranoid because of the day I'd had, but come on!

"Trace." Nixon came up behind me, grabbing my arms as I threw a sweater into the air. "Trace." This time his lips grazed my ear, and I stopped. Not because I wanted to, but because I honestly couldn't move my arms and speak at the same time when he was that close to me. "What are you doing?"

I hung my head. "Looking for hidden cameras."

"What kind of guy do you take me for?" He turned me around in his arms so we were face to face.

I looked down. "The kind who carries guns and sends his friends to babysit me in my own dorm room. The kind who knows the minute I'm done with my paper and magically appears at my door. That kind."

Nixon burst out laughing. "Wow, you are just too much." He reached into his back pocket. I slowly backed away. I mean, what if he pulled out a gun? Or a Taser or . . . crap. A cell phone.

"Ever seen one of these?" He flashed it in front of my face. "Chase texted me ten minutes ago and said you were close to being finished."

"He was sleeping. He—"

"Is a light sleeper and was under strict instructions to tell me when you finished."

"Why?" I crossed my arms. "So you could send in the next shift? Who's it gonna be this time? Tex? Phoenix?"

When I said "Phoenix" he scowled.

"Are you done?"

"Yes, but—"

"Thanks, Chase. See ya later." Nixon pulled me down the hall like a bat out of hell.

"Where are we going? And why are we in a hurry?"

Nixon didn't answer. He swiped his card and the elevators opened. The minute they closed he hit the button for it to stop.

Holy crap. This was how I was going to die.

"Nixon, what the—"

He had me pushed back against the wall before I could finish my sentence. His mouth pressed against mine and he lifted me into the air, pressing our bodies tightly together. The metal of his lip ring sent electrical shocks through my system as it rubbed against my bottom lip. Good lord, I'd never been kissed by a guy like this before. Ever.

With a groan, he released me. I didn't mean to touch him, I just did it. I grabbed his hand but he jerked free. "Please, no touching."

Not okay. So he could maul me but I couldn't even graze him? "Nixon, you can't just—"

"Yes, I can." He folded his arms across his chest and leaned back against the opposite wall. "And I did." He pushed the button again, causing the elevator to descend.

Son of a whore. I wanted to punch him in the face. I think he could tell too, because he kept smiling. Who the hell did he think he was? So, what? People were afraid of him because he was rich? Because his big bad daddy owned everything? That didn't mean you could make out with a girl just because you felt like it. It didn't mean you never had to make excuses for your behavior. And it sure as hell didn't mean you could kiss a girl senseless then order her not to touch you.

"So is that how this works then, Nixon? You take, but you can't receive?"

He bit his lip and stalked toward me just as the doors opened. "Funny. I didn't think I was taking."

"Oh yeah?" My eyebrows shot up.

"Yeah." He grabbed my hand before I could pull it free. "I was giving."

I stuck out my tongue.

"Do it again, see what happens," he threatened.

I kept my mouth shut. Something had shifted between us this afternoon. Something big—I just didn't know what it was. A day ago I was worried he'd look the other way if a car was barreling toward me. Now...Well, now it felt like he would do anything to keep me close—almost as if he'd lost me before and knew what it felt like to be without me. But that was crazy. Clearly I'd never been kissed like that before, because my mind was conjuring up all sorts of crazy stories. I needed to stop reading so much.

We went outside and started walking across campus.

"I didn't know." He swore violently. "About what Phoenix did."

"I thought you'd told him to do that, because of your little challenge earlier about not offering me protection and stuff."

He stopped and pulled me next to him. "Do you really think I'm that much of an ass that I would really drug you, set you up to look like the school slut, and then take away your key card so you were up a creek with no paddle?"

I shrugged. "You said you wouldn't protect me anymore, that—"

"Shit. Girls are so dense sometimes." He ran his hands through his hair. "I was upset, Trace! You're so damn argumentative and you never listen! I was trying to scare you for a few days. I wasn't going to throw you to the freaking wolves!"

"Oh."

He grabbed my hand and kept walking. My hand felt so small in his.

"Where are we going?"

"You'll see."

And he was officially done talking. He picked up the pace when we got behind the gymnasium. Toward the back side of the fence a few trees had been planted in order to make the place look more like a park than a school, which I guess was somewhat typical for a rich university.

Nixon stopped in the middle of the grass and whistled.

Holy football team.

A few lights turned on—almost like a spotlight—and then Tim, the quarterback I'd supposedly slept with, walked out into the spotlight. He looked scared shitless.

I looked behind me. Phoenix and Tex were standing there silently watching. Nixon took off his leather jacket and held it out. Tex slowly walked up and took it from his hands then gave me a wink.

"Tim," Nixon said in a stern voice. "Do you know why you're here?"

Tim nodded, his eyes flickering to mine and then back to Nixon's.

"Words, Tim. I need to hear you say it."

"Yes."

"Yes, what?"

"Yes, sir." Tim's voice sounded strained.

"Tim, did you or didn't you have sex with this girl?" He pointed to me. I wanted to disappear on the spot. Crap, for some reason I felt like it was my fault... If only I hadn't taken that drink from Phoenix....

"No."

"No... what? I'm losing patience, Tim."

"No, sir. I did not have sex with Tracey Rooks."

"Interesting." Nixon moved closer to Tim and cracked his knuckles. "And who told you to spread the lie about Tracey?"

Tim said nothing.

"You hear that, everyone?" Nixon turned around and lifted his hands into the air. The guy who'd kissed me in the elevator and the guy in front of me now were two very different people. His muscles flexed in the moonlight. He pushed back a few pieces of fallen hair. "His answer is silence. Well, at least he's not a rat. Right, Tim?"

Tim didn't say anything. He just stood there. Head held high.

Nixon laughed and then punched him across the jaw. Hard enough to cause Tim to stumble. Blood oozed from his lip, but he still didn't say anything.

"How long will this take, Tim?"

Tim smiled.

Nixon punched him again. This time Tim fell forward, giving Nixon the perfect opportunity to use his knee. Blood spewed from Tim's nose as he cursed and fell to the ground. "Still silent, Tim?"

Crap, why wasn't anyone doing anything? Horrified, I looked back at Tex. He shook his head, as if giving me a silent message not to do anything, but I was too scared to run anyway. My feet were locked in place.

"More?" Nixon asked and then landed another blow to Tim's jaw, and another, and another until I thought he really was going to kill him.

Finally Tim cried out. "Phoenix! One of your own! He said you would be pleased."

"He said I would be pleased?" Nixon laughed. "Tim, do I look pleased?"

"No."

"No, what?" Nixon said in a deadly voice.

"No, sir. Sorry, sir. It won't happen again. It won't—"

"Damn right it won't happen again. Now get off your sorry ass and apologize to Trace."

Tim slowly got to his feet and stumbled toward me. His left eye was beginning to swell and blood was caked on his face. "I'm sorry for any trouble I may have caused you, Trace."

Nixon came up behind him and grabbed his arms, thrusting him into the crowd of football players in front of us. "Clean him up."

An abnormal amount of *yes sirs* came from the guys who helped Tim walk away. People began to scatter. Including Tex and Phoenix.

"One more thing," Nixon said loudly. Everyone froze in place. "Phoenix...come here. Now."

Phoenix's normally smug face paled as he slowly walked toward Nixon, avoiding eye contact. "Yes, sir."

"Why?"

"Because you never—"

The sound of knuckles hitting flesh almost made me puke as I saw Phoenix hit the ground and Nixon shake his hand.

People gasped. My mouth dropped open. Whispering commenced. I wasn't sure if it was normal for Nixon to hit his own friend. I mean, he didn't seem the type. I just ... I didn't know.

"What should your punishment be?" Nixon circled him. "I leave for the night to take care of family business—a business you have interest in—and while I'm gone you betray me by ordering your own hit on the new girl?"

"She was disrespecting you!" Phoenix all but yelled.

Nixon leaned down. "So you thought to disrespect me, is that it? You thought disrespect equaled more disrespect?"

Phoenix said nothing.

"Since when has it ever been okay to drug an innocent girl? Hmm, Phoenix?"

He was silent but then said, "Chase took her."

"He also told me everything tonight and will be carrying out his own punishment over the next year."

I had a sick feeling his punishment had to do with babysitting duty. Kind of like protecting me from what he'd caused. Oh joy.

"What? Nothing to say?" Nixon asked.

Phoenix shook his head. "No, sir. I'm sorry, sir."

"You will be," Nixon mumbled. "You're out, Phoenix. Broken. You're a *cafone*."

"What?" Phoenix surged to his feet. "You can't do that to me! My father will—"

"Son," came a deep voice. "It's already been discussed. Just let it go."

"What?" Phoenix roared. "I gave everything to you! To your family! You promised!" He tried to land a blow on Nixon, but Nixon stepped out of the way. Phoenix was already too hurt to do much damage anyway. "You son of a bitch! I'll kill you!"

A large burly man came up behind Phoenix and whispered something in his ear. Phoenix's eyes grew. I've never seen such hatred behind someone's glare in my life. I was suddenly afraid for Nixon, afraid for anyone near Phoenix.

"This isn't over, Nixon. You can't just break away from this—from us! You're making a huge mistake. I hope you realize what you're doing."

"I do," Nixon said confidently. "And I hope you enjoy working in fast food. Because it's the only kind of place that will hire you if you as much as breathe in her direction again."

Phoenix spat at the ground and jerked away from his dad, disappearing into the shadows of the night.

His dad, who I recognized as the dean, stood there looking helpless. "Are you going to . . . tell—?"

"No." Nixon cut him off. "This is between us, *was* between us. Just keep him away, and it won't go any further."

"Thank you, sir."

Nixon nodded. The dean left.

"What the hell kind of school is this?" I muttered under my breath.

Tex answered. "I thought you'd have figured it out by now. It's his." He pointed at Nixon.

"Says who?"

"The American dollar." Tex put his arm around me as I shivered. "A couple billion of them to be exact . . . Well, that and the Abandonato family."

"So the last name Abandonato covers a multitude of sins. Is that it?"

Tex sighed. "The last name Abandonato either covers the sin or gets you killed. Either way the outcome is the same, I guess."

"And what's that?"

"You're never free."

"Of what?"

He was silent. Which scared me more than anything. When I'd entered the lottery to go to this school, all I could think about was how I would be practically set for life.

Now it seemed like I'd stepped into an action movie where the star had more power than the president of the United States. Just who were the Elect and why was it such a big deal to be kicked out of their ranks?

I needed answers, but I wasn't so sure Nixon would give them to me.

"You okay?" he asked.

"Do I have to say *yes sir* too?" I asked in a shaky voice.

Tex burst out laughing. "She's all yours, man." He walked off into the dark still cracking up, and I was left with the Ultimate Fighter.

Chapter Fifteen

"Y̶ou okay?" I asked in a small voice.

Nixon nodded. "I'm good." Blood was crusted across his knuckles. I wondered if it hurt. With a curse he handed me his jacket and took off his tight-fitting Henley, revealing a tight black sleeveless shirt underneath.

He wiped off his hands with the Henley and then put his jacket back on.

"So…" I shoved my hands in my pockets. "I'm not sure if I'm supposed to say *thank you* or *what the hell were you thinking*."

He shrugged. "They had it coming. Tim should never have listened to Phoenix, and Phoenix should have stayed the hell away from you. He had rules and he didn't follow them."

"There we go with the whole rules thing again," I mumbled.

"Rules make the world go 'round." Nixon laughed and then put his arm around me. "The rumors should die down now, okay?"

"Yeah, but aren't people going to talk about this? And why was the dean so chill? I mean, he's like twice your age."

Nixon shrugged. "We have an understanding."

"Right." I nodded. "What type of understanding? He follows your rules or you shoot him in the face?"

Nixon laughed again. "Wow. Thanks, I needed that." His eyes glistened in the moonlight. "Is that what people do on TV, shoot people in the face?"

"Yes. Well, no. I guess. I don't know." I sighed. "What are you? Some sort of gangster or something?"

"Sure." His fingers moved to the back of my neck, caressing the skin just below my hairline. "Let's go with that. I'm a gangster."

"Have you ever killed anyone?"

"Have you?" he fired back as if offended I would even ask.

Well, that shut me up. His hand moved to my cheek, sending shivers down my spine. "It's not fair," I said breathlessly.

"What?" His eyes were on my lips.

"That you can touch me, but I can't touch you." *That you look like a god and I look like a poor farm girl.* I sighed and stepped away from him.

He tilted his head to the side. "Would you rather I not touch you?"

"No!" I blurted, then covered my face with my hands.

He chuckled and pulled me into his body so my head rested against his chest. "I just don't understand. What's so different? I mean, we're touching now, but..."

"I'm in control of it." He exhaled and tilted my chin toward his. "I know it sounds crazy. I just...I don't like it when people touch me without permission. Ever since I was a kid, after..." He swallowed. "Anyway, it doesn't matter. It's just this thing I have."

"Like the rules?" I whispered.

"Yeah, like the rules." His thumb grazed my lower lip. "You're beautiful, you know."

I laughed awkwardly and tried to tilt my chin down but he wouldn't let me. Why I was letting the guy who put the fear of God into the dean touch my face, I don't know. But... there was something about him. Something that made me want to touch him, made me crave his touch, and I hated that I responded to him, especially after the way he'd treated me at first.

"Don't," he whispered against my cheek as he bent his lips to my ear. "Don't pull away from me, please."

"Okay." My voice was shaky and wobbly and my heart pounded like I'd just run a marathon. Breathe. I just needed to breathe.

His lips found my neck and I let out an involuntary gasp.

"So sensitive," he murmured as his tongue wet his lips and then drew a design just below my ear. "So damn sensitive. Your skin's so soft right here."

I shivered as his mouth met my jaw. His hands moved to clench in my hair, forcing me closer. "Nixon." My voice was weak. "What are you doing?"

His lips met mine. The kiss was brief. He sighed. "I wish I knew."

"You can't just..." I swallowed. "You can't just go around kissing people you hate."

"Who said I hate you?" He released my head and stepped back.

"Well, you weren't exactly shaking my hand and shouting my name a few days ago."

Nixon licked his lips. His hooded eyes blazed a hot trail across my body until I thought I might die from wanting him right then and there. "So you want me to shout your name? Is that what this is about?"

Laughing, I pushed him away. "Stop being such a guy. I'm serious."

"Oh, believe me..." He ran his hand along my shoulder and down my collarbone until his fingers brushed the first few buttons of my shirt. I had no doubt in my mind that the guy probably had an A+ in stripping women of their clothes with one hand. "I'm dead serious."

I swallowed the nervous laughter bubbling up within me and stepped out of his reach. "So, gangster, you gonna tell me why you've taken personal interest in running this school?"

Taking the hint, he shoved his hands in his pockets and fell into step beside me. "I like things to be fair."

"Wow. Then you're at the wrong school for that."

"You know what I mean. I do what I can when I can. Besides, it's kind of one of my jobs, to keep the peace around here, keep the secrets, keep everyone happy. It's exhausting, actually."

"I have a hard time imagining anyone making you do anything."

He laughed bitterly. "You haven't met my dad."

I stopped walking and pulled his hand. "What do you mean? Is he...is he bad?"

Nixon sighed. "Well, he's no Mickey Mouse or Santa Claus, if that's what you're asking." He bit his lip and opened his mouth as if he was going to say more. Instead he grunted and grabbed my hand. "Doesn't matter. Anyway, I was going to ask you earlier but then I got distracted by all your drug money..."

I rolled my eyes.

"Does the name 'Alfero' mean anything to you?"

"Alfero?" I repeated. "Hmm...kind of like Alfredo and without the D?"

"Yes. As in the food." He glanced at my necklace and sighed. "It's on the back of your necklace."

"So?"

"So..." He nodded his head. "You know it's okay for you to tell me. I won't say anything. I mean, I know I'm an Abandonato, but it's not like, you know, I'll set Jimmy on you or anything."

I burst out laughing. "Are you high?"

His eyes narrowed. "No."

"Wow. Then you have to know I have no idea what you're talking about."

"You don't?"

"Nope."

"Good." He sighed and kicked the ground. "That's—wow—that's really, really good."

"I think you must have lost more blood than you realize in that fight." I nudged him with my elbow.

He laughed. "At least I can say I'd freaking bleed for you, if that's what it takes."

"Takes?"

He stopped and reached out to touch my chin, lifting my face toward his. "To keep you safe."

"So you'd die for me?" I joked, trying to break the awkwardness.

"Don't you get it?"

My breathing became erratic as he leaned close enough to kiss me again. "I'd give my life for yours."

"Why? You don't even know me."

His eyes closed, and when he opened them all I saw was pain and regret. "You have no idea what I know, and believe me when I say your life is worth a hell of a lot more than mine. And yes, after tonight, you better believe I know you better than anyone, even better than you know yourself. I hope to God it stays that way, Trace."

Just as I was about to open my mouth to ask more questions, because basically that's all I'd had ever since coming to this school, headlights were on us. The dorm was in front of us, but the road was suddenly blocked by a few expensive-looking cars.

Of course they were all black.

Did no one believe in color around here?

"Trace, go inside."

"But…"

Nixon gripped my arm and turned me toward him. "Trace, I need you to listen to me right now. You take this." He handed me his black key card. "You don't walk. You run until your legs burn. You run into the building, you run into the elevator, you run down the damn hall, and you lock your door until I come and get you. Do you understand?"

Freaked out, all I could do was nod. Nixon gripped my hand closed over the key card and whispered it again. "Run."

I didn't need to be told twice. I ran like hell. And as I ran all I could think of was why wasn't I safe at my own school? And how did the people in those cars get in if they were bad?

I swiped the card and ran into the dorm. Once I was inside the elevator I looked out and saw twelve guys in suits walking toward the dorm. As the doors to the elevator closed, I could have sworn I'd seen Grandpa among them.

God, I missed him. That's why I was freaking out.

The elevator dinged and I ran to the room and locked the door behind me. Monroe was already on the bed.

"What the hell, Trace? You got murderers on your tail?"

I shook my head and gasped for breath. "I don't know. I just... Nixon told me to run, so I ran. And he got into a fight with Phoenix and Tim and—"

"It's fine," Monroe said quickly. "You saw the fight?"

I nodded.

"Then you know Nixon can take care of himself, right?"

I nodded again.

"Great. Let's watch a movie."

"What!" I yelled. "I can't just watch a movie while your brother could be getting murdered!"

Monroe burst out laughing. "Believe me when I say nobody would be stupid enough to murder my brother."

"Are you insane? I—" My phone started ringing. Well, at least it was working. I'd had my doubts after the sugar water incident. I looked at the caller ID. *Oh, good.* "Hi, Grandpa!" I practically shouted into the phone.

He chuckled on the other end. "Sweet pea, how was your first week of school?"

"Oh...you know. Um, boring," I lied. If I told him the truth he'd be on the first plane out here, and I felt guilty enough that I was having as much trouble as I was. I'd relied on him my whole life; now it was time for me to grow up and try to deal with things in a mature way.

"They treating you nice up there at that fancy school?"

Immediately, I relaxed. I missed him so much. I was so freaked out, but if I told him what had happened he'd probably come up here with his shotgun and sit outside my dorm room. He and Nixon had that in common. "Yup, everyone's super nice."

"Oh, honey, I knew it. I'm so glad."

He was quiet for a while and then he added, "Trace? Did you open your grandma's box?"

I sighed happily. "Yes, sir! I haven't looked at everything, but I wore the necklace today!"

"Aw, that does my heart proud! She loved that necklace, Trace."

I was itching to ask him more about it, but my caller ID lit up. "Hey, Gramps, can I call you back?"

"Oh no, don't worry about me, Trace. I gotta go do the night feeding for the cows. You stay out of trouble, okay?"

"Okay! I love you!"

"Trace, I love you more. Good night, sweet pea."

"'Night!"

I switched lines. "Hello?"

All I could hear was creepy breathing on the other end. Awesome. My night was complete. I quickly pressed END and threw my phone against the bed.

"You okay?" Monroe asked. "How's the grandpa? Hmm, why don't we watch *The Proposal* or something?"

"No"—I waved my hand in the air—"to all of that." With a grunt I plopped onto my bed and groaned.

"Hey." The bed dipped as Monroe came and sat next to me. "It's fine, I promise. Nixon is . . . Nixon is. Well, that's the thing. He's Nixon. I'm sure he had a good reason for sending you in here and freaking the crap out of you, but let's not forget how protective brother bear is."

"Right." I shivered, not because of fear, but because I hardly thought Nixon and I were turning into a brother bear relationship. And if that's how he would categorize it, then I had a hell of a lot more problems than men in suits and creepy phone calls.

A knock sounded at the door. I flung myself off the bed. Almost tripping over the blankets, I reached for the door. "Who is it?"

"Nixon."

When I opened it, Nixon was leaning against the frame and looking at his cell phone. Without thinking, I pulled him into my arms and hugged him. There went all the rules about no touching or breathing the same air again. But I was so freaked out and...

Holy crap, he was like a warm statue, but then his arms very slowly wrapped around me. I was pretty sure, in that moment, that Nixon's arms were my favorite place to be in the world, but bliss didn't last all that long. I realized he had no bumps or bruises and he'd been texting—yes, *texting*—before I hugged him.

With a shriek I pulled back and smacked him on the chest. "You scared the crap out of me."

He grinned. "You sure do run fast, Farm Girl. They teach you that in Wyoming?" With a slow wink he walked around me and gave his sister a brief hug as well.

"Something's very wrong with you." I slammed the door and crossed my arms.

"Don't I know it," Monroe muttered. "And what the hell, Nixon? You can't just go scaring my roommate like that. I thought she was going to have a heart attack and tell her grandpa she was witness to your murder."

"Believe me, her grandpa would not have come to my rescue." Nixon snorted.

"Hey!" I pointed. "You don't even know him! He's a good guy."

"Did I say he was bad?" Nixon held up his hands defensively. "I just said he wouldn't come to my rescue."

"If I asked him to he would," I argued.

Nixon laughed. "Your innocence is both aggravating and shocking."

Clenching my fists, I fought the urge to stomp my foot and glared at Monroe. He was her brother. I refused to keep dealing with his mood swings.

"We should watch a movie," Nixon said after I sat on the bed like a normal human instead of stomping around the room like Godzilla.

"She doesn't want to," Monroe said, pointing in my direction. *Yes, because I'm the one who is not being reasonable right now.*

"Who were those guys?" I asked.

Nixon ignored me. "She saw me beat the crap out of two dudes tonight. She should watch something funny."

Monroe nodded. "A chick flick and maybe some chocolate?"

"Hello!" I waved my hands in the air. "I'm right here."

Nixon waved back. *Bastard.* Monroe had yet to look up from the movie selection.

"Nixon." I hissed his name. "Who were those guys and why did I have to run?"

"Guys from work." Nixon shrugged. "They just had a few questions about what went down tonight. I just didn't want you to stay if things got weird, and the less people that they know about who know what happened, the better."

Damn. That did sound convincing. But work? What college student had grown men working for him? It again begged the question, just how old was he? And what type of business...ugh. My brain hurt. "Fine. We'll watch a stupid movie," I grumbled.

"Excellent." Monroe threw the DVD at Nixon, who in turn popped it into the computer. He sighed and laid his head on my pillow.

Angrily, I jerked the pillow from underneath him and beat him on the head with it.

"What the hell was that for?"

"It slipped." I shrugged innocently.

"Slipped, my ass..."

"Children!" Monroe sang. "Behave or I'm not going to give you snacks."

"She started it—"

"Nixon Anthony—"

I pinched him and laughed. "She totally middle-named you just now."

"Trace..." There was a warning edge to her voice, so I shut up and sat as far away from Nixon's body heat as I could. But it was nearly impossible, especially when Chase and Tex showed up halfway through the movie. According to Chase, his back hurt when he didn't have a bed to sit on. Screwy logic, so I let him sit toward the bottom with his back against the wall. My feet would have been touching him, so I sat up. The minute I sat up, Nixon sat up. The minute he sat up, I dipped toward him.

And that was how I ended up falling asleep with my face on his shoulder. At least that's what I told myself when I woke up at three a.m. Nixon was staring at me like a monster in a horror movie.

"Are you trying to give me nightmares?" I whispered grumpily.

"No." His voice was hoarse. His arm shot out, and before I could stop him he had somehow flipped me around so he was spooning me. His hand ran up and down my arm, tracing circles and massaging every inch of exposed skin.

I snuggled back into him, trying to get comfortable.

He groaned low in his throat. "So not helping, Trace."

"Oh."

He brushed my hair aside and kissed my neck as his right hand dipped beneath my shirt. Tiny electrical shocks hummed through my body as his warm hand rested on my bare stomach.

"Nixon—"

"Please," he whispered in my ear. "I just want to touch you."

I fell asleep to Nixon, student body president, all-around bad boy extraordinaire's hand burning against my skin.

It was the best night I'd ever had.

Chapter Sixteen

You drool," Nixon announced the minute I saw him for first period Monday morning. After everything that had gone down Friday night, I desperately needed some calm time. Monroe and I had stayed in bed all day Saturday and watched movies.

She'd had a family dinner Sunday, so I worked on what homework I had left and then plunged into a vampire novel in order to forget the drama in my life.

It must have worked because like a total loser I fell asleep at seven at night and didn't wake up until my alarm went off Monday morning.

Nixon hadn't spoken to me since the night I'd fallen asleep in his arms. I was beginning to think I was the one going crazy and nothing had happened.

Tempted to flip him off, I merely mumbled thanks under my breath as I walked by his desk and sat down. One more week with him as our stand-in teacher, and then I would be home free!

"Movie day." Nixon addressed the class, took attendance, and then flipped off the lights as a documentary about early America began to play in black and white. Great.

"Hey," he breathed in my ear.

"Crap!" My desk moved as I jumped away. I turned around and glared. "Are you trying to kill me?" I whispered.

Nixon smirked. "Not at all. Remember? I'm the one who keeps you safe. I'm the one who would die for you and all that? Why, want me to prove my loyalty?" His teasing smile made me want to smack him with my history book, or maybe my lit book. That one was heavier.

"I'm trying to watch the movie." Oh gosh, nothing about that statement sounded remotely true. My voice even wavered into high-pitched, liar-pants territory.

"No, you're not." He sighed and leaned back. Every other kid was paying attention to the movie. Why was I the lucky one getting haunted by the Gangster of Christmas Present?

"Yes. I am." Flipping my hair, I turned back around and focused on the movie about America. *Ah, Indians. Focus on the Cherokees, Trace.*

A loud yawn interrupted me, followed by two arms that stretched so far beyond the desk behind me that they practically pulled me back with them.

Letting out a heavy sigh I looked heavenward and shook my head. Ten minutes later Nixon had maneuvered his hands underneath my mop of hair, and was in the process of massaging my neck.

In class being massaged by the substitute teacher. So not how I'd planned my second week of school going.

But dang, if my neck wasn't sore. I leaned heavily against his hand as he pushed against the tight muscles, and then I felt his other hand move beneath my shirt. No, no, he wasn't. No. No.

One strategically sinful hand massaged while the other one dove beneath my shirt. If he was going to cop a feel, his balls would be on the opposite end of my pencil.

However, whatever his other hand was doing, it felt good. He had moved down my back and was playing with the fastener on my bra. I tried to wiggle away. He laughed softly, much to my horror, so I stayed put.

"Hmm. I took you for more of a comfortable type of girl. Is this lace?" His lips tickled my ear.

Unable to use words, because clearly I'd forgotten an alphabet existed, I nodded.

"It's sexy."

Heat pooled in my stomach as his lips touched my ear again. This time his teeth came out and tugged slightly on my ear, almost making me gasp. His hand shot out from beneath my shirt as someone turned around.

Great, now it looked like political history turned me on.

That was just what I needed to be spread around the school: New girl moos in front of student body and orgasms during Freshman Politics.

Awesome.

I felt my face heat with embarrassment as a guy from class looked from me to Nixon and then back to me.

Nixon must have done something scary from behind me because the guy's eyes widened and then he turned around, his back ramrod straight.

I wasn't sure if I was irritated that Nixon kept his hands off me throughout the rest of class, or excited. By the time class ended a half hour later, the jury was still out.

After stuffing my politics book into my new Prada bag, I yawned and made my way toward the door.

"Where do you think you're going?" Nixon asked the minute my toe stepped over the threshold.

"To my next class?" I refused to turn around, and why the heck was I always last? My hand moved to my cross necklace. Touching it had become one of those things I did when I was nervous. I grabbed the necklace and rubbed the cross. Great, now I needed supernatural power just to be in the same room as Nixon.

"Come here."

"I didn't hear *please*." I smirked, but still didn't turn around.

A moment later his breath fanned my neck. Out of the corner of my eye I saw one muscular arm lean on the door frame as he slowly closed the door with the other. "Please."

I counted to three and turned around, expecting one of two things. Either he was going to murder me or kiss me. There really wasn't any other logical option, not with Nixon.

"Sit," he commanded.

I dropped my bag to the floor and crossed my arms.

"Please." He smirked.

"Fine." I went over to the desk closest to me and sat on it, careful not to let my skirt hike up. Tempting the devil wasn't the smartest thing to do, considering we were alone.

"I need you to do me a favor."

"I won't have sex with you. I'm not that kind of girl." I tilted my head and basked in the glory of taking Nixon by surprise, and also getting my revenge after he'd blurted all of that out in the middle of the dance floor last week.

"I deserved that." He leaned against the teacher's desk.

"And more."

"Care to punish me?"

"I'm leaving." With a huff I pushed away from the desk and grabbed my bag.

"Wait." Nixon's hand was on my arm. "I just, I wanted to warn you. Be careful, okay?"

I nodded.

"I'll see you at lunch?" His voice almost sounded insecure.

"Yup, remember? I've got your key card." Something I'd noticed this morning when I rode the elevator down to the first floor of my dorm—and did a fist pump!

"Keep it." Nixon's eyes fell to my necklace again. "Another favor?"

"Wow, you're just full of requests this morning, aren't you?"

Wrong thing to say.

Nixon's eyes heated as he stepped forward and with a little tug had me flush against his body. "Oh, I can think of some more favors. How bad do you want an A?"

"Not bad enough to see you naked."

He laughed softly and tilted my chin toward him. It was becoming a habit, looking into his eyes. I hated that I was getting used to him touching me. I hated it even more that I liked it.

"Don't wear expensive jewelry during the school day. I would hate to see you lose something important to you." His eyes darted to my necklace. "Please? That's something even my money can't replace."

Stunned that he would care, I could only stare at him with my mouth open. Nixon licked his lips and then looked behind me, before very gently tilting my chin toward his and brushing his mouth against mine. "Have a good day, Trace."

Uh-huh. Holy hell, my day was going to be all kinds of good if I got kissed like that. I opened my mouth to say something, but Nixon's two fingers pressed against my lips. "Don't ruin it by saying something. Now. Go to class."

Nostrils flaring, I stepped back, grabbed the door and flung it open, stepping out of the room and into the noisy hallway. *Straight lines, Trace. Just walk in straight lines.*

Chapter Seventeen

Straight lines were overrated. I decided this as I almost tripped over my own feet twice and face planted into some guy as I hurried to my next class.

I almost made it to the door before I remembered what Nixon had said. With a curse I pulled off the necklace. It caught on my hair. "Crap!"

I brought my rat's nest of hair in front of me so I could pick through it. When the necklace finally broke free it crashed to the floor and managed to skid a few feet away from me.

Okay, so maybe Nixon was right, and I'm a freaking accident waiting to happen. Rolling my eyes, I walked over to where it had fallen and knelt. A pair of shoes met my reaching hand.

"Allow me," came a familiar voice.

Frozen in place, I watched as Phoenix knelt down and picked up the necklace. "Pretty."

"Thanks." I held out my hand.

"What? I can't be nice?" He smiled and flipped the necklace over reading the name on back. "Hmm, pretty cool. Family heirloom or something?"

"I guess."

He nodded and plopped it into my hands. "I don't bite, you know."

"No, you just drug girls."

He held his hands up. "I guess I deserved that, but are you really going to side with the same guy who last week embarrassed you in front of the entire student body?"

He had me there. I took a step back and shrugged. "He apologized."

"Nixon Abandonato apologized to a farm girl from Wyoming?"

I nodded.

"Hmm." Phoenix crossed his arms. "Now, why does that sound suspicious?"

"What, that he'd be nice to me?"

"No. That he'd apologize to a nobody."

"A nobody?" Furious, I was half tempted to throw my book bag across my shoulder and hit him in the face. "At least today when I eat lunch I'll be sitting with the Elect. Where will you be?"

"Don't you worry your pretty little head about where I'll be... but good to know whose side you're on. It makes what I have to do so much easier."

I didn't like the way his eyes looked, as if he hated me almost as much as he hated Nixon. I took another step back and another until I was close to my classroom.

Phoenix smirked, and walked off in the other direction.

Sighing, I leaned against the wall by my classroom. Nixon had asked me to do two things, and five seconds after he'd asked me, bad things happened. Great. *Note to self. Listen to the Godfather.*

* * *

Lunch felt weird. Mainly because I could tell Chase and Tex felt awkward not having Phoenix there. I'd found out from Monroe that the guys had all been friends since the first grade. This was the one and only time any of them had fought, and clearly, it hadn't ended well.

Nixon showed up late. I played with the food Monroe ordered for me and pushed at my temples. A headache was coming on, I just knew it.

My phone sounded.

Curious, I picked it up. "Grandpa?"

"Sweet pea!" His voice was a bit hoarse. "How is your day?"

"Fine." I mouthed *Grandpa* to Monroe, stood up, and walked a few feet away from the table. "Are you okay? Has something happened? Are the cows out?"

"Oh, I'm fine, I just miss you. Which was why I was calling. Do you think you would mind seeing your old man tomorrow night? Grandma's life insurance company needs a signature, and well, you know how I get with doing things over the phone and faxing, so I was going to fly in and take care of business."

"Life insurance? Shouldn't that have been taken care of a while ago?" I asked.

Grandpa coughed. "Yes, well, I wanted to add you to my plan as well. I'm going to kill two birds with one stone." He chuckled.

I didn't.

Something was off.

"Grandpa, are you sure you're okay? You never go to the city. Aren't there some branches in Cheyenne?"

"Listen, I gotta go do the milking. Tomorrow night at seven, okay?"

"Sure, um, yeah—"

The phone line went dead. He didn't even say he loved me. My stomach clenched. Grandpa wasn't the type to just up and fly somewhere. Shoot, he wasn't even the type to take out insurance on anyone.

Dread pooled in my stomach. Nauseated, I didn't really want to go back to the lunch table and answer questions about Grandpa.

I bit my lip and sighed.

"Everything all right?" Nixon whispered from behind me. How he was always able to sneak up on me I'll never know.

For some reason I felt like blurting out my feelings to him. Go figure: the one person I should probably steer clear of and I just wanted a hug from him.

"Grandpa's acting weird," I mumbled.

Nixon tensed. "What did he say?"

"Something about my grandma's life insurance and stuff. I don't know, Shouldn't he have taken care of that months ago when she died?"

Nixon shrugged. "Who knows, Trace? Sometimes it takes a while to get death certificates and stuff. You just never know."

I nodded. "He's, um, he's flying into Chicago tomorrow."

"When?" A muscle flinched in his jaw.

"I don't know. He said he'd see me at seven."

"Shit," Nixon mumbled.

"Huh? Why is that bad? He's my grandpa. He's—"

"I know, I just..." Nixon grinned. "I had plans. I wanted to take you out."

"Well, you can take me out tonight."

Holy crap, did I just say that?

"Did you just ask me out?" He grinned.

"Uhh…"

"Intelligent as well as beautiful. Whatever am I going to do with you?" His thumb rubbed my lower lip. "Fine, Trace, I'll go out with you. How about six, tonight? Sound good?"

"No, no, not good, wait—"

Apparently I didn't get a vote. He sauntered off like he'd just won an Olympic gold while I returned to the table with a stunned expression on my face.

"Sorry." Chase poured me some water. "Nixon can be a little…"

"A lot." I nodded. "He can be a lot. A lot of the time."

Chase threw his head back and laughed. "Yes, yes he can."

Monroe threw a napkin at his face, or at least tried to. "Hey, watch it. He may be the devil, but he's my brother."

"I'm right here," Nixon said, sounding irritated.

"So? He's my cousin, which gives me familial rights."

"What?" I shrieked.

All eyes turned to me. Chase shrugged. "I thought you knew."

"What, through mind reading?" I threw my hands up in the air. "Unbelievable. Are all of you related?"

"Oh God, I hope not." Tex winked at Monroe. Overshare.

"Nixon said you met my dad." Chase took a swig of water.

"Anthony?" I looked really closely at Chase; it made sense now. Why he and Nixon were so close, and why they had similar features. Chase had dark hair and a muscular build, but nowhere near what Nixon had. He was also missing the lip ring and the all-around wicked glint in his eyes.

Chase cleared his throat. "Uh, could you not stare like that? I'm not as used to it as Nixon is."

"What do you mean, you're not as used to it?"

Chase shrugged. "Simple. I'm not the man-whore of the group. Women don't gawk at me as much when he's around. I mean, come on. Look at him. He's trouble with a capital T."

Nixon rolled his eyes. "If you weren't my cousin I'd think you were hitting on me."

"If I wasn't your cousin I just might."

"And too far." I threw my hands over my face as I felt it heat. The guys all started laughing while Monroe patted my back. "You are trouble, though. Hmm..."

"What?" Nixon grinned. "Tell me."

Was it possible for someone's head to heat so much it fell off their body? "No, no, it's no..." I bit my lip.

Now all the guys were watching me.

"Tell us." Tex clapped his hands.

"Fine, it's just, Nixon reminds me of that Taylor Swift song 'Trouble.' You guys heard it?" I laughed as they all shook their heads. "Yeah, well, if I didn't know any better I'd think Nixon dated her, dumped her, and she wrote a song about him."

I kept laughing.

The guys all stopped, including Monroe.

You could hear a pin drop in the lunchroom.

My eyes widened. "Shut up. No way! Did you date Taylor Swift?"

Nixon chuckled and pointed at Chase, who in turn opened his mouth to say something, and then pointed at Tex.

Tex turned around and pointed at an empty chair. "Damn. I have nobody to blame."

"What. You *all* dated her?" I crossed my arms.

"What happens in the Elect, stays in the Elect." Chase gave Nixon a high-five.

"This isn't Vegas."

"Drugs, gangs, sex, money, and guns? You sure about that?" Nixon winked.

Okay, he had me there. I mean, if it was possible to name a second Vegas, Elite would be it.

The bell rang in the distance. I quickly grabbed my bag and moved toward the door. A hand came out and tugged my bag, successfully making me fall back into strong arms. "Where do you think you're going?"

"Class?" My voice squeaked.

"Hmm..." Nixon's arms tightened around my body. He rested his chin on my head. I could feel the muscles beneath his shirt flex against my back. A million different sensations ran through my body in that moment. It was nearly impossible to breathe.

"How about you skip?"

"I can't just skip class!"

He released his hold and turned me to face him. "But you kind of want to, don't you?"

"No." I looked down at my shoes. Brave. I know. But whenever I looked into his eyes it was impossible to deny him anything! It was both aggravating and exhilarating. Sometimes it hurt to look at him.

He wore his perfection differently than most guys. The beauty of Nixon was in his imperfection. His crooked smile. The lip ring drew attention to his lips, making them look larger. Then his nose—it looked like it had been broken once, but it was in that tiny crook at the bridge that you saw something fierce about him. And his eyes. His ice blue eyes would warm within an instant when he was amused. His hair would fall across his brow, giving him a rough yet vulnerable look.

Agh! I needed to stop. It sucked that if you took all of those perfections in one by one he wouldn't be perfect, but together they made a masterpiece.

"Fine." He sighed and released his hold on me. "But don't forget about tonight. No faking illness or saying you have homework, okay?"

Still looking at the floor, I grinned and nodded my head once.

"Okay, off you go." Nixon stepped in front of me and opened the door. Head down, I walked through. I should have known better. I mean, it was Nixon. The minute I breezed by him, he smacked my butt. And then slammed the door in my face, so I couldn't yell.

However, I did hear his laughter on the other side of the door, which just infuriated me more. With a curse I stomped off to math. At least that would take my focus off Nixon, which was really all I'd been thinking about lately.

I couldn't figure him out.

I don't think he even had himself figured out.

He was like a giant puzzle with missing and broken pieces.

And, as much as I knew I would live to regret it... I was on a hunt, for the missing and damaged ones. Every. Last. One.

Chapter Eighteen

Ready?" Nixon held out his hand. After much coaxing, Monroe had convinced me to wear a short black dress with nylons and the boots from Chase. I added a short jeans jacket and wore my necklace. I mean, I was with Nixon—nothing would happen to it.

I'd like to see someone try to mug me with him around.

"Yup." I took his hand.

And so the date with the devil began.

"Still hate me?" he asked once we were in the Range Rover.

"Still not telling me who you are?" I replied.

"And off we go!" He laughed and started the car. "So, you may have noticed we don't have security tonight."

Telling myself to stop sweating so profusely, I nodded and tilted my head toward him. "Why not?"

"Other than the fact that I'm packing?" He lifted his eyebrows at me and let out a bark of laughter.

All signs pointed to him not kidding.

"Chill." He turned the car to the right as we passed through the campus security gate. "It was a joke."

"So you aren't packing?" I gulped.

"Not technically."

"Right." I turned the air conditioning on in the car and closed my eyes. "So where are we going? I'm guessing it's safe since we're not having to worry about security?"

"Absolutely."

"Cool."

"Want to know where?" Geez, he was grinning like a little kid.

"You want to tell me, don't you?"

"So bad." He leaned over the steering wheel and laughed. I'd never seen him so animated or excited.

"Surprise me."

"I get too excited when it comes to surprises," he grumbled. "Okay, I'm going to try, but you can't talk to me, or else I'm going to blurt everything and ruin it, okay?"

"Not talk to you? Whatever will I do?"

His smile turned wicked. "I've got a few ideas of other things you could do with your mouth—"

"And I'm pretty sure if I searched hard enough I could find a gun and shoot off your man parts, so... Say that again, I dare you."

He gulped. "Silence it is."

"That's what I thought."

"Damn." He shook his head. "Well played."

"I know." I smirked and leaned against the window, trying not to be too obvious about the fact that I was watching every single move he made.

Seriously, the guy made even driving sexy. In that moment,

watching him lick his lips and every once in a while suck on his lip ring, I realized, if he ended up in Hollywood, he'd be a hit. He'd make millions and women would cry in his presence.

If he went to work in corporate America, he'd be the hot CEO who secretaries would stab one another to work for.

No matter what Nixon decided to do, he'd be successful, and it wasn't just his good looks, although they helped. It was the confidence behind his good looks. I mean, I knew I wasn't supermodel gorgeous, yet being with him didn't make me feel insecure. Instead, it made me feel like I could do anything.

If he told me I could be a rock star, I just might believe him.

It was scary when someone's presence had more than enough power to alter the way you felt about yourself. What could happen if you lost yourself in that person? Would you disappear, or would you just mold yourself into how they viewed you?

Too many deep thoughts for a first date.

"Almost there." Nixon reached over and touched my thigh. His hand stayed there, warming my skin until his touch was almost searing.

Holy Superman, even his touch seemed to have magical powers.

"Okay." Nixon pulled down a dirt road. "Close your eyes."

I did as he said, totally noticing before I closed them that we were nowhere near the city. "Are you going to kill me?"

"No." He laughed. I relaxed until he added, "I didn't bring my silencer."

Stiffening under his touch, I tried to jerk away from him. His laughter made me want to give him a black eye.

"Trace, calm down. This is supposed to be fun, remember?"

"Yeah," I said breathlessly.

The car's engine went off. Cold air hit me as his door opened and then shut again. Seconds later, my door was opened, my seat belt unbuckled, and Nixon was picking me up in his arms.

I rested against his firm chest and told myself to stop sighing like the hormonal teenager I was. I swear my estrogen spiked just being around the guy, as if my feminine body was begging me to do more than touch him.

Clearing my throat, I licked my lips and waited.

Finally, he set me on my feet. "Open your eyes."

I did.

And almost collapsed into blackness. Not because he'd hit me on the head, or because what he'd done was so incredible, but because it was the most thoughtful thing anyone had ever done for me. The devil had given me the one thing I missed more than Grandpa.

Home.

"Are those—" I forced myself to swallow back the tears.

"Cows." Nixon laughed. "Yes, real live cows. I hear they even moo from time to time."

"And this"—he pointed behind us—"is our picnic under the stars."

"With the cows," I added, still stunned.

"With the cows. Though I've heard a few goats live out here, too. Don't want to leave out any farm creatures and take a chance of offending them."

"Right." My lower lip trembled. Crap. I was going to cry.

Nixon didn't say anything. He simply pulled me into his arms and kissed my head. "I know you miss it. I know you miss your grandpa." He sighed and ran his hand across my chest where my cross necklace lay. "And I know you miss your grandma. But being at Elite, it's where you belong. As much as you miss all of this." He pointed at the pasture. "You're home. Right here." *In my arms* is what was implied, and I still couldn't figure out why I believed him. I mean, I'd known him for less than two weeks. So why did it feel like I'd known him all my life?

"Hungry?" Nixon released me and walked over to the basket.

"Starved." I went over to help him, but he shook his head. "Nope, you sit right here." He clicked a button on his keys that opened the back end of the SUV and then picked me up and sat me on the edge of the Range Rover's tail. "There now. Stay put while I get this all ready."

Getting it all ready involved him laying down at least four layers of blankets—apparently it had rained here the night before—and setting out different containers filled with lasagna and spaghetti.

After the food was laid out, he lit a cylinder candle and held out his hand. "Your dinner awaits."

I jumped off the back of the car and took his hand. "Thank you."

We sat in silence on the blanket while he poured me what I assumed was sparkling wine and put food on my plate.

I liked that he expected me to eat a lot. Maybe it was because he was Italian, or at least his last name said as much. *Must be like our family, where not eating is a cardinal sin.*

You feel sick? Eat.

You feel tired? Eat.

You feel happy? Eat.

The food looked delicious. I tried the lasagna first and moaned aloud—totally by accident, I might add.

"Shit." Nixon dropped his fork and splattered lasagna onto the blankets. "Sorry, it's just…" He looked away from me and gulped his wine. "Ah, slippery fork and all."

"Right, because of the rain." I rolled my eyes and took a bite of spaghetti. This time my moan was totally on purpose. Talk about foodgasm. Every flavor was perfect.

Nixon began choking.

"Are you okay?" I leaned over and hit his back.

He nodded and stole my wine, drinking half of it. "Yeah." His voice was hoarse. "I just...was...choking."

"Right." I offered him my most disbelieving look.

Was he blushing?

Impossible.

"Who made the food?" I mentally patted myself on the back for my smooth subject change.

"I did."

Laughing, I pushed him with my free hand while I took another bite and chewed. This time, I did not moan. I mean, I didn't want the guy to die or anything.

"You don't believe me?" His eyes widened a bit, then narrowed. "You think I'd lie about something as important as food?"

I put my hands up in the air in mock surrender. "Sorry, Nixon. Yes, I believe you, and if you ever get tired of running around in your little gang, you could become a world-renowned chef."

"My little gang," he repeated. "You sound like Ma."

"How?"

"She used to call us guys her little gang." He pushed some food around with his fork. "Not so much anymore."

Clearly he was uncomfortable. Another subject change already? "Did she teach you how to cook?"

"Oh yeah. My father hated it." Nixon's eyes softened as he leaned over and licked his lips. "I spent all my early years in the kitchen holding on to my mom's skirts and testing all her food. She cooked a lot."

A fuzzy memory ran through my head of a tiny little boy screaming at me in the kitchen because I got dough in his hair. I laughed. I'd forgotten all about it!

"What?" Nixon urged.

"Nothing." I shook my head. "Or, well. It's just, I don't remember much from when I was little. Grandpa said everything was too traumatizing with my parents dying and all, but I remember being in a kitchen with this little boy and getting in a food fight."

He chuckled. "What happened?"

"I think he got mad because the cook let me have a taste of the cookie dough first. Anyway, all I remember is that he threw dough at me, and I threw it back at him. We fought, and I think he tripped and hit the side of his head on the counter. I'm sure it left a scar."

"Wow, you were a terrible child." Nixon nodded his head. "I'm impressed."

I only then realized that he had scooted closer to me.

Slowly, I reached over and grabbed his hand.

"Do you remember anything else about your parents?" he asked softly. "Or would you rather not talk about it?"

"I don't really know how I feel about it." I shrugged as a breeze picked up, making me scoot closer to him. "I mean, the memories are so scattered."

"Like a movie you can't remember?" he asked.

"Something like that. I see pieces..."

"Tell me one..." He kissed my cheek. "If you don't mind."

"All right. Um...I remember things being really loud when I

was little. We always had people over, lots and lots of people. I remember the dough thing...and a really pretty woman."

Nixon's head lifted. "I like pretty women."

"Very funny." I squeezed his hand. "I don't know why I always remember her. I know it wasn't my mom because I've seen pictures and remember her face a bit."

"What did this pretty woman look like, hmm?" Nixon released my hand and began massaging my neck.

I focused on the memory, begging for it to be more clear, but all I could remember were her eyes. "She...she had really blue eyes. Like yours."

He stopped massaging.

"And she had a really pretty laugh. It sounded like..."

"Church bells," Nixon finished.

I jerked away. "What?"

He very sadly dropped his head. "I read minds. Why? What were you going to say?"

I didn't want to tell him that he was spot on. But only because I remembered actual church bells close by. Another one of my flickering memories. I bit down on my lip. I knew it was a lucky guess.

"Dance with me." Nixon stood and held out his hand.

"In front of the cows?" My voice squeaked.

"Uh, yeah." Nixon looked from the cows to me. "I don't think they'll mind. Why, what kind of dancing were you thinking of doing? Were you hoping to embarrass the cows and get them to moo?"

Narrowing my eyes, I swatted him with my hand.

"Come on." My body was flush against his before I could protest.

Chapter Nineteen

Nixon smelled like *hot guy*. Seriously, they should bottle him up and put him in stores. He'd make millions—not that he needed it.

My stomach clenched. Everything he had done...I shook my head. It didn't compute. Why was he helping me, including me in his Elect group?

"Nixon." Pulling away so I could look into his eyes, I stopped myself from throwing up from nerves and just blurted out, "Are you leading me on?"

His blue eyes widened and then he reached out and grabbed my shoulders. "What?"

"L-leading me on." I looked down at my shoes again. There went my bravery. "I mean, are you doing all this so you can just—I don't know, throw me to the wolves later?"

"You don't trust very easily, do you?" he asked.

I shook my head.

"I don't blame you." Sighing, he pulled me back into his arms and began swaying. "And no, I'm not leading you on. I've told you before. I want to protect you...In the beginning, you were just another new kid, but now..."

"Now?" I repeated.

"Now you're the girl who moos?" he offered, chuckling.

I tried to pull away from him, but it was impossible.

"You're..." He stopped swaying and looked away from my face for a few seconds. "You're beautiful. In a way, I've been searching my whole life for you."

"Wow, easy on the corny movie lines." I laughed.

He didn't. "I'm serious." His eyes darkened and I was reminded again of how protective and unpredictable he could be. "I just wish you would re—"

His lips were on mine before he finished the sentence.

With a growl he picked me up and wrapped my legs around his body and laid me down on the blanket.

Nixon's body hovered over mine. A moment of indecision flickered across his face as he pulled away and cursed. For some reason, I didn't want to allow him to think about what we were doing. I just wanted to feel him. I wanted this moment to be ours, away from the school, away from the drama, away from everything.

I leaned up and my lips touched his. With a sigh, he leaned his forehead against mine and ran his fingers through my hair as his teeth grazed my lower lip.

"You have no idea..." He breathed across my lips as his hands moved to my neck and lifted me closer to his body. "How much I want you."

My breathing was ragged as his lips crushed against mine. All I could taste was him. All I could smell was Nixon. A mixture of the outdoors and spice invaded my senses as his tongue slipped around mine, making my world explode with pleasure and sensations I'd never experienced before.

Shaking, I moved my hands to the loopholes of his jeans and tugged at his lower body until it met mine with such force that I let out a gasp.

Taking full advantage of my mouth being open, Nixon's mouth pressed against mine so hard it almost hurt. My fingers clenched against his hip bones as he settled between my thighs.

I'd never made out with a guy before, but everything felt so good I didn't want to stop, nor did I really care that there were cows nearby or that we were outside on our first real date.

I just wanted him all to myself.

Nixon swore as I kissed him back as hard as I could, my teeth biting down on his lips. He paused and growled against me. With little effort, he flipped us around so that I was straddling him.

My hair fell across my face as I leaned down and kissed him softly on the lips.

His hands moved to my hips and then he gently pushed me back and stared. His icy blue eyes nearly glowed in the dark. My chest rose and fell, and he moved his hands to my jacket and nodded, as if asking permission to peel it from my body.

Um, yes please. I held out my arms as he pulled it off, leaving me in nothing but my nearly see-through dress and lacy bra.

For a minute, I thought he'd died. His breathing turned shallow. He closed his eyes and murmured, "It was always supposed to be like this. Always."

"Like what?" I whispered.

"Like this." His fingertips skimmed my breasts and moved across my hips until they finally settled on my backside. "Like this," he repeated as his hand reached for my face and traced the outline of my lips with his fingertips. "And like this..." That same hand moved to my chest. My heartbeat had to be erratic—I couldn't even think clearly. But he seemed too intent, so serious about us being together. There had to be more, not that I cared. I mean, I had Nixon at my mercy, and really, all I wanted to do was take advantage. He was so beautiful.

"I—" Nixon swallowed. "I have to kiss you. I have to have you—all of you."

I felt my eyes hood with desire as I nodded my consent. And then he tugged me down to him and kissed my neck. I arched against the sensation of his hot lips on my collarbone and then...

I heard sirens.

"Stay," he mumbled as he continued kissing me. "They won't see us."

"Okay." I pushed his head out of the way and started my own assault on his neck. He chuckled and cursed as he pulled me harder and harder against him. I clenched my thighs around him as his hands moved to my dress, slowly lifting it until I felt the cold night air.

The sirens sounded closer, but I didn't care. I wanted more.

I nodded as he lifted higher and higher until a car door slammed.

His hands froze where they were.

Footsteps approached.

"Shit." He rolled his eyes and gently pushed me away as he stood.

Chapter Twenty

I knew my skin was flushed. I mean, come on! I'd just been straddling the hottest guy I'd ever had the pleasure of seeing in real life. Who wouldn't be blushing?

The minute my dress dropped to its appropriate length and I was set to rights, a cop got out of his car and approached with a flashlight. Wow, thought they only did that in the movies.

"This here is private property." The cop sounded pissed. Great. I was going to get arrested on my first real date. Hopefully, Nixon wouldn't feel threatened and pull his gun. *Down, boy.*

"I know," came Nixon's cool reply.

Aw, crap. I wondered if Grandpa would bail me out.

"Then what the hell are you kids doing out here?"

Nixon threw his head back and laughed.

I felt my eyes widen at his response, was he *trying* to get us arrested or something?

"I know the owner," Nixon said. "I'm sure he won't mind."

"Won't mind?" the cop repeated. "Son, do you have any idea whose property this is? I can guarantee you he'll mind! In fact, if he finds out you kids are out here this late at night even I can't protect you from that son of a—"

The flashlight fell on Nixon's face. He squinted and put a hand in front of his face. The cop swallowed but didn't finish his sentence. Nixon chuckled. "Go on. *That son of a . . . what?*"

"Uh...gun. Son of a gun. Sorry, Mr. Abandonato, I didn't realize..."

"That's okay." Nixon stuffed his hands into his pockets. "You didn't realize. Right?"

"My badge number is—"

Nixon waved the officer off. "That won't be necessary. I'm not going to report you. You were just doing your job. Though it's a damn shame it had to be at this very moment."

The officer's eyes flickered to mine as he lifted the flashlight to my face. "Damn shame, sir."

I rolled my eyes and put my hand on my hip. Embarrassment complete, my only option was to pretend to be irritated, when really all I wanted to do was crawl into a very tiny dark hole. Preferably with Nixon, but whatever. I knew I couldn't get everything I wanted.

"So..." The officer nodded his head awkwardly. "I'll just be on my way. Say hi to your old man for me, will ya? He still having trouble with—"

"Thank you." Nixon shook the cop's hand and walked him back to his car. "Have a good night."

The cop's brows furrowed, but he did exactly as Nixon said and drove off. This time there weren't any sirens. Just crickets and some mooing.

Nixon turned around and grinned. "Well, that didn't go as planned."

"Oh really?" I crossed my arms, suddenly a bit chilled since I was missing my jacket. "And how was it supposed to go?"

He crooked his finger and like a love-drunk reject, I stumbled into his arms. He kissed me softly across the lips. "Hmm." His hands tangled into my hair. "Like this." He chuckled when I let out a small moan. "And a bit like this." His hands slid down to my butt, lifting me against him. "And a lot like this." His tongue plunged into my mouth.

I felt something buzz against my thigh. *What the heck?* Nixon froze and pulled away. I swear my mouth felt naked. The warmth of his lips was absent, and I found my body missed the fact that he wasn't pushed against me anymore.

"Shit. I um…" Nixon glanced at his phone. "I have to take this. Hold on."

His eyes got a little crazy, as if he couldn't believe his phone had actually gone off, but what did he expect? I mean, he had brought it with him.

He walked a few feet away from me and leaned against the fence. "No. That's impossible. Not until tomorrow." He glanced over at me.

I offered a weak smile. He gave me a tight one in return and then cursed into the phone. I strained to hear, but all I could make out was that he was speaking softly in another language. Was he doing that so I couldn't understand him? After a few seconds where it seemed as though he might be getting ready to punch one of the cows in the face, he hung up and stalked over to me.

"We have to go."

That was it. No kiss, no hug. Nothing.

"What the heck? No 'please' this time?" I grabbed my jacket from the ground and dusted it off before putting it on, while he made quick work of cleaning up our little picnic.

"Not this time," he grumbled. "It's more of an order. As in, get your ass in the car."

Horrified, I was frozen in place. "W-what?"

"Get. In. The. Damn. Car. Now." Every word was said with such irritation and anger that my eyes welled with tears. Biting my lip, I nodded once and jumped into the car.

The trunk slammed and then he was in the driver's seat mumbling to himself. I scooted as far away from him as I could. What was wrong with me? Minutes ago we'd been making out and well on our way to doing more, and now he was pissed all over again. It seemed my worst fears were coming true. Was my fairy-tale ending going to be Nixon having the last laugh? I closed my eyes and willed the tears to stay in. What if this had all been a setup? And like an idiot I'd fallen for it, fallen for his charm just like everyone else.

"Hey." Nixon reached across and grabbed my hand. "I'm sorry about…" He hit the steering wheel. "Damn. I'm just sorry I freaked out. But we needed to get out of there."

"But it's your property," I pointed out in a shaky voice.

"Which the cop had no problem explaining to his other little friends who were out patrolling tonight."

"Whatever." I shook my head. "I don't even know why that matters. Why would you care? It's not as if they were going to come watch us make out, too!"

At that, Nixon laughed. "I wasn't worried about them, Trace."

"I don't understand."

"Protection. I promised to protect you, right?"

I nodded.

"So trust me. What I'm doing right now? This is me trying my damnedest to protect you. Okay?"

"Yelling at me and ordering me around is protecting me?"

"I said…" Nixon pinched the bridge of his nose. "I said I was sorry. You're right. I shouldn't have been so rude, but we needed to get out of there, like fast."

Biting my lip to keep from saying anything else, I simply allowed us to fall silent in the car. Once we got closer to the school, I saw two Suburbans turn onto the street and get in front of us.

Nixon's hands clenched the steering wheel until his knuckles were white. His eyes darted to the rearview mirror.

I turned around in my seat.

His arm came flying across my chest, holding me in place. "Don't look."

Okay, now I was freaked. "Nixon, what aren't you telling me?"

His arm jerked back as he gripped the steering wheel and took a hard right. "Nothing you need to know…yet."

I glanced into the side mirror and noticed a similar Suburban was tailing us really close. The windows were tinted so it was impossible to see inside. My breathing picked up speed the minute I saw a window open and a gun attached to an arm come out.

"Um, Nixon. Nixon…The car behind us—they have guns. Nixon, they have guns!"

"Shit!" Nixon reached into the console and pulled out a black gun. Holy crap, I was officially in my own TV drama! "Trace, I need you to lay low. Can you do that? Just lean down in your seat, all right, sweetheart?"

Trying not to cry or pass out, I leaned as far down as I could while still staying buckled in. Nixon took a hard left and another hard left. I glanced in the rearview mirror. The car behind us sped up. The guy's face appeared from the car, and something looked vaguely familiar about him. We weren't close enough to see them clearly, though. Nixon was driving like the devil, something that might have made me laugh if I wasn't so afraid we were going to die.

"Trace, how are ya holding up?" Nixon's voice wasn't worried. He sounded calm, which in turn calmed me, but only a bit.

"I'm...fantastic." I clenched my hands together and sighed.

We hit a bump. Or at least I thought it was a bump, but when I edged up and looked into the side mirror I noticed that the car behind us was trying to hit us.

"Are they trying to kill us?"

"Possibly. I'm guessing they just want to see who I'm with and why I'd go to such lengths to hide you."

What the hell? "Why are you smiling?" I screamed.

"Because we're almost to the school. They know we're on our way and no chance in hell are those guys coming within a hundred feet of the place. We're almost there, sweetheart."

The car jolted again. I screamed.

Nixon turned the car hard, causing it to screech under the pressure and speed.

"Oh my gosh, oh my gosh!" I closed my eyes. This had to be a dream. This couldn't be real! "I'm going to die a virgin!" I blurted and then began to truly hyperventilate.

"What?" Nixon shouted.

"A virgin," I repeated as I greedily tried to suck more air into my lungs. "I'm going to die a virgin! I'm going to die without ever going overseas! I've never even been naked in front of a man before! Oh my gosh! I'm never going to have kids! What if I want kids? What if—"

"Trace..." Nixon tried to interrupt me, but I was freaking out and couldn't stop talking.

"Nixon, you have to promise me that if we live through this—and that's a giant *if,* considering we're literally trapped between two death machines—you have to take my virginity. Take it!"

"Trace, I don't think this is the time to—"

"Promise!"

"Trace—"

"Promise me, damn it!" Well, it was official. I had lost my mind. I clenched my eyes tightly closed as our car ripped through something and then sped over bumps large enough to be people.

"Crap-crap-crap!" I covered my face with my hands, and suddenly the car skidded to a stop.

I peeked through my fingers.

Nixon was coolly setting his gun back into the console and opening his window. We were at the security gate. He gave a rundown of what had just happened to the security guard.

Aside from the shaking, I wasn't sure I could move, let alone speak. Had I just begged Nixon to steal my virginity?

Horrified, I clapped my hands over my burning face all over again.

The car moved again and we drove in silence.

Finally, we pulled to another stop, and Nixon turned off the car.

I still refused to look at him or take my hands off my face. He was going to have to use the Jaws of Life on my hands. No chance in hell was I going to—

"Hey!" I shouted when he pulled my hands free of their grip.

I closed my eyes again. Maybe if I couldn't see him, he couldn't see me? You know, like when you play hide and seek when you're little?

"Trace." Nixon's voice held little humor so I opened one eye, then two. "Are you okay?"

"No." I shivered. "I'm not okay! We could have died! Who were those people? Why did they have guns? Is it like this all the time when you're out and about in public? What the hell, Nixon! I need answers!"

"As well as a volunteer..." Nixon chuckled.

"Come again?"

He burst out laughing. "Yes."

"Yes, what?"

"My answer." He winked. "Just name the time and place. I'll be there."

Oh my gosh. He didn't mean...

"It would be an honor." He bit down on his lip and happily hit the steering wheel. "I mean, I would love to be the one guy going into uncharted territory and..."

"Shut up! Just shut up!" I clapped my hands over my ears, convinced they were so red they were going to literally fall from my head. "Oh my hell. I'm so embarrassed."

"Hey, that was a real bonding experience back there," Nixon whispered as he neared my face and then very gently removed each hand from my head and kissed the insides of my wrists. "And don't worry...We'll wait until you're ready."

"You'll be waiting a long time."

"It's not like you didn't," he retorted, and before I could come up with a snappy reply his lips were crushing mine—*devouring* them was more like it. Instinctively I wrapped my hands around his neck.

"Now is good, too." He groaned as I opened my mouth to him.

A knock jolted us away from each other.

I turned around and was immediately face to face with Grandpa.

An entire day early.

Pointing at me with a frown on his face.

Make that two of my most embarrassing moments in one night.

Chapter Twenty-One

Grandpa did not look pleased. In fact, if people's stares could set clothes on fire...Nixon would've been doing the stop, drop, and roll right about then.

We both faced him like teenagers who'd just got caught making out. Which, to be fair, was kind of true, considering I was only eighteen. But still, I didn't think of Nixon as being in college. Maybe it had something to do with him being so protective? Or with adults being afraid of him? Or the gun? Yeah, the gun probably had something to do with it, too. Grandpa would have a stroke if he knew the truth.

Not that I knew the truth, either.

But I'm pretty sure whatever Nixon's deal was, it had to be bad. I mean, why else would people be chasing Nixon and pointing guns out of their cars at him? I was surprised at how well I was handling everything, but at that moment my embarrassment was trumping my fear...which was probably a good thing.

"Hey, Gramps, you're early." I got out of the car and gave him an awkward hug, then waited for the yelling to start.

He hugged me and then shot daggers at Nixon. "You."

Uh oh. Grandpa didn't know who Nixon was. He had no idea

that cops called him "Mr. Abandonato," and that women nearly fainted in his presence. He didn't know this world, so he didn't know that narrowing his eyes at Nixon was probably like a death wish.

"Me," Nixon repeated. "Great to finally meet you, *Mr. Rooks*."

"I didn't catch your name." Grandpa crossed his arms, refusing to shake Nixon's hand.

"Really? I could have sworn you knew it already." Nixon was almost chest to chest with Grandpa now. Crap. They were going to kill each other. I tried to step between them, but the minute I moved, both of their arms shot out and pushed me gently out of the way.

Weird.

"I'm old." Grandpa let out a hollow laugh. "Tell me again, what's your name...*son?*"

Nixon's jaw flexed. "Nixon Abandonato. But most people around here just call me 'sir.'"

"You're too young to be a sir."

"And you're too old to be protecting your granddaughter."

"I've been protecting her for her entire life." Grandpa poked Nixon in the chest, but Nixon didn't budge. "And last I checked I don't take orders from a mere child."

"Maybe it's time to let someone else protect her."

I raised my hand and cleared my throat. "Um, just FYI, I'm standing right here, and I have no idea why you two are being so idiotic right now, but I really want to go inside. I mean, I did almost just die back there."

Grandpa's nostrils flared. Without warning he reeled back and punched Nixon in the face.

I groaned into my hands. "Grandpa, he saved me. He—"

"He"—Grandpa pointed at Nixon, whose nose was gushing blood—"is bad news, Tracey! I don't want you seeing that boy anymore!"

"No!" I yelled. "Why are you being like this? Grandpa, I miss you. I haven't seen you in weeks, and you just punched my boyfriend in the face! Are you insane?" *Whoops.* I may have dropped the "boyfriend" word too soon. Nixon probably thought I was so stupid. One date did not mean we were boyfriend and girlfriend.

"Boyfriend!" Grandpa wound up his arm to punch Nixon again, but this time I stepped in front of my bleeding date, making Grandpa drop his hand. "Trace?"

"I like him." I leaned back into Nixon's frame and sighed as his arm came around me and held me against him. "He even beat up a guy who bullied me. He's good. And I was going to tell you all about him over dinner tomorrow. Actually, I was going to invite him, but now that you've punched him in the face—"

"Trace." Nixon's voice was raspy. "It's fine. You should spend some time alone with your grandpa tomorrow. Don't go to class. Take a day off. Really, it's probably best that you do, all things considered. You've had a rough night."

Perplexed, I turned in his arms and stared at him. His eyes were ice cold. No emotion was behind them. It was like staring at a statue. "Why are you doing this? Come with us tomorrow; it will be—"

"It will be best if you do as your grandfather says," Nixon finished and licked his lips. Blood was still slowly trickling over them. "It was...*interesting* meeting you again, Mr. Rooks. Be sure to keep an eye out for the shadows tomorrow evening. They've been lurking."

I didn't turn around in time to see Grandpa's expression, but when I did he suddenly seemed very old to me, as if his wrinkles had taken on enough lifetimes. He looked away, tears welling in his eyes. "And tonight?"

Nixon released me. As he walked away he said, "The dove's existence is not yet known."

"What?" I yelled. But Nixon was already jumping into his car and driving off. Grandpa wrapped his arm around me.

"Are you sure you're okay, Trace?" he whispered as his hug tightened around my shoulders.

"Yes, but..." I looked back at Nixon's taillights. "I don't understand."

Grandpa chuckled. "He's an interesting boy, that Nixon. But you cannot see him anymore. It isn't...smart. You're such a young girl and—"

"Gramps." I pulled out of his embrace. "Did you really come all this way to do insurance stuff and talk me out of dating my boyfriend? Or did you want to spend some time with me?"

His worried face broke out into a smile. "I wanted to spend time with you, of course." He walked me to the door of my dorm. "Why don't you skip tomorrow? I'll pick you up around eight for breakfast?"

I nodded. "Grandpa." I licked my lips. "Things are weird here. They...I don't know, sometimes I feel like everyone knows me better than I know me. Does that make sense?"

"Yes. And I promise I'll do what I can to clear things up. But not tonight. Now, off you go. It's late." He shooed me inside. I watched him walk away into the darkness and climb into a waiting black Mercedes. Weird. His rental car arrangement must have been upgraded. There wasn't any other explanation why Grandpa would drive something so nice. It wasn't like we were made of money.

*   *   *

I tried to get in touch with Nixon but two hours later he still hadn't texted me back. Monroe had gone out with Tex and then decided to "stay over at his place," whatever that meant. So I was alone and still a bit freaked out. It was around eleven and I still couldn't sleep.

I tried Nixon again.

You gonna tell me what happened tonight?

I threw my phone onto the bed and groaned. Finally, two minutes later he responded.

Sure! You offered me your body—I'm free if U R?

I laughed.

U R an ass and that's not what I'm talking about!

If evasiveness was a sport, Nixon would be an Olympian, seriously. Now that I really thought about it, even in the car he had changed the subject, to my embarrassment, and then kissed me.

Well, either I was really easy, which could be true considering Nixon did crazy things to me, or he didn't want me asking questions.

My phone went off again.

I'm an ass? That's not what you were saying when we were kissing. Want me to come over?

I stared at the text message. Did I? Grandpa would be ticked, but he didn't have to know. And I was lonely.

Will you answer my questions?

He responded immediately.

Maybe.

I smiled and typed, *Bring popcorn.*

Chapter Twenty-Two

I tried to get into the latest zombie novel I'd bought on my e-reader but every time the author described the hero's eyes, I thought of Nixon. Every time the couple kissed, I thought of his lips.

Really, I was pathetic.

A half-hour after I received Nixon's last text, I heard swooning women in my hallway. Okay, so maybe I couldn't hear them, but I did hear Nixon. He was laughing.

I sighed, held my e-reader close to my heart. I loved his laugh.

Seriously, someone needed to come in here and smack me with my e-reader. I was acting crazy. I'd known him for what, two weeks? Not even.

I was worse than a twelve-year-old Justin Bieber fan with Bieber Fever, or whatever they called it.

My door swung open.

"Do you have access cards to every room or something?" I jumped off my bed and fought the urge to tackle a smiling Nixon.

"Of course." He grinned in a way that said, *I'm important, so there.*

I rolled my eyes. "I don't see popcorn."

"About that." He scratched his head. "Chase was bored so…"

"The party is here!" Chase shouted from the doorway, loaded down with enough groceries to feed a small country. "Move over, Nixon. It's chick flick time and I've got the goods."

"Is he high?" I crossed my arms and examined Chase's eyes.

"No," they said in unison.

"I'm my normal awesome self. I have had two Red Bulls, though, so my bad for the loudness. Damn, I was bored. You saved my life." Chase winked and set the groceries on the shared desk in our dorm. I always seemed to forget how attractive he was. I almost felt sorry for whoever ended up with the guy. Next to Nixon he was the hottest guy here and probably just as much trouble to deal with. Well, maybe not just as much, but close. After all, they were family.

Nixon slammed the door to my room shut, much to the disappointment of the waiting girls in the hall, who were eyeing me like I was the harlot of the century.

"So..." I began unpacking the groceries. I didn't even want to know how much security detail the guy had taken with him in order to obtain them. "What movie did you guys bring?"

Chase chuckled. "Well, funny that you ask that."

"Chase," Nixon warned, but Chase kept talking.

"Nixon here was pouting about your ruined date, and I thought to myself, wow, what would make him feel better? What would inspire him to be more romantic? I mean, cows, man? Really?"

"It was romantic," I defended Nixon and walked into his arms, unable to keep myself from being near him.

"Cows. Cows are romantic?" Chase shook his head. "I think not. And in my opinion, or that of my dear mother's, Nicholas Sparks is the shit. Therefore, we're going to watch...Drumroll, please."

Nixon and I just stared while Chase bounced his hands against the desk. "*The Notebook*!"

"Shoot me now." Nixon grumbled.

I smiled. "Hey, it's a good movie."

Chase smirked at Nixon. "Say it, dude. Say it."

"Say what?" I asked.

"V-vampire?" Nixon guessed, totally quoting *Twilight*. He put Chase into a headlock and cursed. "Fine, you were right to choose Nicholas Sparks. Good job. Too bad you can't use any of that romance on finding your own girl."

Chase pulled away and shrugged. "I've already found my girl."

Nixon narrowed his eyes.

Chase stalked toward me and put his arm around me. "You see. I have it worked out perfectly. The minute you screw up—and let's be honest, you're like a time bomb—I'm swooping in for the kill."

"Romantic." I picked Chase's arm off of my shoulder and stepped away.

Nixon's eyes turned icy again as he glared at Chase. "Not in this lifetime, dude."

"You never know," Chase fired back.

Wait, when did this turn into something serious? Both of them looked ready to throw punches.

"Okay, too much testosterone!" I stepped between them. "Let's just watch the movie, all right?"

Chase snapped out of his funk and smiled. "Sure, let me just get the chips and dip out. Oh yeah, and popcorn. I also got some licorice and Skittles."

"Skittles?" I repeated.

"He wants you to taste the rainbow." Nixon groaned. "It's one of his lines, and then he puts the Skittles in his mouth and kisses you. It's a very tired line that he can't seem to let go of, huh, Chase?"

"Bastard," Chase joked and went about putting our snacks together.

Nixon lay on my bed and held out his hand for me to follow him. I snuggled into his side and within minutes felt my eyes droop.

"It's okay," Nixon whispered into my ear. "You can sleep. I know it was a rough night."

"But…" I didn't open my eyes. "We were supposed to talk about tonight and why you have guns and…Skittles."

"Skittles?" He chuckled. "What, are you trying to taste *my* rainbow?"

"I love rainbows." I smiled.

Huh? I must have been dreaming, because I could have sworn I heard Nixon say. "I've always loved you."

"You too," I said back, because you know, I was dreaming and it was totally okay to say that back in your dream.

Nixon's warm lips were on my neck. "I'm glad you're safe, Trace. Now sleep."

He felt so good. I snuggled as close as I could and tucked my head into the crook of his arm. It was an amazing dream, being in his arms, being at peace.

*   *   *

The sound of my alarm jolted me awake. Almost falling off my bed, I stared at my phone. Who'd plugged it in?

I had a text from Nixon. Wait—Nixon? Where was he?

Set your alarm for seven just in case your old man was coming early. Cleaned up snacks but Chase wanted to leave you the Skittles. Use them wisely! Have fun today please be safe.

My grin was so huge I'm surprised my face didn't hurt. I quickly texted him back.

Thanks for not tasting my rainbow while I was sleeping. Promise to be safe. Plus nobody would attack me without you around. You're the gun magnet! See you tonight?

I anxiously wrung my hands together while I waited for him to respond.

Leave the lights on ☺

With a happy sigh, I sent him a smiley text back and looked at the time. It was just after seven. I had plenty of time to shower and make myself presentable.

I grabbed my shower tote and threw on my flip-flops and bathrobe.

The dorm bathroom was pretty busy. Luckily, one of the showers was open. I snatched it before anyone else did and washed my hair. The hot water was therapeutic against my sore neck. Why would my neck be sore? I rolled my head around and gasped. Nixon. I'd fallen asleep against his arm. No wonder my neck hurt.

I was still smiling when I toweled off and gathered my stuff to go back into my room. At the bathroom door I pulled it open and nearly ran into one of my dorm-mates.

"Skank." She pushed past me.

"Excuse me?"

"You heard me." She sneered. "You're a skank. Two guys in your room last night? Really? You know Nixon and Chase are just messing with you, right? They're Elect and you're a nobody. A charity case. Besides . . . word around school is that you'd give it to anyone."

"Hmm." I put my free hand on my hip. "I wonder what Nixon would say about that."

Fear flashed in her eyes for a brief moment before she shrugged. "Tell him whatever you want. Because in a few days it won't even matter anymore. He'll get bored. They always do. You're like the shiny new toy, and believe me when I say, Nixon really loves to play. Good luck finding any guy who will talk to you after he breaks you and puts you back on the shelf."

Stunned, I stared as she stomped off. Girls shoved past me. But I couldn't move. Dread filled my stomach. What if she was right? I hadn't known him very long, and wasn't it kind of weird how close we had gotten? It wasn't normal. Even I wasn't backwoods enough to think anything about our relationship was normal. It was odd, but it worked, right?

I chewed my lower lip and walked back to my room.

Monroe was sitting on her bed looking like she'd been thoroughly kissed the night before.

"I take it Tex was attentive?" I decided not to tell anyone about my run-in with the chick in the bathroom and put my stuff away while I waited for Mo to answer.

"He's so . . ." She sighed happily. "Perfect."

"Tex?" I laughed. "We are talking about Tex, right?"

"Shut up!" She threw a pillow at my head and giggled. Oh gosh, she had it bad. Right, like I could talk. I did in fact just sigh while reading a text not even a half hour ago. "He's just so sweet and my family totally approves, which is a huge deal!"

My hands froze over my bathrobe. "Is your family kind of strict?"

"Kind of?" She snorted. "The last guy I dated ran away screaming, and I'm not joking. My family is all about appearances and connections. Luckily, Tex is everything my dad actually likes."

"What do you mean?"

"Well, for starters, his parents just bought out a multimillion-
dollar software company, and Tex is supposed to take over the family
business in a few years. I mean, not like Nixon. I guess things happen
faster than you realize, but Tex is next and—"

"Wait." I put my hand up. "Nixon runs your family's business?"

"Businesses." She chewed her fingernail. "He kind of oversees
everything. Like the CEO to the CEO, you know what I mean? Or I
guess just the owner-operator. Whatever. Anyway, Tex—"

"Wait, one more question. Why is Nixon even in school?"

Monroe laughed. "I thought you'd been hanging out with my
brother for the past couple weeks. You know just as well as I do that
he doesn't actually go to school."

Oh my gosh. My boyfriend was a dropout. "He quit?"

She gave me a confused look. "Um, he's technically already grad-
uated. He was so many credits ahead that this year he decided to take
enough credits to be student body president, but that's it. Why do you
think it seems like he's always roaming the halls and has all the access
cards to everything? They wouldn't just give that to a student."

"But…" Confused, I began to pace. "Why hasn't he told me?"

"Chill." Monroe jumped up from the bed and pulled me into a
hug. "It's not like it's a secret. Everyone knows about it. I'm sure he just
assumed someone already told you."

"Right." I smiled even though it felt forced, and hurried through my morning routine. It bothered me that Nixon hadn't said anything. But what bothered me more was the fact that I had been blindly trusting him for the past few days without ever forcing him to answer any of my questions.

The main one being... Who the hell was he?

Chapter Twenty-Three

As promised, Grandpa was waiting outside my dorm at eight o'clock sharp. "Looking good," I shouted at him once I stepped outside.

The minute he turned around I froze.

All his white facial hair was gone. He was wearing a really nice suit, like the type you see on Armani ads, and his smile seemed... worried.

Was nothing real in my life anymore? My grandpa was a farmer! A farmer! What would he need with a suit?

I approached him and the same black Mercedes I'd seen him driving last night. "What's going on?"

"Trace." He licked his lips. "Let's just spend the day together and we'll talk, okay? But not here, honey."

I nodded. I mean, I really didn't have any other choice. The car smelt like Grandpa, which was weird considering it was a rental.

The doors were heavy, too heavy to be normal, and the glass seemed thicker than normal. Not to mention that the windows were so darkly tinted it would be impossible to see in. I had no idea you could rent cars like this.

"Good news first or bad news?" Grandpa asked once he started the car.

"Bad. Always the bad first."

Grandpa coughed. "Let me start with the good."

"Why ask if you were already going to start with the good?"

He chuckled and shrugged. "The good news is that I'm going to be in town for a few months."

"What!" I shrieked. "Grandpa, what about the cows! You know Wilbur won't like being left without anyone familiar, and Matilda is—"

"I still regret letting you name some of the animals," Grandpa grumbled. "And Wilbur and Matilda will be fine. They've got Scott. He's going to watch over operations for a while."

"Scott. As in, our cousin Scott?"

"Yes, Scott." We joined the main road traffic. "He's a good man and wanted some extra money, so I'm going to pay him to watch over things while I'm here."

And then it hit me. Grandpa was sick. He had to be. Why else would he move? "Are you dying?"

Grandpa shook his head and sputtered. "Why would you think that? Do I look that awful clean-shaven?"

"No." My breathing returned to normal. "I just…Well, why would you move here for a while?"

"Now, for the bad news." Grandpa looked pasty white as he got on the freeway.

"What?"

"Everything you've ever known…is about to change."

*   *   *

For some reason his words didn't really hit me as hard as I guess they should have. After all, everything had already been slowly changing since Grandma's death. I just didn't know how or why.

Things were too weird not to change.

Maybe that's why I didn't ask any more questions. Instead, I tried to concentrate on what Nixon and I would do later. I had to. Because if I thought about the fact that Grandpa was driving me outside the city in an expensive car, wearing a suit, I would freak out.

I closed my eyes for a few minutes in order to conjure up Nixon's smile, his face. When I opened them, Grandpa seemed to be immersed in his driving.

I snuck out my phone and sent Nixon a quick text.

I'm kind of freaked.

He didn't respond right away, but when he did, I pretended not to hear the vibration. Grandpa was clueless. I pulled out the phone and looked at the screen.

U R safe and U have nothing to be afraid of.

I smiled and texted back.

Why? U following me?

My phone went off again.

Gotta run!

I glanced in the rearview mirror just in case I was right. But I didn't see Nixon's SUV. Clearly I was reading too much into things.

Grandpa took the next exit. We were on the outskirts of town in some sort of subdivision I'd never been to before.

"Where are we?" I asked as we passed some large houses and

land. I could still see Lake Michigan, so I knew we couldn't be that far out of Chicago.

"Lake Forest," he answered.

Something about Lake Forest seemed familiar. I just didn't know what it was. Maybe it was just because I'd seen lots of signs for it? Wait, hadn't Nixon taken me out in this direction for our date? Granted, we hadn't gone this far. Or had we? Gosh, it felt like it took forever to get back, but I could have sworn it was only a twenty-minute drive. Or was it?

I wracked my brain. "This kind of looks like where Nixon took me for our date."

"Date," Grandpa repeated. "With what, pastures?"

I looked around at some of the pretty farmland. "Yeah, kind of."

Grandpa didn't say anything for a while as we headed down a paved road into what looked like private property. "He was probably trying to get you to remember. I should shoot him for doing that to you."

"He'd probably pull his gun on you, too, Grandpa." Whoops, that slipped.

Grandpa slammed on the brakes. "You saw his gun?"

"Kind of hard not to with people chasing us." I shrugged.

Grandpa cursed in the same language Nixon often cursed in, and I couldn't help it. I started laughing. This was too strange. Like something out of a movie. Clearly I was losing my mind.

"What's so funny?" Grandpa asked.

"You sound like Nixon. What language is that, anyway?"

Grandpa was silent again as we drove to the gate of the property. Across the railing it said ALFERO.

"That's on Grandma's necklace." I pointed at the sign as the gates opened, revealing a gorgeous expanse of grass and water fountains with trees lining the driveway. As we neared the end of the driveway, a three-story house came into view. It was a freaking mansion. My mouth dropped open as Grandpa pulled the car to a stop.

With a sigh he pulled the key from the ignition and looked at me, sadness dancing across his face. "Welcome home, Trace."

Chapter Twenty-Four

Home?" I repeated in a small voice.

Suddenly a man with an earpiece pulled open my door. "Miss Alfero, an honor. Just this way."

I gawked at the man and looked back at my grandpa. He was getting out of the car and walking toward us.

The guy with the earpiece gave a curt nod to Grandpa. "Mr. Alfero. Welcome home, sir."

Grandpa gave the man a swift nod in return and put his hand on my lower back as he led me up the steps to the giant entryway of the house.

Nothing could have prepared me for what was behind those doors. Nothing. I wasn't sure if I was supposed to be happy or sad or pissed or shattered...I could only stare as Nixon stood in the entryway in my supposed house, with at least fifteen armed men. Chase and Anthony were by his side.

"Ready?" Nixon asked, not once looking in my direction but rather over my shoulder to Grandpa.

Grandpa answered with a gruff *yes* and continued coaxing me through the giant hall.

Feeling heartbroken and so totally betrayed, I didn't know what to do. All I knew was that the one person I'd wanted to trust had lied to me, big time.

My legs almost gave out on me before I could sit on the couch. Nixon sat directly across from me. All of his armed men were behind him, and then I turned around and noticed that we had twice as many men behind us in that large entryway.

Everyone had guns.

And every single gun from Nixon's group was trained on Grandpa. Every single gun from Grandpa's group was trained on Nixon.

It was like a bad mafia movie, only every time I blinked it just became more real.

"You broke the rules," Grandpa said, leaning back in his seat.

Nixon smirked. "What? You think I actually knew right away?"

"You grew up with her!" Grandpa yelled.

"She was six!" Nixon all but shouted.

"You may as well have pulled that trigger. Your father..."

"Is dead." Nixon smirked. "Cold and lifeless, lying right next to my mother."

"What?" I shrieked. "You said that—"

"Monroe doesn't know, Trace." Nixon's eyes softened for a brief second. "He'd been sick a while. It's..."

"None of her damn business." This from Anthony, who was staring at me as if we hadn't shaken hands and spoken a few days ago.

"Gentlemen." Chase cleared his throat. "Back to the reason for meeting."

Grandpa bristled next to me. Clearly he didn't like taking orders from people younger than he was, but then again how was I to know they weren't lying about their ages, too?

"As I was saying…" Grandpa put an arm around me and squeezed. "The poor girl lost her parents when she was six. That's still old enough to recognize people. You should have known, Nixon."

"I told you the minute I did," Nixon defended himself. "And it wasn't like I could have done anything!"

"You took her outside school property."

"Before I knew." Nixon sighed heavily. "I didn't even guess until I saw the damn necklace with 'Alfero' on it."

"Then you should have stayed away."

"Careful," Anthony said from Nixon's left. "You may be within your rights to call him out, but he's still the boss. Has been for some time. So tread carefully, old man."

Grandpa cleared his throat. "Excuse me, Mr. Abandonato." He spat out the words like they were venom. "But the minute her cover was blown—the very second—you should have locked her in her damn room."

What? Why would Grandpa say that? I tried to shrug underneath his arm but he held me firm.

Nixon's icy eyes pierced through mine. "She's just a teenager, Frank. What did you want me to do? Blow everyone's cover? Ruin everything? And for what? Precaution? We've been in this for four damn years." His eyes fell to Anthony. "Some of us longer. How was I supposed to know you'd drop her directly into the fight? Your own granddaughter? We were doing just fine until you did this to us!"

"And you still have no proof!" Grandpa shouted.

"We're close!" Nixon fired back. "We just need more time."

"Time doesn't give Trace her parents back," Grandpa said softly. "Time doesn't heal a broken heart, and time will not fix the fact that you have successfully helped expose my innocent granddaughter to our world. I only meant to appease my dying wife, while at the same time allowing Trace to be used as bait only if necessary, and what do you do? You claim her for your own! An Abandonato!"

"All I can say is I'm sorry. I didn't know. But would you rather have me leave her helpless? Admit it. She would have known something was up if I locked her in her room, and honestly we weren't even sure she was exposed until last night when we almost"—Nixon swallowed—"got killed."

"Until it was almost too late!" Grandpa nodded his head. "So what are you going to do now? How do you hope to make amends?"

"Easy. We'll let things die down, and work faster to infiltrate the De Lange family."

Grandpa nodded his head as if satisfied. "She must be protected."

"We've been protecting her." Chase's teeth clenched. I thought he was going to break a tooth.

"And she almost died," Grandpa repeated. "Last night. Isn't that right? Or wait, were you too busy sticking your tongue down my granddaughter's throat?"

In an instant Nixon had his gun out and pointed at Grandpa. "Disrespect your granddaughter in front of my men and yours one more time and I will end you."

Holy freaking shit.

Grandpa scowled. "I would never do such a thing. I love her. I put her into hiding. Twelve years of work gone just because of you!"

Nixon put his gun down and cursed. "She wasn't supposed to get into the school."

Grandpa joined in with the cursing. "Her grandma was the culprit. She told me on her deathbed it was time for Trace to know the truth. I thought I could give my wife her dying wish and at the same time appease my granddaughter. Allow her to experience the luxury she should have grown up with. The life that was stolen from her. Like I said, I did not think she would be recognized and figured even if she were, we could use her to pull out the De Lange family."

Nixon looked from Grandpa to me. "Using your own granddaughter, even if things came to that? I think we're done here."

"I think so." Grandpa rose from his seat. Nixon and Grandpa embraced each other and kissed each cheek before saying something in that stupid language they were always speaking in.

Nixon took one last look at me and shook his head slowly. My heart was in my throat. I felt tears start to pool in my eyes as I looked from him to Chase. At least Chase mouthed *sorry* before turning back around and following Nixon out.

"One more thing," Grandpa said.

In a flash he pulled out his gun and shot at Nixon's feet. I covered my mouth with my hands to cover my shriek. Nixon didn't move. He just stared at the ground then gazed back up at Grandpa with cool indifference.

"Noted." Nixon nodded and his group left.

Chapter Twenty-Five

If I hadn't been so horrified, I might have laughed that my backwoods grandpa had just fired a crazy-looking gun at my boyfriend's feet.

But it wasn't funny. What the hell kind of alternate universe had I just walked into? My legs suddenly felt heavier than before. Spots appeared in my line of vision. I tried to steady myself by holding on to the table next to me, but my arms weren't doing what I wanted them to do. Instead they flopped near my sides, hitting the table. Then my legs gave out... and everything went black.

*   *   *

"Trace? Sweetheart?" Grandpa was hovering over me with a cold compress against my cheek. "There you go, take some deep breaths. You fainted."

I licked my dry lips and looked around. Several men in suits were standing behind Grandpa as he held the compress against my face.

"I don't understand."

Grandpa swore. "Give us a minute."

A man put his hand on Grandpa's shoulder This time Grandpa stood and very calmly spoke in what I was now beginning to assume was Nixon's and everyone else's native language. It wasn't Italian, that much I knew.

"What language is that?" I sighed heavily and leaned against Grandpa as he helped me to my feet.

"Sicilian."

My blood ran cold as memories flashed through my fuzzy brain. Memories of a life I had long ago forgotten. The woman in the kitchen speaking to me in a language I now thought foreign. A language I actually knew.

"I think...I think I know it."

"You should. It is all we spoke when you were young, but after the accident..." Grandpa cleared his throat. "We chose to forget in order to protect you. After all, we could take no chances."

I swallowed the dryness in my throat and followed him back to the couch.

"How are you feeling?" Grandpa set the compress onto the table and poured me a glass of wine. I examined the glass, feeling somewhat awkward that my grandpa would serve me alcohol, but if it helped my nerves I was all for it. I took a few careful sips, hoping it would take away the nightmare in front of me.

"How do you think I'm feeling, Grandpa? Really?"

He chuckled. "Always straight to the point."

My nostrils flared as I watched him play with the thick white hair near his ear. The room was eerily quiet now that the men with guns had gone outside for a timeout. My fingers itched to pull out the cell phone in my pocket. Nixon. How could he have lied to me like that?

Answers. I needed answers. Nixon had always evaded my questions. Perhaps it was for my own protection, perhaps not. But that ended now.

"I want answers." I gave Grandpa a steely look.

He nodded once. "Your full name is Tracey Angelica Alfero. You are the daughter of deceased mafia hit man Mario Adele Alfero. Your mother's full name was Nicola Alessandro De Lange."

"De Lange? As in Dean De Lange? And Phoenix De Lange?"

Grandpa nodded.

"So...I'm related to Phoenix?"

Grandpa laughed. "No, not technically. I guess very, very far down along the line you would be cousins a few times removed."

"And they were killed?"

Grandpa clasped his hands together in front of him and leaned forward. "A hit was ordered on your parents without my knowledge or your father's. To understand why, you need a bit of a history lesson."

I nodded, fully ready for any information he could give me.

"The De Lange family is the weakest of the mafia families still located in the Chicago area. That is to say, they are the weakest in the states. In Sicily, it is quite another situation. At any rate, your mother was promised to one of the Abandonatos. Nixon's father. They wanted to make a sort of truce, combine powers. The Abandonatos were, and still are, the most powerful family here and in Sicily. They are also the wealthiest. When it came time for their betrothal announcement..." Grandpa swore. "Your father would not see reason. He had fallen in love with your mother. So he ran away with her. When they returned there was nothing we could do. They were already married, honor-bound to each other."

At least that part of the story wasn't traumatizing. I always knew my parents loved each other. They were constantly hugging and kissing, and they were always laughing.

"So what did the Abandonato family do?" I wasn't sure I liked that Nixon's family were the bad guys.

"Nothing." Grandpa chuckled bitterly. "And that, my dear girl, was the problem. They weren't the ones in need of an alliance, nor were they going to force a woman to divorce her husband in order to do so. After all, we do not look kindly upon divorce. It is simply not done in the Catholic church, my girl."

"So the Abandonato family let them live in peace?"

Grandpa nodded. "They allowed them their space. After a while everyone forgot the scuffle. Angelo, Nixon's father, married a woman soon after. She resembled your mother, but that was the end of it. Unfortunately, Angelo had always been an angry sort of man. The De Lange family was a constant burden to the Abandonatos. There wasn't a week that went by where they didn't try to rob one of the businesses or even beat up cousins at the school. It got out of hand, and Angelo began to blame your mother for everything. Soon, he took out his anger on his own wife... and his son."

Feeling like I was going to puke, I clenched my stomach and told myself to keep breathing in and out. Was that why Nixon couldn't handle anyone touching him?

"Nixon?" I asked, not wanting to hear the truth.

"Suffered greatly at his father's hands." Grandpa swore. "One evening, the evening of your sixth birthday, your parents were coming home from one of their nights in town, when they were stopped on the road. Your father wasn't able to pull his gun out fast enough. They shot your mother in front of him and then shot him."

Sobbing, I bit my lower lip so it wouldn't tremble. "Who did it? Who? Angelo?"

Grandpa rose from the couch and retrieved a box of Kleenex and brought it back to me. He sat down and cleared his throat. "Nobody knows. Angelo wasn't in the country at the time, and he swore up and down he would never do such a thing, but by that point nobody believed him. After all, his sweet wife had died just a few months before from a brain hemorrhage.

"So, you see, his word was worth nothing. His empire was at the point of crumbling because he was unable to control his anger. And on top of that, fingers were pointing in his direction that he could no longer control his own businesses. This continued until Nixon was around the age of eighteen."

"And then Nixon took over?"

Grandpa sighed. "His part of the story is not mine to tell. But had I known history would repeat itself, had I known another Abandonato would fall in love with one of our girls, I would have put a stop to it."

"Love?"

Grandpa closed his eyes. "Yes. That boy. He would die for you. Yes?"

I wanted to deny it. But I couldn't so I just looked away.

"Who killed my parents?"

"Angelo believed it was the De Lange family. He believed it was a setup. The gun used was engraved with the crest of the family, but there was no proof. We were afraid for your life, not knowing who we could trust. Your grandmother and I decided it would be best to protect you, to put you in hiding until you were of age. But as the nightmare of that night faded and your eighteenth birthday loomed closer, I hadn't the heart to tell you the truth. Not the heart that she had.

"Four years ago, it was discovered that the De Lange family was in debt to another family from Sicily. It seemed some bad investments were made. Nixon and the others formed a plan to not only bring the family down, but to expose the De Langes for their treachery."

"And has he?"

"What?" Grandpa took the wineglass from my hands and set it on the table.

"Exposed them?"

"Not yet." Grandpa sighed. "And the longer it takes, the more I wonder if the Abandonato family wasn't behind it. But we will never know. There has been too much killing, and now my only grand-daughter is in the middle of it."

I covered my hand with his. "Gramps, you can't change that any-more." I knew he was going to be pissed but I had to ask. "How can I help?"

"You've already done what I needed you to do. You've drawn attention to yourself. But now that you know who Nixon is, you are in more danger. I never meant for you to discover who he was. I trusted him to stay away from you. No." Grandpa swore. "No, you will return to school, you will forget this happened, and you will forget about that boy."

I sighed. It would be impossible to forget to breathe, to forget I had a heart, so what made him think it would be possible to forget Nixon?

"I can't, Grandpa."

"Why not?" Grandpa jumped to his feet. "What has the boy done to you? Has he—" His face flushed red as his hands did a weird sort of flailing in front of my face.

I chuckled. "Um, no, he didn't do...that." I copied his hand ges-tures and shook my head.

Grandpa let out a sigh and laughed. "I do not know why the

Good Lord left me alone with a girl. I do not think my heart can take it. I go to bed, I worry. I eat my breakfast, I worry. I see a cow, I worry."

Swallowing my tears, I exhaled in relief, glad to see part of my old grandpa in front of me. I pulled him into a hug and closed my eyes as I inhaled his familiar scent.

"Grandpa, you can't control everything."

"I can try."

"No, you'll die of a heart attack and where will that leave me? Without any family."

"You are like your grandmother." He sighed. "So wise."

He released me and stepped back. I still had a question, but I wasn't so sure I would like the answer. "Gramps." I scratched my head. "Who's the leader of the Alfero family?"

Grandpa's grin was wide. "Are you asking me if I'm the mob boss?"

I nodded.

Grandpa shrugged and with a loud laugh walked to the door. "I'll send Adrian in to show you to your room so you can freshen up before luncheon."

Awesome. Add Grandpa to that list of people who ignore questions. I was beginning to realize that if Grandpa or Nixon didn't answer something, it was usually answer enough. Jerks. Avoidance meant yes, and addressing something meant no.

I pulled out my phone in vain, hoping Nixon would have sent something—anything!

One new message.

I quickly hit OPEN and saw Nixon's number and next to it two words I'd been holding my breath to hear.

I'm sorry.

Can you come back? Need to talk, I texted back.

He responded immediately. *Sure, give me a minute to find a bulletproof vest. U do realize I was shot at last time I was in that house?*

Without thinking, I dialed his number. I had to hear his voice.

"Trace—" he answered, but I interrupted.

"Please, Nixon. Please."

He sighed long and hard. Cursing ensued, and I could have sworn I heard Chase laughing in the background. "Give me an hour."

"Thank you."

"Oh, and Trace?"

"Yeah?"

"Do me a favor. Tell your grandpa you invited me so that they don't shoot me on sight. You don't want innocent blood on your hands."

"Are you?" I whispered.

"What?"

"Innocent?"

"No." His voice was shaky. "Not since the day I was born, not since the first day my dad raised a hand to me, not since the first time I watched my mom huddle in the corner, and definitely not since the first time you let me kiss you. No, Trace. I'm anything but innocent."

I didn't know what to say.

He cleared his throat. "Do you still want me to come?"

"Yes."

"See you soon, Trace."

The phone went dead. I put it in my back pocket just as an attractive man in his twenties waltzed into the room. "Miss Alfero? Your grandfather would like me to show you to your room."

"Great." I managed a small smile and followed him out of the sitting room and up the grand staircase. Once we reached the room, I turned to Adrian and gave him the biggest smile I could manage. He staggered backward but soon regained his composure.

"Tell my grandfather we'll have company for lunch."

"And who will we be expecting?"

I grinned. "Mr. Abandonato. My boyfriend."

Adrian's mouth went slightly ajar. To his credit, he only swore three times before giving me a curt nod and stalking off.

This was going to be interesting.

Chapter Twenty-Six

Not ten minutes later Grandpa barged into my room. "Tell me it isn't true. Tell me you didn't invite that boy to—"

I held up my hand. Surprisingly, Grandpa stopped sputtering, and the red glare from his face faded to more of a pink.

"He will be dining with us. You will be civil. There will be no guns."

"Why?"

"Because." I swallowed. "I deserve answers from him as well. Don't you think?"

I knew Grandpa couldn't argue against that. He gave me a curt nod, then turned toward the door, but not before saying under his breath, "I promise not to shoot him."

"Good."

"Today," he finished and slammed the door behind him.

Well, that was progress. One day where Nixon's life didn't hang in the balance. Good things were coming, that was for sure.

I walked over to the bed and sat down. I didn't remember this house. It looked too big, too regal to be mine. The room they'd put me in looked like a girl's room. Everything was pink and white.

Curious, I walked over to the desk and opened a drawer. A small diary was lying on top of a few crumpled up pieces of paper. I dug around and pulled out some of the pink papers and laughed. Pictures of horribly drawn unicorns and cats stared back at me.

I'd already cleaned up, so I had at least a few minutes to waste. Grabbing the diary I went and sat on the bed and opened it.

The front page said, *To my little Tracey girl, love Father.*

Was it weird that I didn't remember getting the diary? I didn't even remember writing in one.

I turned the page and nearly fell out of my chair.

Mrs. Abandonato. Tracy + Nixon = Love.

And, I was going to burn the diary. Like now.

The rest of the pages were basically the same thing. Horrible drawings of what appeared to be a cat and then a cow with no udders. Clearly, becoming an artist had not been in my future. As I flipped the pages, one thing remained true: I was constantly misspelling my own name and Nixon's as I tried to write our names together. I could only imagine my mom must have helped me. No way had I known how to do any of those things at almost six.

Either that or Nixon had helped me.

I shuddered.

Forget burning the diary. I needed to shred it, then burn the pieces of evidence.

I flipped to the last page and a picture fell out.

It was of me and Nixon. We were holding hands. He was looking at the camera grinning from ear to ear, and my head was tucked in his arm while I clutched his hand for dear life. The little boy staring back at me was the one I always remembered. When I fell and scraped my knee, he kissed it and made it better. When I cried because my mom wouldn't let me have a pony, he laughed and told me ponies were stupid and that I should do something cool like learn how to be a spy. When his mom stayed over, I—

Crap. I remembered.

The last time I remember seeing Nixon was about a week before my sixth birthday. He'd come over to my house with a bag. His mom followed us indoors and sobbed to my mom at the kitchen table while I took Nixon into the back room.

He'd always been so tough, so strong, so it freaked me out that he was crying. And then I noticed he was bleeding, too.

"Nixon, what happened?" I reached out to touch the cut above his eye.

He shrugged. His shoulder slumped as he sat in the middle of my floor. His tears fell onto the carpet as he played with one of the toy cars he had brought.

"Why are you sad?" I asked, taking a seat across from him.

"I hate him."

"Who, Nixon? Who do you hate? Isn't hate bad?"

He shook his head. "You're too young. You don't understand." He slammed the car against the floor, again and again, until it broke.

I was scared, not because I thought he was going to hurt me, but because I knew he was hurting. So I did the only thing I knew how to do.

I hugged him.

I reached my skinny little arms around his neck and held him while he continued to cry.

"Don't worry. I'll save you, Nixon. I'll save you."

"Girls can't save boys."

"Can too!" I squeezed him harder. "I promise. I'll take you away from what makes you sad."

"Tracey…" His sobs grew louder. "I'm so scared."

"If you're scared, I'll be scared too, Nixon. Until you feel safer, I'll be scared with you."

"Promise?" He pulled away from me.

"I promise. Because you're my best friend in the world, Nixon. I want you to be happy."

He nodded and we played until we fell asleep on the floor.

"Tracey?" I heard Grandpa's voice. "You almost ready?"

"Yup!" I tossed the diary back into the desk and opened the door. "Sorry, I was just thinking."

"That's never a good sign," Gramps muttered.

I looped my arm through his as we made our way down the stairs to the marble entryway.

"He's here." A man approached Grandpa and nodded.

Grandpa lifted his eyes heavenward, made a cross over his chest, and then said, "Let him in."

The door opened, revealing Nixon. To me he looked like my normal Nixon. He was wearing hip-hugging jeans and a tight t-shirt that showed off his chest tattoos and the half sleeve on his left arm.

His eyes fell to mine and he smiled. I almost lunged for him, but Grandpa held me tight so I couldn't budge.

Grandpa nodded to the two men beside us. They went to Nixon. He lifted his hands in the air and turned as they patted him down.

Was this really necessary? They pulled a gun from behind his pants, a knife from his boot, and a set of steel knuckles from his pocket. My eyes widened. He just shrugged as if what was happening was completely and totally normal.

Once unarmed, his hands fell to his sides. I looked to Grandpa. With a curse he released me and I ran into Nixon's arms.

The tension was so thick you could cut it with a knife. Nixon politely accepted my hug but as soon as our chests touched, he let out a hiss of air and gently pushed me away, creating immediate distance between us.

Confused, I reached for his hand but he pulled it away and shook his head.

Hurt, I looked from him to Grandpa. Nixon looked like he wanted to shoot Grandpa, and Grandpa looked like he was about three seconds away from castrating Nixon. Great. Lunch should be stellar.

The sound of stiletto heels hitting marble interrupted their tense exchange. A lady cleared her throat. I looked in the direction of the sound and was surprised to see a very pretty woman with straight black hair smile at me and announce, "Lunch is ready."

Grandpa turned on his heel and followed her out of the room. I guess I was supposed to go too because Nixon stepped ahead of me.

What had just happened? Why was he acting so weird? It had to be Grandpa. Right? It had nothing to do with me. Dread filled my stomach. What if he was faking it? What if…what if it really was about protecting me, about promises made when we were little? My heart clenched, because a week after those childhood claims I had broken my promise to him, leaving him and his mother with a monster of a father.

I silently wondered how many beatings he'd suffered at the hands of the man who should have been protecting him instead of striking him.

Suddenly, I wasn't hungry anymore.

We walked into a large medieval-looking dining room with a long wooden table. The bright flowers in the middle of the table gave the room a cheery look, which was a nice contrast to the paintings of gargoyles decorating the walls. Everything was wood paneling and dark wallpaper, which made me feel like at one point the dining room might have been a place my family used to take people to kill them.

Cold pastas were set on either side of the table, along with a few pieces of salmon and bruschetta.

The same woman I'd seen before filled each of our glasses with water, and then our wineglasses with a red wine.

So being in a mafia suddenly meant I could drink now? Was that it? This was the second time I'd been offered wine in one day. Funny how, under the circumstances, it seemed so natural that I would need some sort of alcohol to get through the stress.

The silence alone was going to kill me.

My eyes pleaded with Nixon as I reached for his leg. I needed to know we would talk, that we were okay. I mean, wasn't I the one who'd been lied to? Shouldn't I be the one giving him the cold shoulder?

His nostrils flared the minute my hand made contact with his thigh. He cleared his throat, but didn't move my hand away.

We ate lunch in silence. Well, if you considered Grandpa swearing in Sicilian while drinking wine silence. I swear I never realized how loud I chewed until that moment.

Finally, everyone was finished.

"Grandpa, may we be excused?" I asked politely.

He nodded his head. I reached for Nixon. "I need to talk with you."

Nixon looked from me to Grandpa.

Grandpa cleared his throat. "Remember the terms, Nixon."

"How could I forget?" He sneered and grabbed my hand. Without thinking, I led him up to my bedroom and quickly locked the door behind me.

Chapter Twenty-Seven

Good God, I forgot how pink this room was." Nixon chuckled, taking one of the stuffed animals off the bed so he could lie across it.

"I must have really liked pink." I laughed.

"You hated it." Nixon put his arms behind his head and sighed. "In fact, I distinctly remember your mom putting you in a pink dress and you taking it off in front of the entire dinner party."

"Please tell me you weren't—"

"I was nine!" Nixon laughed. "Trust me, I was horrified. I thought girls had cooties. I closed my eyes and pointed, though."

"Rude. You should have saved me." I lay down next to him, and my breath hitched when I realized what I'd just said.

"I was always saving you. Even when you didn't know I was there, I was saving you."

"Did you ever visit Wyoming?" I asked in a small voice, scooting closer to his body until my head rested on his chest.

He sighed. "Trace, you're putting me in a hard spot. I can't tell you everything, because it will just make you sad. I can't be completely honest and it kills me. It makes me want to scream, but I have responsibilities—not just to you—to my family, to your grandpa…"

He cursed. "Everything is pretty screwed up right now. I didn't know you were going to find out this way. Believe me, if I did I would have..."

"What?"

He licked his lips. "I would have kissed you harder. I would have fought for you more. I don't know. I would have stolen you away, taken your virtue, made myself so permanently etched on your person that every time you took a breath it was my scent that was permeating the air."

Well, what was I supposed to do with that? Rip his shirt off? I'm not gonna lie, that's exactly what was racing through my mind when he pressed a kiss to the top of my head.

"I never visited Wyoming. My father wouldn't let me and at that time I wasn't in charge of anything so I couldn't bully my way into it."

"When you came to be in charge, you were eighteen?" I asked.

"Yup. Father wasn't doing well. He wasn't able to make good decisions. He developed pneumonia and was never the same after that. Always out of breath and whatnot. So I took over some of the operations, and then more and more, until I was running everything while he stayed at home and drank whiskey."

I winced.

"At any rate, that's done with now." His hand clenched on my arm and he seemed to realize how tense he was. His fingers relaxed. "I'm sorry, Trace."

"For what?"

"Not telling you the truth. I knew the day we went shopping, and then when you took out all that money. Damn, I knew for sure then. I had Anthony do a background check on you. Apparently Tracey Rooks doesn't exist. So I went through all the Traceys in our school and there you were, Tracey Alfero, eighteen years old, granddaughter of the second most powerful mafia boss in all of Chicago. The same mafia boss who still blames us for his son's death."

"You forget. Technically I have De Lange blood in me, too," I muttered.

"Right. Which means I really should have killed Phoenix." He scowled and pulled his arm away from me. With a curse he sat up on the bed and rubbed his hands over his face. "He can't ever find out who you are. If he does . . . Trace, he's dangerous, seriously. We've been keeping tabs on him. He's lost his freaking mind. He's next in line after his father dies, and his father's too much of a coward to tell Phoenix when he's out of line. I have no doubt that family is into some shady business."

"Do I want to know what 'shady business' is?"

Nixon took a deep breath. "Probably the sex trade, cocaine, money laundering—typical things you'd see on TV, but definitely not what this family is about, that's for sure."

I don't know why I felt so relieved. It wasn't as if I could help who I loved, even if he was involved with terrible things. I couldn't just pull away from family.

"What do you do?"

"A little of this and a little of that." He smirked. "Nothing too illegal. We aren't desperate for money, unlike some people."

"I'm sorry." I huffed, feeling tears start to burn the back of my eyes. "For leaving you. I'm so damn sorry, Nixon. I remember. I saw a picture of us when we were little and . . . I left you! I promised I would keep you safe and I left you!"

Full-on sobs were escaping my throat now as I hunched over and hugged myself.

"Trace, sweetheart." Nixon lifted me closer to him and pulled me onto his lap. "Those were pretty big promises coming from a six-year-old. There was no way you could have protected me—or Monroe—from him."

"But I promised—"

"And I promised I'd find the people who killed your parents. So I guess we both failed, Trace."

"You'll find them," I said through my tears. "You won't give up?"

"No." He kissed my cheek and then my lips, gently licking the salt from my bottom lip before pulling back. "I just...Trace, I have to keep order between all the families here. The three families have been just fine for the past ninety years. If something happens...If the balance is thrown off, or God forbid, if any of the originals hear about the happenings with Phoenix..." He trembled against me. "Believe me, you do not want any of the Sicilians traveling to the states."

"They won't." I kissed his mouth. "Phoenix hasn't done anything yet and when he does...you'll be there."

Nixon's eyes closed briefly. When he opened them they were full of sadness. "Yes, but so will you."

"By your side," I confirmed.

Nixon didn't say anything. His mouth found mine and I fell against the bed as his body hovered over me. His lips saying what his words couldn't. I wrapped my arms around his neck and coaxed him toward me. With a grunt and then a masculine groan he swept his arms around me and under my shirt.

"Damn." He growled the minute his hands came into contact with my bra.

"What?" I kissed his neck.

"Your grandpa's going to shoot me if he finds out I'm doing this right now...I promised..."

He didn't finish the sentence because my hands had already found his lean, muscled stomach. I was drawing circles with my fingers across his hip bones. He closed his eyes. "I need you to remember something, Trace."

"What?"

He kissed me softly across the lips and stared directly into my eyes. "When I make a promise I keep it. Regardless of whom it hurts, even if it means it hurts me or someone I care about the most. Sometimes... sometimes in life we're asked to sacrifice something for the greater good."

"Okay, you're making me nervous. Can't we just make out?"

Nixon's smile was sad. "I love you, Trace. I always have. Just remember that, okay? Hold on to it. No matter what I say or what I do...and trust me, I'll do some terrible things. Just know. I love you. With every fiber of my being."

Tears clouded my vision as I nodded and brought him in for another kiss. "I love you too," I said across his lips.

"I have to go."

"Don't!" I didn't mean to yell.

Laughing, he lay back down on top of me, careful to keep his weight off so I could still breathe. "Trace...your grandfather's not a patient man. Let's not give him a heart attack."

"Seeing us make out would not give him a heart attack," I argued. "You taking me up on my whole virginity offer? Yeah, that would do it."

Nixon froze above me. His eyes were wild. "Please. Just please don't ever. Trace, you have to promise—shit, you have to promise that no matter what happens, you wait, okay? You wait until it's with someone you love."

My smile widened. Because I knew he was talking about him. After all we'd basically just declared ourselves. I nodded just once and kissed him on the cheek. "I promise."

His chest rose and fell as if he'd just run a marathon. He nodded once, his eyes welling with tears. Had I said something wrong? I pulled his face to mine and kissed him, this time slowly memorizing the way his lips slid past mine, creating the perfect amount of friction as they teased and taunted. His tongue. Good Lord that tongue could make a girl throw caution to the wind.

Nixon didn't kiss as if it was something to pass the time. He kissed as if there was nothing in the world he'd rather be doing. He kissed like I was his oxygen, and I knew in that moment there was no way I was ever letting him go for a second time.

A knock sounded on the door. Nixon jerked away from me so fast I thought he was going to fall to the floor.

After a staggering breath, I went to the door and unlocked it.

Grandpa stood, arms crossed, and glared at Nixon. "It's time to say good-bye."

I rolled my eyes and turned to Nixon. I latched on to his arm as we walked slowly down the stairs to the front door. "I'll see you at school tomorrow, Nixon."

His eyes still looked teary, as if he was going to lose it at any minute. Nixon collected his gun, knife, and brass knuckles, and gave me a quick hug. "Remember what I said, Trace. Remember."

With that he left.

Chapter Twenty-Eight

I slept like crap. Visions of a scary-looking Phoenix chasing after me made it so that I literally got two hours of sleep, and that was an optimistic estimate.

When Grandpa dropped me off at the dorm that night, I found Monroe crying on her bed. I hoped to God it had nothing to do with me. I wasn't sure I could handle any more drama.

"What's wrong?" I asked, rubbing her back.

"My father died."

Yeah. Not the time to tell her I already knew. "I'm so sorry…"

"Don't be." She snorted. "I'm not crying because he died. I'm crying because the last thing the bastard said to me was that he wished I would have been born a boy."

"So he was a jerk." I reacted without thinking about how that may or may not sound.

She stopped crying, and then the tears turned into laughter. "What would I do without you, Trace?"

Wow, loaded question, that one. I shrugged. I knew that Nixon hadn't told her who I was yet. I wasn't sure she would remember me anyway. I didn't remember her at all, but Grandpa had let it slip that the minute she turned six she was sent off to a boarding school, making it so I'd only seen her at Christmas once or twice before I was taken away.

This morning I sighed heavily and looked to my right. Mo was still sound asleep. Not wanting to wake her, I tried to get ready as fast and as quietly as I could.

"Ugh, what time is it?" Monroe asked sleepily.

"Time for class in about an hour," I announced, throwing a pillow at her.

She looked back at me through swollen eyes. "I'm going to need a tub of cover-up."

"Or kickass sunglasses?" I threw her a pair of aviators.

"I shall rock the hungover look." Monroe punched her fist into the air and staggered out of bed. "So how did yesterday go?"

"Good." I cleared my throat and pretended to still be straightening my hair, even though it was already as straight as can be.

"That's it. Good? Where'd you guys eat?"

"Um..." I didn't want to lie but I had no choice. "Grandpa's kind of going to stay longer than we thought, so we ate at the place he's renting while he's in town."

"Hmm, isn't that kind of weird?" Monroe brushed her teeth at the sink and then smacked on some lip gloss. "I mean, don't get me wrong. I'm glad he's here. I know how much you missed him. But he has a ranch, right?"

"Yeah, I don't know. Grandpa's always wanted to hang out in the city. And one of the ranch hands needed the money, so I think it's a win-win."

Monroe nodded and threw on a baseball cap. Impossible. She had on tattered jeans, a rock-n-roll sweatshirt, aviators, and a baseball cap, and she still looked better than me. "No uniform?" I lifted my eyebrows.

"Crap. There went my idea to look cool." Monroe kept a loose shirt on, threw a cardigan over it and pulled on her skirt and knee high boots. "This, my friend, is as good as it's going to get."

"Hey, still looks good to me."

We ate some breakfast and walked to our first class. She waved while she ran off to the science section of the building. I walked slowly to my politics class and was somewhat stunned to see an actual teacher sitting at the desk. Where was Nixon? Didn't he have a few more days left to teach?

I sent him a quick text. *Where are you?*

And sat down.

An hour went by and still there was no text from Nixon. I kept the phone in my hand just in case it vibrated. I didn't want my only form of communication stripped from me, and for some reason it made me feel safe. The mafia was only one phone call away, literally. So if Phoenix decided to mess with me, I could run and call for one of the other families, through either Grandpa or Nixon, to smack him upside the head.

Oddly enough I didn't feel any better about the whole gangster thing. I mean, the mafia is the mafia. And I wasn't one of those ignorant girls who hadn't seen her fair share of mafia movies. Not that I knew if they were realistic, but still.

After a few more minutes of torture, class ended. I made my way down the hall to the next class. This was always the part I hated because kids were standing around talking to one another, texting, and pointing. I still couldn't figure out why the school gave us ten minutes between classes. It seemed extreme to say the least. You could get into a lot of trouble in ten minutes.

I looked down at my phone and sighed. Still no text. The minute my gaze lifted to look down the hall, it was too late.

I ran smack dab into muscle.

Reeling back I realized it was Nixon. I sighed with relief and wrapped my arms around him for a hug.

He froze beneath my touch. Cursing, he gripped my arms in his hands and pushed me off of him. "What the hell do you think you're doing?"

"Huh?" Probably not the best response.

"Why are you touching me?" Nixon sneered.

"Because…" My gaze moved to all the students around us. The expressions on their faces were a mixture of amusement and horror.

"Because?" He took a step toward me and tilted his head. "What, cat got your tongue? Or I guess in your case it would be a…cow?"

"A cow?" I repeated. "Nixon, what the hell is wrong with you? Last night…"

Gasps resounded around the hallway. I refused to back down.

"Was clearly a mistake if you still think I want more from you." His eyes were steel. The tightening in my chest increased so much I thought I was going to stop breathing.

"But you said…"

"Are you deaf?" He shouted. "I don't want you, Farm Girl. Not now, not last night…never." He laughed. And with each echo of his laughter off the walls I felt my heartbeat slam into my chest like a hammer. "Let me put it into a way you understand. I will never want you. I mean, look at you. You're nothing like us, and you won't ever be. So do yourself a favor; leave me the hell alone." His hands shook as he looked away, a muscle twitched in his jaw.

I refused to move. I could only stare as tears streamed down my face.

"Get the hell away from me." Nixon was inches away from me. Those very same lips that had promised me forever were driving a knife into my chest. "Leave. Now."

Somehow I forced my legs to move past him but not before I heard him yell after me. "Moo."

Sobs wracked my body until I couldn't breathe, or see straight for that matter. I didn't even know in which direction I was running. I just knew I had to get out of there. Away from him and away from my broken heart, that had just shattered at Nixon's feet.

I turned to make sure nobody was following me and again slammed into someone, but this time it wasn't Nixon, and it wasn't anyone friendly.

Phoenix grinned. "Nice show. Good to know he's finally put you in your place. Maybe now that the whore's out of the picture, we can go back to the way things were before you polluted this school."

"Screw you!" I spit in his face and jerked away from him, running into the first available classroom I could find.

Unfortunately, it was occupied by a few students, but I didn't care. I just had to get away from him…away from everything.

I crumpled to the floor in front of everyone as I tried to keep my breathing even, but it was impossible. I was dying. I knew it. I tried to breathe. I really did. But each breath was shallower than the last, until I started seeing black spots.

Chase's face was suddenly in front of mine.

Wordlessly, he lifted me into his arms and carried me out of the classroom, damning the mafia to hell the entire way.

Chapter Twenty-Nine

By the time we'd reached the Bat Cave, aka the Elect hideout, I felt like I'd lived through a thousand lifetimes. In a word, I felt old and grumpy and bitchy. And really all I wanted to do was punch something—*anything*—in the face.

Why would he do that to me? And in front of everyone? My fuzzy brain tried to come up with excuses. Maybe that's how pitiful I had become in the way I felt about him. I tried to justify his actions. By replaying everything he'd said to me the night before, I succeeded in only making myself more sick.

He'd talked of protecting me, loving me, doing things he didn't want to have to do. But what the hell? I mean, I get having to make rough choices. But if his plan all along had been to make me look like shit in front of the student body, couldn't he at least have warned me? Any girl, even if she knew the plan all along, would have been in tears.

I was pathetic because I had almost convinced myself that Nixon had done all of that on purpose. That he wasn't actually using me like Grandpa said.

"Damn it, Trace, listen to me!" Chase was in front of me,

examining my face and swearing so much I would have blushed had I felt anything but numb from the pain. The boy had a mouth on him.

"What?" I licked my lips and refused to make eye contact.

He grabbed my chin with his hand and jerked my face toward his. "Do you need to go to the hospital? Lie down? Need a drink of water? Want a sedative? These are all the things I asked you on the way over, and again when I plopped you on the couch. Shit." He released my chin and ran his hands through his hair. "What the hell was that? Are you out of your freaking mind? You can't just..." He pushed away from me and began pacing.

"You can't just break down at school like that. You can't let people see weakness. You're better than that. I don't care if the freaking president of the United States waltzed in here and told everyone you were a terrorist. You're an Alfero, for shit's sake. Start acting like one!"

Chase had just given a whole new meaning to the words *tough love*. My mouth gaped open. I was too shocked to be hurt anymore. *Did he just reprimand me for getting my heart broken?*

I felt the sting of tears but I refused to let any more fall. Instead, I flipped him the bird and may or may not have dropped a really inappropriate word.

His stone face broke into a small smile. "Better, Trace. You can do better than flipping me off and telling me to go screw myself. I know this blows. Believe me, I know. But it's the only way."

"The only way?"

Chase nodded. "You and Nixon. You can't happen. There's too much history—too much drama, and with Phoenix lurking around campus, you can't be the catalyst that brings this entire operation down. Believe me, you don't want that and you don't want Nixon to be tempted to do that."

"Nixon." I spat. "He can do whatever the hell he wants."

"Good to know," came the familiar voice.

My head jerked up to see Nixon in the doorway. His eyes were uncertain as they flickered from me to Chase and then back to me.

Concern laced his eyes as he began walking toward me. "Are you okay?"

Rage boiled within me. Before I knew what I was doing I jumped from the couch and tackled him, banging my fists into his chest as anger and hurt coursed through me. Chase had to pull me off him and even then all I could do was crumple into Chase's arms while the hot tears poured out of my eyes.

"I—" Nixon's voice cracked.

"You're making it worse, man," Chase whispered. "Just go. She doesn't want to see you. Hell, I don't even know if I want to see you. I know why... I just think... this can't be fixed by your badass mafia mojo."

"But—" Nixon cleared his throat. "Trace?" It was a question.

"Just go to hell." My voice was muffled in Chase's shirt.

Chase swore. "Nixon, you had to choose. And I think you made it pretty clear to everyone within a fifty-mile radius who you chose."

"I just don't know if I want to live with the consequences," Nixon said.

"I guess we'll see what this family really is made of."

"Chase." Nixon's voice was hoarse. "Take care of her, please. Just—"

"Go!" I yelled, interrupting them.

Chase held me tighter and nodded his head once. I heard the door open and close, and I squeezed my eyes shut.

Exhausted, I didn't protest when Chase lifted me, for the second time that day, into his arms and carried me back to the couch. I tucked my hands under my chin and closed my eyes. Within seconds the lights in the room were off. I heard a door lock and then I felt a warm body next to mine.

The couch was big enough for two people, so I scooted over while Chase lay down behind me and tucked me into his body. He pulled a blanket over the both of us and sighed.

"Chase?" I sniffled.

"Hmm?"

"Why are you helping me?"

"Because you're hot." He rubbed my arm and let out a laugh. "Trace, I'm kidding. Don't get your panties in a bunch. I'm here because there's nowhere else I'd rather be. Because I hate to see chicks cry, and although popular opinion states I don't possess a heart, I actually do. So color me weird, but when I see a friend—and don't scowl, I can hear it from here—when I see a friend, a good friend, upset, I would freaking bleed myself out before letting them go through shit alone."

"That was a nice speech. Did you practice it?" I found myself smiling even though my heart was still breaking and thumping in my chest as if it had permanently lost its rhythm.

"Very funny." Chase pulled me tighter to him.

"Chase?"

"Yeah?"

"Why can you help me but Nixon can't?"

"Loaded question, Farm Girl." His hand moved back to my arm and he rubbed up and down in slow strokes. "He's the mob boss. I'm the cousin. It's different. I'm not even next in line. I've always done my own thing. I mean, yeah, I work for the family. I guess you could say I'm lower on the totem pole, so I don't really matter as much. If anything, you're better off with me than Nixon anyway. At least with me you won't be a target for murder."

"How...reassuring."

Chase's warm chuckle relaxed me. "Hey, you asked. Now, please try to get some sleep."

"Will you be here when I wake up?"

"Always."

I tried not to let his promise affect me. After all, Nixon had promised a lot of things, too. I hated that my distrust and confusion of what Nixon had done might totally spoil any other relationship I had with my friends, but I was still terrified that Chase would leave me just like Nixon. In the end I'd be stuck with nobody. Because one thing always seemed to be certain in my life...everyone left. My parents, Grandma, even me....It was only a matter of time before those I loved left me, too.

Chapter Thirty

I woke up in Chase's arms. Not exactly the way I had planned my Wednesday to start.

His oven of a body was seriously overheating me; add that to the viselike grip he had on my person and I was feeling slightly claustrophobic. With one hard tug I fell to the floor. And Chase, of course, fell on top of me.

"What the hell, Trace?" His eyes opened as he braced his body over mine, looking from the couch to me in confusion. "You could have at least told me before you tried to kill me!"

"Kill you?" I lifted an eyebrow. "Right, because if the one-foot fall wouldn't have done it, what? Your tiny heart would have burst?"

His eyes narrowed. "Look, I know you're heartbroken and you're upset—blah, blah, blah—but do you have to be mean to the guy who helped you when you were having a nervous breakdown in front of the entire student body?"

"Valid point," I ground out.

He grinned. "Knew you'd see it my way. Now, no attacking. I'm going to get off of you, help you to your feet, and attempt not to stare at your ass as you bend over to grab your bag."

"Such a gentleman," I grumbled as I took his hand and he helped me to my feet.

Chase whistled the minute I went to retrieve my bag. "Sorry, Trace, I lied. No wonder Nixon was—"

"Can we just...*not* talk about him." I threw my bag over my shoulder and crossed my arms.

Chase nodded and put his hands in the air in surrender. "Good deal. Let me just grab my key card and I'll walk you to your dorm."

"You don't have to do that. You've already let me hide out in here for most the morning and—"

"I insist. Besides, it's kind of my job."

"Your job?"

"Chase Winter at your service. Get used to it, babe, I'm your official bodyguard."

"Says who?" I yelled.

"Um, Nixon? Your grandfather? Mo? Just about everyone who loves you..."

"Nixon doesn't love me."

Chase sighed. "I refuse to get into that with you right now. Believe what you want, but that boy would flipping cut his own arm off before he let someone harm a hair on your head."

Tears threatened again. "Sometimes, Chase...it's the emotional wounds that hurt the most." I pushed back the anger and sighed. "I'd rather he beat me. Cuts heal, bruises fade—but broken hearts? They carry scars for a lifetime."

With a heavy sigh Chase stuffed his key card into his pocket and pulled me into his side, kissing my head. "I don't think any guy can promise not to break your heart. But I do promise that the next jack-ass who tries it will be on the other end of my fist."

I nodded.

"Come on, Trace…" His blue eyes danced. "One smile. Give me one smile before we walk the plank."

I rolled my eyes.

"Please?" Chase jutted out his lower lip.

My pathetic attempt at a smile probably looked more like a gri-mace, but it was enough for Chase to nod his head in approval and walk me out the door.

Once we stepped outside, I took a soothing breath of fresh air. People were walking around campus and nobody seemed to be the wiser that I was coming out of hiding.

"See?" Chase whispered in my hair. "Smooth sailing."

He really shouldn't have said that, because the next few minutes became what I would like to refer to as *hell on earth*.

People began whispering and pointing, which really wasn't all that bad, until some girl yelled *skank* and another guy started to chant *whore*. Naturally, because boredom promotes stupidity, the rest of the kids joined in until Chase and I were literally walking to the beat of the chants.

He squeezed my shoulder, told everyone to F off, which to be honest made me cringe more, and kept a straight face.

Once we reached my dorm, he swiped his card. And that very same she-devil from the bathroom walked out the door.

"Told you." She smirked. Her eyes fell to Chase. "Nice of you to take over Nixon's sloppy seconds."

I tried to pull Chase in after me. I'd had enough *skank* remarks to last me a lifetime, but he refused to budge.

"Sloppy seconds?" Chase repeated. *Uh-oh.* I knew that tone of voice. It was the same voice that had taunted me on the first day of school. That girl had just opened up a box that really should have stayed closed.

Chase released my hand and began to circle her.

Scratch that. The box should be nailed shut and buried so deep it reached the Seventh Circle of Hell.

"Cara..." Chase threw his head back and laughed. "I forgot how entertaining that little mouth of yours is, which is crazy because I could have sworn it was wrapped around Phoenix's junk last week."

I was way past blushing.

Cara's mouth dropped open.

"Aw baby, was that an invitation?" Chase chuckled. "I wonder how your boyfriend would feel about you screwing Phoenix behind his back? Hmm? I wonder what Deacon would do. No, actually..." He snapped his fingers. "I know exactly what he'd do. He'd drop your fat ass and move on to the next *skank* ready to spread her legs for him. Then again, maybe he likes that you're easy. Hey, why don't I call him right now and see if he wants to join us for a threesome? Hell, make that a foursome, since you clearly like what you see. I'll play."

Cara's lower lip began to tremble. I wanted to tell Chase to stop, but I was too horrified by the stuff spewing out of his mouth to say anything.

"Don't tell him. Please, just..." Cara looked to me for help. I immediately looked to Chase.

"You know what girls like you are worth?" Chase sneered.

"Nothing. Absolutely nothing. You're a dime a dozen. I won't call Deacon, because I truly believe he's your free ride to hell. Your future is clear as day to me. You'll be his perfect Stepford wife, stand back and smile politely while he screws every prostitute available to a man of his tastes, and you'll do Phoenix and whoever will give you the time of day on the side."

Tears streamed down her face.

"Wake up." Chase was directly in front of her now. "You will never be as good as Tracey. You will never be good enough to freaking lick the pavement where her shoes have been. Now listen and listen very closely."

She nodded.

"You will never look her in the eyes again. If I hear that you do, I'll ruin your perfectly caked up face. If you breathe the same air as Tracey without my permission, I'll show you what it feels like to suffocate to death, and if you spread any more rumors about her or the Elect..." He chuckled. "You won't make it to Christmas break, without at least one of your pretty manicured fingers missing from your hand. Do we understand each other?"

Cara was full-on bawling now. She nodded lamely and ran off.

"Have a good day!" Chase called.

Stunned, I just stood there staring as Chase happily sent off a text and began whistling.

"What the—"

"What?" He shrugged. "Hey, let's go inside. I'm cold."

"Right." I numbly followed him into the building and to the elevators where he swiped his card and kept whistling.

I'd always thought Nixon was the scary one. The one everyone was afraid of.

It's possible I had underestimated Chase...big time.

We stood in silence. I really didn't know how to start that particular conversation. You know, the one that starts with..."What the crap just happened?"

Instead I just went with, "So, you can be scary."

Chase shrugged. "It's a family thing."

No crap.

"Great." I kept eyeing him. He was as cool as a cucumber. Sure, I hadn't even been involved in that little exchange and I still felt like I was going to throw up. It wouldn't surprise me at all if I saw Cara on the evening news because she'd attempted to murder Chase in his sleep.

The elevator doors opened. Chase waited for me to walk by him, then he followed me to my room and glared at any girl who dared to give me the stink eye. No doubt rumors of his run-in with Cara would be around campus by dinner.

"Thanks for walking me home." I opened my door.

Chase followed me inside.

"Um, what are you doing?"

"My job." He grinned and lay down on my bed. "Now get your homework done so we can watch a movie."

"We?"

"Yeah. As in you and I? What. You have a cow hidden in here somewhere?"

I blinked.

"Holy crap, *do* you have a cow? That would be awesome."

"Yeah, Chase. I have a cow under my bed. It's invisible, though, so you can't see it. But sometimes at night it comes out to play. What the hell is wrong with your brain?"

He winked and pulled my vampire novel off my bedstand and began reading. "Homework," he ordered, sounding bored. "Now."

"Okay, *Dad*."

"Oooh, say it again. Only this time call me 'daddy' while you're—"

"CHASE!"

Cackling, he licked his lips, blew me a kiss and opened the book again. If he was my permanent bodyguard, I hoped to God that Nixon or Grandpa would figure out what to do with me while I was at school. No way could I handle Chase's presence day and night.

Chapter Thirty-One

Oddly enough, my life fell into a sort of routine. I'd go to class. Chase would threaten anyone who looked cross-eyed at me. After three weeks of his insufferable presence we had become friends, if one could call Chase Winter a friend. I was still trying to figure him out. All things considered, I had no doubt in my mind that if I told him I needed someone killed, he wouldn't even ask questions. He'd simply ask who and jog away.

Wow. Never was there ever a truer friend.

To be honest, though, I felt suffocated. If I as much as coughed, Chase freaked out, called Nixon and Grandpa, and informed them that I was coming down with a sickness and needed to be taken to the hospital.

Sometimes I coughed just to get him to move away. I think Chase had a thing about germs.

Once I tripped and Chase swore up and down that if I didn't learn how to walk like a normal human being he was going to lose his mind with worry. What? Because a scrape was going to be the end of me?

When I asked him if we could go out for ice cream, he said it wasn't safe. No, instead he brought ice cream to me. Not in typical boy fashion. No. Because that would be too easy, and Chase did things the hard way. I had forgotten about asking him until later that night. He showed up with one of those hard stones used for mixing ice cream and a guy who worked at the local ice cream shop. The worst part was he set up shop in the dorm room lobby and ordered the dude to make me whatever I wanted. We had enough ice cream to feed an army.

I probably gained five pounds in two days.

I clicked my pen and waited for class to start. I just wanted things to be back to normal. My heart still hurt. I mean, there was no way that crap was going to heal, especially since Nixon avoided me like the plague.

Chase said I dreamt about him, that sometimes I called out to him.

It embarrassed me for a little while, but now I was bordering on pathetic, especially when Mo had to constantly wake me out of my sleep and hold me while I sobbed my eyes out.

I seriously needed to look into taking sedatives at night.

I pulled out my U.S. History book and nearly swallowed my gum when Nixon walked into the room.

It was the first time I'd been this close to him since the incident when he'd trampled over my heart and ruined any chance I had of falling in love. I know it sounded severe, but it was all or nothing with him. I still loved him, and I hated that I had feelings for him when he clearly felt nothing for me.

Even after thinking through what had happened that day, it occurred to me that even though he could have been doing it to protect me, he could have at least texted me in private or made it so we could hang out. I mean, come on. He was a mafia boss. He could make anything happen. Couldn't he?

Maybe that was the worst part. He didn't love me enough to even make me his dirty little secret? He didn't love me enough to even try to make something work. He didn't use his many connections. He didn't have any weak moments. The bitterness just kept getting worse until I felt like I was going to explode from it all.

"Dr. Stevens is out sick today, so I'll be filling in." Nixon's eyes scanned the room and fell on me. Without breaking eye contact he instructed everyone to take notes on the movie assignment. Papers were passed out and then the lights went out.

I closed my eyes. Not because I was tired, but because I figured if I couldn't see him it wouldn't hurt so badly. I thought I was done crying. I thought wrong, as a single tear slid down my cheek. It still cut deep; it still hurt so much.

"Trace," Nixon whispered behind me. I stiffened. Refusing to turn around, I pretended I didn't hear him.

"Trace, don't be like that…"

Was he for real?

"I miss you." His lips grazed my ear. "So damn much, and I wish…I wish I could tell you…Damn it, I wish I didn't promise, but I did. I have to protect you. Being with you. It isn't safe. You have to understand that now."

I swallowed the lump in my throat and still refused to acknowledge him.

"Please, sweetheart. Just please remember what I said." The metal from his lip ring sent a tingle down my spine as it connected with my ear. "I always keep my promises. If I don't—people die. Do you understand? I can't have innocent blood on my hands, especially when it could be yours."

He sighed heavily, sending tremors through my body. "I had no choice, Trace."

That was it. I was done.

I flipped around so fast he jerked back and cursed.

"No, you listen." I pointed my finger at him and whispered so nobody else could hear us. "There is always a choice. I refuse to allow you to justify your actions by saying your hands were tied. You're Nixon Abandonato. You had a choice, and you made it. Screw your excuses. I'm so tired of it, Nixon. All of it. I'm done. I'm…" I swallowed. "I'm not coming back next semester. You're right. I can't do this. It's not my world. I don't belong here."

He reached for my hand but I jerked it away.

"You do, though, Trace. You belong here just as much as anybody else and—"

"No." I shook my head. "I don't. I can't tell them who I am, and even if I did, what would happen? I'd earn respect because of my family, but it would all be fake. Meanwhile you'd come up with another excuse to break my heart into a million pieces, saying you had no choice. Go to hell, Nixon. Actually…" I laughed. "Don't. Because I've been living there for the past three weeks. Just stay away from me."

I grabbed my books and left class. The last image I had of him was his forehead pressed against his hands as his face contorted into a mixture of pain and regret. Good. Let him hurt as much as he'd hurt me.

Once in the hallway I reached for my necklace. Maybe I was being ridiculous, but since Nixon had warned me not to wear it, I found great pleasure in doing the opposite of one of his orders.

I pulled the cross from beneath the collar of my pressed white shirt and sighed. "Grandma, I wish you were here."

"Grandma?" A dark voice came from beside me.

Oh no.

I looked up and directly into Phoenix's eyes.

His smile was pure evil. "Grandma?" he repeated. "Would that be Grandma Alfero?"

I laughed at him and briskly started walking past him. "I have no idea what you're talking about."

I quickly pulled out my phone and sent Chase a text that said "911."

"Where do you think you're going?" Phoenix moved to stand in front of me. I turned around and started walking in the other direction, but he jogged in front of me. His arms came out to brace my shoulders. His fingers dug into my flesh as he slammed me against a wall. Why did I have to leave class!

"Talk." His lips almost brushed mine. I tried to jerk away from him, but it was impossible. He was too strong.

"Or not." He grinned. "We could always do some other things... Word around the school is that you're used goods. Once I'm done with you, you'll forget all about Nixon and be screaming my name instead."

I kicked him, but he just laughed and grabbed my arm, dragging me down the hallway with him.

I began screaming for help but the kids in the hallway just laughed when Phoenix added, "She likes it rough."

"No, no! Please! Please help me!" I was frantic, clawing at his arms as he used all his strength to pull me out of the building and toward the Elect headquarters.

"Stop! Phoenix! STOP!" I dug my heels into the ground, but he just laughed and pulled me harder. I tripped over my own feet and went sailing into his arms.

"That's more like it," he said gruffly. "You think you're so perfect just because of who your family is? Do you even know who I am?" He jerked my head close to his mouth and yelled it into my ear. "And all because of you I've lost the chance to be with Nixon's family! My connections? Gone. My money. GONE! Wanna know why?"

I tried to shake my head.

"Because the De Langes aren't a for-sure thing. Our money isn't good enough. But Nixon's? His name? It's freaking gold and you went and ruined everything by batting your damn eyelashes. You're a freaking whore just like your mom."

He slapped me across the face and pulled me through the door into the Elect headquarters.

I hoped in vain Tex would be in there with Mo. They'd been inseparable since they'd started dating. But it was empty. I started pressing buttons on my cell in hopes that it would call someone, anyone.

"What are you doing?" Phoenix grabbed my phone just as it rang. "Answer it. Tell him you're fine."

I shook my head no.

Phoenix pulled out a knife. "Answer it or I'm going to make a permanent mark on your face."

With shaking hands I took the phone and answered. "Hello?"

"Trace?" It was Chase. "Are you okay? Nixon said you left class and... Trace, are you crying?"

"No." I tried to keep my voice chipper.

"But you texted 911. Usually that means you're either upset or someone called you a whore again..."

I gulped, my eyes on Phoenix's knife. "Um, Chase, I gotta run. I'm going to go back to my room to take a nap."

Chase was silent. "Trace."

"Yeah?"

"How hot is it in Arizona?"

"Scorching," I answered, tears blurring my vision.

"Shit." Chase hung up.

I handed the phone back to Phoenix, who threw it against the wall, shattering it into pieces.

"Think you know all our little secrets just because you're an Alfero?" Phoenix pushed me against the wall and laughed. "Where's Nixon now? Is he going to save you? Where was he when your parents died? Oh, right. He was too young, unable to do anything. Just like he won't be able to do anything now."

"Why?" I choked out, trying to buy time. I had no idea what he was going to do; I just knew that for some reason he hated me and wanted to hurt me.

"Why?" His eyebrows rose as he licked his lips and then spat on me. "Because you're a dirty whore. Because you've ruined everything I've worked for years to build. Because from the minute Nixon broke me away from the Elect, nobody in town will do business with us. I've been ordered by my father to take care of things in any way possible. This is my way of doing that. Can't have family secrets rearing their ugly heads just because Nixon decided he had a heart, now can we?"

"Nixon will kill you," I said in a shaky voice.

Phoenix punched the wall above my head. "Not if I kill him

first." His laugh was dark, crazy actually. Was he high on drugs? His hands moved from the wall to my shoulders and in an instant he was ripping my sweater from my body. With sickening dread I knew exactly what he was planning to do.

He wasn't going to kill me. No. That would be too kind.

He was going to make me into the whore everyone already thought I was, and he was going to destroy me. Take the one thing that was only mine to give.

"A thousand bucks says you're a virgin…" His hands moved to my blouse and very slowly he began undoing the buttons until my shirt fluttered to the floor along with my sweater. I'd never been so scared or embarrassed in my life.

He leered at me.

Frantic, I clenched my fist and let it fly, hitting him in the jaw. Staggering back, he cursed and then grabbed my leg as I tried to run away.

"I like a girl who's rough."

I tried kicking him in the stomach, but he pushed my leg against the ground and then jumped on top of me, lifting my skirt in the process. I couldn't help the tears streaming down my face, or the fact that my scream wouldn't come out of my mouth. It was like I wasn't actually living through this, like my soul had left my body and I was watching it happen to another person.

His hands touched my thighs and I prayed to God that he would knock me out before any more of him touched me.

With one final surge I tried to buck him off me, scratching his face and whatever else I could do. He hit me repeatedly across the face until it no longer hurt.

My head fell to the floor. My strength was gone. I couldn't fight. My brain told me to, but my muscles wouldn't work.

He pulled my skirt up past my waist.

I prayed again.

Phoenix blew me a kiss and then moved his hands to my underwear.

Someone pounded on the door and then I heard cursing. My eyes were blurry from tears, my face swollen from being Phoenix's punching bag.

Two blurs entered the room shouting and threw Phoenix off me.

Chase was immediately by my side. He threw a jacket over my exposed body and tucked my head into his shoulder while Nixon threw Phoenix against the wall.

"I'll kill you for touching her," Nixon seethed. "You lowlife." His fist sailed into Phoenix's stomach. "Piece of shit!" His other fist connected with Phoenix's jaw and then Nixon pulled a knife from his back pocket and kicked Phoenix in the stomach. As he bent over in pain, Nixon jammed his knife into Phoenix's right hand.

Phoenix screamed.

Everything happened in slow motion until someone else entered the room—Grandpa.

His gaze took in the mess and me lying in Chase's arms. Murderous rage reflected in his eyes as he slowly walked up to Nixon, who had just pulled his knife from Phoenix's hand.

"Get a place ready," Grandpa said to the man who had followed him in. He nodded quickly and left.

Grandpa and Nixon were both circling Phoenix. Crumpled on

the floor, he was still holding his one hand, and blood poured from the wound.

"Your decision, Nixon." Grandpa said, his voice cold.

"Hammer." Nixon didn't flinch, didn't even think about it.

Grandpa nodded and looked to me and Chase. Chase pointed to one of the cupboards. Within seconds Grandpa had located a hammer and brought it back to Nixon's outstretched hand.

"You should close your eyes," Chase whispered into my ear, his arms so tight around my body I almost couldn't breathe. I also couldn't look away, even though I knew I should.

Grandpa grabbed Phoenix's hands and tied his wrists together. "You look at her without asking—you lose an eye. You touch her with your dirty hands?"

A pregnant pause caused me to gasp.

Nixon held the hammer over his head. "You lose your hands. And I promise, this is just the beginning." The hammer came down and smashed against Phoenix fingers. The sound of bones crunching almost made me puke. I did look away then. I tucked my head into Chase's shoulder and blacked out.

Chapter Thirty-Two

Trace, look at me."

I moaned and shook my head.

"Trace!" The voice was frantic.

My eyes fluttered open to see Nixon leaning over me. "Trace, I need to..." Nixon's eyes were wide with panic. "I need to know if anything happened, if he—" Nixon swore, biting down on his lip as his eyes pleaded with mine.

"No," I said in a scratchy voice. "You guys came just in time." I wanted to yell and scream that even though nothing had happened, that I was so traumatized, so scared that I didn't know what to do. My entire body felt numb. I was torn between wanting Nixon to kiss me and tell me everything was okay, and wanting to cry myself into a pitiful coma in order to erase what had just happened.

I tried to calm my shaking body. But it had been close, so close to being something irrevocable.

I gave another involuntary shudder as Nixon said something in Sicilian to Chase, who was still holding me.

Grandpa stood over us. Nixon stood, spoke to Grandpa again in Sicilian. Grandpa nodded once in agreement.

"Trace, baby girl, I—" Grandpa's eyes welled with tears as he knelt down. "I should have done better. I don't know what I would have done if Nixon and Chase…" He swallowed. "I can't lose you. Do you understand? I can't, Trace. You're my life."

I gave him a shaky smile. "I'm not going anywhere, Grandpa."

He sighed in relief and stood. "Nixon, would you please stay with her?"

Nixon looked as shocked as I felt. What had happened to wanting to kill him? He nodded once. Grandpa looked over to Phoenix, who had passed out from pain. "I'll have everything ready for your arrival…sir."

It was the first time I'd heard my grandpa address anyone younger than him as "sir" and actually put the respect behind the name. The shock must have hit Nixon, too; his eyebrows rose just briefly before he gave Grandpa a curt nod and a handshake.

"Family sticks together," Grandpa said, shaking Nixon's hand.

"I'll protect this family until I breathe my last breath, to that I swear."

"I know that now." Grandpa's nostrils flared. "Tracey, I love you, sweet girl. Please listen to Nixon in my absence. I'll be only a phone call away, but as you can imagine, I have something to take care of." His gaze flickered back to Phoenix. Two men were lifting his body into their arms.

"When you're ready." Grandpa slapped Nixon on the back and walked off.

"Ready?" I asked, voice still hoarse from exertion. I wasn't even that curious. It was just that I needed something else to focus on. If not, I was pretty sure I was going to lose it.

Nixon swallowed. "Ready to rub him out."

My eyebrows furrowed in exhaustion as Nixon chuckled darkly and leaned down to the ground, his knees popping in the process. "Kill him. When I'm ready to end his life, Trace."

"Oh." I wasn't sure how I felt about that. I mean, I knew Phoenix was bad. I knew he would have raped me and possibly killed me, but did that make killing him okay? A life for a life?

I struggled to my feet and nearly toppled over. Nixon caught me and motioned to Chase.

Chase hesitated for a second.

Nixon's brow furrowed. "Chase, you can go."

"But…" Chase licked his lips, his hand reaching for my back.

I sighed and stepped back into Chase's arms. It was Nixon's turn to look confused and a little pissed off.

"Thank you, Chase." I wrapped my arms around his neck and closed my eyes. "I love you." Yes, Nixon had helped save me. But Chase had literally saved my life with his perceptive question. Tears burned at the back of my throat as Chase's blue eyes warmed.

"Love you too, Farm Girl." He pulled away and held my chin in his hand. "You call me if you need me, okay?"

I nodded as he stepped back and walked out of the room.

The minute the door closed, my body started slumping to the ground. Nixon's strong arms came around me. In an instant he was lifting me and carrying me to the bathroom.

"No, please, no. I just—" I fought against him as he carried me to the room and gently placed me on one of the small benches in the bathroom.

"Trace." Nixon cupped my face. "Look at me."

I squeezed my eyes shut.

He exhaled. And finally with tears streaming down my face I opened one eye, then the other. Nixon had tears in his eyes as his thumbs rubbed my falling tears away. "Thank God, I don't have experience in this sort of thing..." His nostrils flared for a brief second. "But I figured you'd want to take a bath or shower or something."

I nodded and broke down into more sobs. Everything hurt on my body, even my skin. Again, I wanted Nixon to touch me, to tell me that I was still pretty, that what had happened to me wasn't my fault, that Phoenix's ugliness hadn't tainted what I had.

"You're beautiful, Trace," Nixon murmured as he kissed my forehead. "And Phoenix is a monster. You know that, right? What he did—it's unforgivable, and I promise you, I will make it right."

"By killing him?" I asked in a small voice.

Nixon shook his head. "It's your call, sweetheart. I don't want to upset you more, but believe me when I say your family and mine won't let this slide without a severe punishment. We don't typically turn people over to the authorities, but if you want him to rot in a hellhole all his life, just say the word. I'll link his accounts to prostitution and a drug ring in five seconds. Hell, I'll frame him for murdering a politician. Just say the word."

I chewed my lower lip and slowly lifted my arms toward Nixon. If he rejected me—I'd be broken forever. I needed him more than I needed to shower, more than I needed to deal with Phoenix. I just wanted to forget. And though I told my heart to stop loving Nixon— it never listened. He was all I wanted, all I cared about.

My arms went around his neck. He stiffened, then hugged me back.

"Will you help me?"

Nixon sighed. "Whatever you need. I'm here, Trace."

"You aren't going anywhere?"

"No."

"You aren't going to pretend to like me today and hate me tomorrow?"

"Hell no."

"You aren't going to say you love me and then take it back?" My voice was raw with emotion as new tears found their way down my face. What the hell was wrong with me? I knew I was stronger than this! I looked at Nixon and waited.

Nixon jerked away from me and his gaze met mine. "Listen to me because I don't want you to ever forget this."

My body swayed in his arms as he tightened his grip around me. "Remember what I said about making promises?"

I nodded.

"I promised, Trace. As a man I promised your grandfather that nothing would happen to you. He believed the longer I was with you, the sooner Phoenix would put the pieces together. He already blamed you for everything. If he saw us together..." He swore and looked down for a brief second before meeting my gaze again. "I had to make you believe me. I didn't know what else to do. I thought the day before when we'd talked—damn, Tracey, I thought you knew me better than that. I'll protect you until the day I die, even if it means I have to protect you from myself. Because in protecting you from me, I was protecting you from them."

"But you weren't."

"I know that now. And I'm not leaving, but Chase—"

"I love him, too." I shrugged. "He was there for me when you weren't."

"Do you love him like you love me?" Nixon asked.

"Who said I loved you?" I fired back.

"You did."

"When?"

"That night when—"

I smirked.

"Glad to see you still have your sense of humor." Nixon rolled his eyes as he leaned his head lower. "I'll understand if you're not ready. Shit, I don't even know if I'm ready, but Trace, I really want to kiss you."

I nodded. "First a bath. I don't want any part of him on me when you touch me."

Nixon nodded and backed away as I stood in front of him. He gently helped me take off the jacket Chase had given me.

"Son of a bitch!" He looked like he was ready to punch a wall. I looked down and noticed a bruise making itself known around my stomach. Nixon's eyes glittered with tears as he brushed my hair away from my shoulder and examined my neck. I'm sure there were bruises there, too.

You would think standing in front of Nixon in nothing but my skirt and bra that I would feel exposed and vulnerable, but instead everything felt comfortable, normal. As if he was the only person I could stand naked with after going through such an ordeal, and feel safe.

He closed his eyes and pinched the bridge of his nose. "Breaking his hands wasn't enough. Not by a long shot. I'm going to cut out his tongue and—"

"Can we not talk about him?"

"Sorry," Nixon muttered. He reached for the faucet on the bathtub and turned on the water. He threw in bubbles, which earned an eyebrow lift from me. He just muttered not to ask and something about Chase and naked time. I made a mental note to ask Chase about this the next time I saw him.

My heart clenched. Thinking about Chase made me feel funny. It was weird, but I missed having that guy around. I missed his sense of humor, the easy friendship we had and his protective, crazy no-bull attitude. I missed him right then, because I could have used his humor to drive away the demons that Phoenix had brought into my life.

Confused, I shook the thoughts away and waited for the tub to fill. The water smelled heavenly.

Nixon turned to me and rubbed the back of his neck before gently turning me from him and unzipping my skirt. It fell to the floor.

His hands moved around my thighs, gently examining the bruises, then he turned me back around. He swallowed a few times and motioned to the bath.

"I'll turn around while you get in. There should be enough bubbles to cover you up."

"And if there aren't?"

"Then I'll pretend I can't see," he said through clenched teeth.

I quickly peeled off my bra and underwear and got into the tub. However, I wasn't counting on it being slippery. With a shriek I nearly slipped into the bubbles, but strong arms caught me and of course grazed my breasts.

Nixon, of course, always the hero, stood behind me, holding me in place while I leaned on him.

"You okay?" he asked, voice rough.

"Yeah. Sorry; it was slippery."

He groaned and very gently released me as I slowly dipped into the water.

His eyes never left mine as I sank beneath the bubbles.

"Damn bubbles," he mumbled as he sat on the chair next to the tub and ran his fingers through his hair.

"You've got something against bubbles?"

"Yeah. I do." Nixon pointed at the tub. "They're practically kissing every naked part of your skin while I sit here and watch." He laughed darkly. "I had someone rip a nail from my finger once… This…" He swallowed and looked away. "Is so much worse."

"Because of the bubbles?" I tried not to laugh, but it felt good after the hell I'd just been through.

"Yes, because of the damn bubbles. Are you done yet?" He twitched in his seat.

"I just got in."

Nixon swore and hung his head in his hands. "Right. Well, can't you… just… be faster?"

"I thought you wanted me to relax? I was just attacked."

He moved so fast I jerked in response. His hands dipped into the water and he grabbed the loofah from my grip and began leisurely washing my back. His Adam's apple bobbed as he swallowed slowly with each stroke.

The whole damn bathroom could have burned down around me and I still wouldn't have been able to take my eyes off of his face as he dipped the loofah in the hot water and then tenderly ran it over my bare skin, washing away the soap as well as the remnants of what had happened an hour ago.

"That feels good." I closed my eyes as his warm hands replaced the loofah and began massaging my neck and shoulders.

"Just so you know," he croaked with his hands kneading into my flesh, "I've never had to practice so much restraint in all my life."

"It builds character," I mumbled, my eyes flickering open.

Nixon's hands froze as his gaze fell to below my chest.

Note to self, bubbles tend to disappear when you've been in the bath for too long. His grip tightened on my body just slightly before he closed his eyes and pressed his lips together. A tiny whistle of air escaped his mouth.

"Sorry." I moved to cover myself up but the bubbles were quickly disappearing.

His eyes flashed open. "Don't be." Nixon swallowed slowly. "Don't you ever apologize for being beautiful—for being perfect. You are…" He moved one of his hands to cup my chin. "Exquisite."

Maybe it was the stress of the day, or the fact that I felt anything but exquisite. I still felt dirty, ugly, used. All in all I felt like the whore everyone had been calling me, as if what Phoenix had done was somehow my fault. At any rate, I began to sob all over again, this time without shame as I looked into the eyes of the one person who made me feel like I was whole, even when inside I felt a bit broken and beaten up.

"Trace." Nixon wrapped his muscled arms around me, not caring that I was getting him drenched, and lifted me out of the tub.

Without a word, he grabbed the nearest towel and wrapped it

around my shivering body and again lifted me into the air as if I was a little kid. He brought me into another room.

There was a bed in one corner and a tiny desk; my guess was that the guys took naps here whenever they could get around to it—either that or the Bat Cave really was his secret hideout. I mean, the man was perfect. He probably had superpowers or something.

I didn't have to ask Nixon for anything. It's as if he knew exactly what I needed and when I needed it. He brought me a t-shirt and a pair of sweats that smelled like him.

When I moved to put on the t-shirt, he closed his eyes like a gentleman even though I didn't ask him to.

Once I was done putting on the sweats I kissed him on the cheek. My way of telling him "thank you," and that I was done dressing.

He dropped the towel to the floor and scooped me into his arms again. With a grunt he had me on the bed tucked into his body.

I didn't realize I was still crying until he wiped away a few stray tears.

"I won't let anything happen to you—I swear on my life, I'll protect you until the day I die," Nixon whispered hoarsely.

"That's a pretty big promise."

"Well, you're a pretty important person. Important people deserve big promises—and you, Trace—you deserve the world."

I shook my head. Why was I suddenly feeling so insecure? Did having Phoenix's hands on me really mess me up that much? I wasn't used to this feeling, as if I didn't deserve anything anymore.

With a curse Nixon tugged me closer. "You deserve the white dress, Trace. And the flowers and the music. You deserve that first dance with your husband. The stars in his eyes when he sees you walking down the aisle. You deserve the castle and the prince. A man who adores you, a family who sacrifices for you, friends who take care of you. Trace—you deserve it, but you have to believe it."

I sniffled. "What if I just want you? What if I just want that one thing?"

"Damn it, Trace, I'm the one who doesn't deserve you. The messed up part is I know it, but I want you anyway."

"Want?"

"Need." He croaked. "I need you like I need my heart to pump blood through my body, like I need air to breathe, like we need gravity. Hell, Trace, you are my gravity. Being with you makes me feel centered and whole, and I'm too screwed up to convince you to want any different. I'm too selfish to push you into someone else's arms when I know mine may be the worst ones for you to be in."

"But I want…" My lower lip trembled. I bit down hard so I could finish my sentence. Taking a soothing breath I started again. "I want you."

His breath hitched and then his lips were on my neck. Warmth exploded at his touch. I leaned into him. Nixon murmured something in Sicilian and gently turned me on my back. He didn't get on top of me, even though I wanted him to. Instead he stayed right by my side and continued kissing my neck, and then my chin, and finally my eyes.

"Where did he touch you?"

"Huh?"

"Where?" Nixon prodded gently.

I pointed to my neck where Phoenix had held me. Nixon kissed the exact spot where I'm sure a bruise was going to start showing. I pointed to my arm. Nixon's lips met the place where Phoenix had gripped me, and so went the next ten minutes as Nixon restored every single place that Phoenix had corrupted.

"And here." I pointed to my mouth.

Nixon smiled, and then devoured—not kissed—my lips. His mouth covered mine completely as his tongue slipped in and pushed against mine.

My hands reached around his neck as I pulled him more firmly against me. After a bit of hesitation he slowly moved on top of me, careful to keep his weight from crushing me. His hands dove into my hair as he deepened the kiss. I bit down on his lip and sucked his lip ring.

A growl escaped his mouth as his hands gripped my face. My body still didn't feel close enough to his, so I arched up to meet him but was pushed gently back against the bed.

"You're killing me, Trace." Nixon groaned against my neck. With another groan he pulled back. "And I'm probably going to hate myself later tonight for saying this, but after everything..." He shook his head. "I can't... I can't—" I licked my lips and leaned forward.

"Ah, hell." Nixon's mouth was on mine in an instant. Eager and hot, his kiss met mine. He pushed, I pulled, he tugged, and I gripped. My body melted into his. I wanted to rip my clothes off, to lose myself in him in order to forget the nightmare of what had just happened to me.

My hands moved to his shirt, lifting it up his torso.

The loud sound of a throat clearing nearby destroyed the moment.

Nixon jerked away from me and snapped. "This better be good, Chase, or I'm going to strangle you."

Chase's eyes met mine and for a second I felt guilty. I looked at the position I was in: underneath Nixon's body, out of breath, and flushed with excitement.

All after Chase had said he loved me and covered me up with his jacket. I licked my lips and saw Chase's blue eyes narrow. He blinked a few times in my direction and gripped the door frame with his hand. His knuckles turned a few shades whiter before his gaze left mine and fell on Nixon.

"I just thought you should know that Mr. Alfero has everything set up and ready. Seems he was a bit overzealous about getting some of the men together. I didn't think you would want Phoenix to die without letting Trace have a crack."

"A crack?" I repeated.

"At Phoenix." Chase's smile didn't reach his eyes. "You do want to slap him, don't you? Because if you don't, I sure as hell will. Shit. I'll break both his legs for you."

I knew he meant it. I also knew that if I let him and everyone else unleash on Phoenix I'd have a murder on my conscience. Was this how they dealt with everything in the mafia?

"How are you?" Chase walked into the room. Nixon held up his hand for him to stop where he was.

"She's fine," Nixon answered for me. His teeth clenched as he narrowed his gaze on Chase.

"She can answer for herself," Chase argued. "Trace, I—"

Nixon leapt off the bed. "I said she's fine. You aren't needed anymore. All right? Text me the address and we'll be there in a few. I've gotta get her some clothes to put on."

Chase's nostrils flared. "Maybe you should have been thinking about that before you started taking her clothes off."

Nixon lunged for Chase. I scrambled off the bed to intervene and nearly tripped over my feet in the process. "Guys, stop!"

Were they insane? There was way too much testosterone flowing through that room and I'd endured enough fighting for the day. My voice cracked when I yelled again, gaining their attention.

Chase reached for me first, but it was Nixon who tucked me into the crook of his arm and kissed my head. "Sorry, Trace. I'm just... shit, I'm just a little messed up after seeing everything go down today."

I swallowed the lump in my throat and locked eyes with Chase. His eyes burned through mine briefly before he shook his head and walked out.

My heart clenched and shattered into a million pieces. Everything hurt all over again. What was wrong with me? I truly loved Nixon, but Chase... Well, Chase had been my best friend for the past few weeks while Nixon was off fighting Phoenix and his evil family.

I was tired and stressed. That was it. It wasn't anything more. I tucked the feelings I had for Chase into the back of my mind while I hugged Nixon back.

"Now what?" I asked.

"Now..." He sighed. "You decide if he lives or dies. Just know, my vote is death."

"And if I want him to get punished but live?"

Nixon didn't respond for a few seconds. Finally, he released me and walked toward the door. "I'll try to listen."

Chapter Thirty-Three

My hands were sweating. I had to keep wiping them on my jeans. Nixon hadn't said a word to me during the drive to the location, or *spot* as he called it. I wasn't sure if he was deep in thought or just pissed off that I wanted to let Phoenix live. At any rate, I was ready for this nightmare of a day to be over.

My clothes even felt uncomfortable, as if they didn't belong there, just like the rest of me.

How had I ended up in this predicament in the first place?

Oh right. Grandpa, my parents...ugh. I guess the old saying is true: You can't help what you're born into.

After a few minutes' drive, we finally turned down a street behind an old restaurant and stopped.

"You ready?" Nixon said without emotion.

I shook my head. I wasn't ready. How would I ever be ready for this? To face the guy who'd tried to rape me? Especially in front of other men? I wasn't ready for any of it, and I wanted nothing more than to stick my head in the sand and pretend that none of it had happened.

I didn't realize I was shaking until Nixon grabbed my hand and brought it to his lips. "You'll do fine. I promise. I won't let anything happen to you."

His eyes were like ice. I touched his face. He blinked and heaved a sigh. This was just as hard for him as it was for me. I knew it. Because I knew, if anyone ever messed with my family or those I loved, I wouldn't think twice about hurting them, but it was entirely different when it was you and when it would be on your conscience. I knew Nixon wanted to rip Phoenix's arms from his body, but I couldn't fathom how I could sleep at night if I knew everything had to do with me and that it was my fault.

I turned away from Nixon and opened my car door. Two steps. I took two steps before I had to stop, close my eyes, and tell myself it was going to be okay. Nixon called out to me and I walked around the car to join him. His hand grasped mine and he pulled me into the shelter of his body as he walked with me into an old building that looked as if it had been abandoned.

Had my sense of humor decided to visit me in that second I may have made a sly comment that the building and his last name were one and the same. Instead, I licked my dry lips and swallowed the lump of fear in my throat.

We walked down a dimly lit hallway and then turned left into a space where a few men were gathered around, laughing.

Laughing.

What?

I looked around me.

The room wasn't as dimly lit as the hallway. Phoenix wasn't in chains. Instead, he was sitting calmly in a chair with his broken hands zip-tied in front of him.

The men were eating food and drinking wine. Holy crap, they were feasting!

As soon as everyone noticed our presence they dropped whatever food they were holding and put their wineglasses down. Out of the corner of my eye I saw Grandpa make his way toward me.

I would have looked at him or maybe even acknowledged him had Phoenix not looked directly at me and smirked.

Bad idea.

I lunged for him and before anyone could stop me, slapped him so hard across the face that he cursed and fell to the concrete floor. My hand throbbed.

The room fell silent.

"Is that it?" Phoenix taunted.

I made another move to kick him in the head, but Nixon gently pulled me back into his arms while a few men helped Phoenix back into the chair and began tying his arms down.

Grandpa cleared his throat. "Will all members of the commission please stand?"

"Commission?" I repeated, still not taking my eyes off of Phoenix.

Nixon held me close. "Each family is represented by one person. It's how we hold court. Each family has a representative, and each representative gets a vote."

"Are you one?" I asked, looking into his eyes.

"Unfortunately, no. Since I'm one of the bosses I elected someone else from my family."

"Who?"

Nixon bit down on his lip, causing his lip ring to shimmer from the light in the room. "Chase."

"Oh." I nodded. "That's good, then."

"Great," Nixon said dryly. His gaze went to the door, where Chase was now walking in.

"Everyone's present," Grandpa announced. "Each representative of the commission is allowed to speak on behalf of their family. I'll go last, considering the subject matter."

This was followed by several grunts and nods.

"I'll go first." Someone stepped forward. I didn't recognize him, but I felt like I should. He looked to be a few years older than me, most likely Nixon's age. His eyes scanned the room and then fell on me. "Trace, is it?"

His voice held a slight accent. I wasn't sure if he was mocking me or if that was just the way his voice sounded. I nodded my head anyway.

Nixon tensed next to me as the guy approached. "Faust Assante, at your service." He gave a wide smile and bent over my hand. His lips were warm against my knuckles as he brushed a kiss across them. I could have sworn I heard Nixon growl next to me. "Now." Faust stood to his full height, which towered over me, and tilted his head to the side looking skeptical and methodical. Had I not had my fair share of hot guy run-ins this year I would have probably swallowed my tongue. The guy was as good-looking as they come, only something about him was cold.

"Your side of the story, if you don't mind." He nodded. "When you're ready, Trace."

"My side?" I squeaked. "Does that mean even he gets to have a say?" I pointed a shaky finger at Phoenix. "After what he did to me? Well, Faust…" I said his name as if it was an expletive. "My side is pretty much summed up in one word. Rape. That guy sitting over there beat me, bruised me, and then tried to rip my clothes off me. When I said no, he said yes, when I pushed, he pushed back. So yeah, that's basically my side. He would have killed me had Chase and Nixon not intervened."

"You don't know that." Faust's eyes flashed. "After all, if what you're wearing now is any indication of what you wear on a day-to-day basis, I'd say you were a tease."

Nixon pushed me behind him and stood in front of Faust. "You've got to be kidding me. Who the hell do you think you are?"

Faust smirked. "I am merely stating a fact. If a woman is asking for something and not careful—well, she will get exactly what she deserves."

Nixon swung hard and hit Faust across the jaw, sending him sailing to the ground. "Anyone else care to tell Trace what she deserves? Be my guest." His breathing was ragged as he stood there and waited for someone to speak. Grandpa moved to stand next to him, as did Chase. The rest of the men in the room shifted on their feet and looked to me. I wanted to die on the spot. What was so bad about a t-shirt and jeans? I self-consciously pulled my shirt lower so that it covered my butt. Maybe Faust was right. Maybe I did somehow ask for it. I looked down at my shaking hands. Warm arms came around me and I knew in an instant whose they were. Not Nixon's, not Grandpa's, but Chase's. I leaned into him. His scent—everything about him—was familiar.

"I have something to say," Chase said, still holding me.

All eyes fell on him.

"I should have killed that bastard the minute I saw him on top of Trace, to be honest. The only reason I didn't was because I was saving the honor for her. So if anyone else has anything to say, say it now. We're just wasting time, and honestly every breath that asshole breathes offends me so much that I want to crush his windpipe."

The rest of the members of the commission whispered to one another and nodded. A man stepped forward. "We do not need to hear anything else. Mr. Alfero?"

Grandpa looked ticked. He moved away from Nixon and stood in front of Phoenix. "You've hurt this family for the last time."

Phoenix smirked. "I seriously doubt that. After all, it's only a matter of time before they figure out who she is. And when they do, there won't be anything that can save you. Not your power, not your money, and not your name. They will come for you all. And I'll be smiling from hell."

Grandpa was handed a bat.

I felt myself pale.

He swung hard and hit Phoenix in the head, sending him to the ground with a grunt.

Grandpa turned. "Your choice, Trace. Make the call."

I looked at all the expectant eyes around me. Chase's arms still encircled my waist. Slowly, I pried myself free and approached Phoenix's limp form. One swift kick between his legs was really all I needed. I'd like to think I made it impossible for him to have children and poison the earth with his offspring. He was already passed out, but I smiled at the thought of him waking up in such excruciating pain he'd wish for death.

"He lives," I whispered, turning to Nixon. "Remember what you said about the whole setting-him-up thing?"

Nixon nodded once. "Done."

Exhaling in relief, I walked over to Nixon, but he had turned to talk to Faust, who had at that point regained consciousness and stood.

Chase held open his arms. I walked into them and laid my head against his chest. "You should have let me kill him."

"Sorry to ruin your fun," I mumbled.

Chase sighed. "Not fun. Just pleasure."

*   *   *

What felt like hours later, Phoenix awoke, screaming in pain. Nixon had contacted Phoenix's father and asked him to meet us at the site.

Dean De Lange walked in and swore. "Phoenix, what have you done?"

"Yes," Nixon sneered. "What have you done?"

Phoenix smirked. Blood stained his teeth where he had been punched repeatedly. "You think you can silence me?" He laughed. "Father, guess who our little Tracey is? You should know, after all. You killed her parents."

"What?" Mr. De Lange paled and gaped at his son. "What the hell are you talking about?"

"It's over. And I'm not stupid." Phoenix spat. "You set them up. I know everything and now they do, too."

"I didn't—" his father repeated, but his words were silenced by the crack of a gun. I gasped as he fell to the ground. Blood was everywhere. I looked to Nixon, but he seemed just as shocked as I was.

But Grandpa wasn't shocked at all. In fact, he was the one holding the gun.

"It is over," Grandpa said hoarsely.

Phoenix laughed from his position on the ground, blood trailing down his chin. "Oh, it's far from over. Do you have any idea what you've just done?"

"Killed the man who murdered my son!" Grandpa yelled.

"I lied." Phoenix grinned. "And now you'll never know. By the way, congratulations on killing the one man standing in the way of making me the boss. You just bought me my freedom."

"Like hell he did!" Nixon stepped forward, but Grandpa held out his hand to stop him.

"War is coming," Faust said from behind me.

"The Sicilians are coming." Phoenix laughed from the ground.

"God help us all." Chase swore and tugged me out of the room, swearing in Sicilian the entire way.

Chapter Thirty-Four

I didn't hear from Nixon all the next day. Chase was eerily quiet as he walked me back to my room. For once I was okay with him having his gun out as he searched around me for any sketchy people.

Once we reached my room, I asked. "War? And the Sicilians?"

Chase swore. I'd never seen him freaked out, but he looked about ten seconds away from losing it. "Our family's been in charge of keeping the peace for over a hundred years, Trace. Your grandfather just shot the De Lange mob boss in cold blood. Who the hell knows what's going to happen to Phoenix? We either have to kill him or buy his silence. You can't just go around shooting people for the hell of it. I know it may seem like that to you, but there has to be a reason."

"Yeah, got that part. But aren't you the mafia? I mean—"

Chase swore. "Trace, listen, you clearly don't understand. We don't want the Sicilians here. Hell, I don't even want them in Sicily. If they come, and if they find out everything that's been happening... Shit!" He kicked the bed.

"But they won't find out. I mean, who's going to tell?"

Chase looked at me like I was insane. "Trace, did you see all the men in there? Do you realize how desperate some of them are for money or to get on the good side of one of the originals? You can't control people, and you sure as hell can't keep them from looking out for themselves."

"What does this mean, for … for all of us?" I asked, numbly sitting on the bed.

"It means we face them. Together," a voice said from the doorway. I gasped and looked up. Nixon had a black eye and a bloody lip.

"What happened?"

Nixon shook his head and winced. "Don't worry about it. Pack your stuff; you're leaving."

"Leaving?"

He ignored me and looked at Chase. "Get a bag."

"Hold on one second!" I threw my hands into the air. "You can't just make me leave!"

"Trace." Nixon pinched the bridge of his nose. "Your grandfather and I decided it's safer for you to be with me at all times. I can't exactly shimmy into your dorm room at all hours without people finding out. It's just not safe."

"So I'm going to be a prisoner in my grandfather's home?"

"Of course not." Nixon smiled. "You're going to be a prisoner in mine."

Chase snorted.

"What was that?" Nixon snapped at Chase.

"Air. I coughed. Found a bag." He handed Nixon my small duffel and saluted me. "Love ya, Trace. I'll be waiting at Nixon's. I think it's best if we all powwow together."

"Okay." I waved good-bye and turned back to Nixon. "You've lost your mind."

"Probably." He pulled me into his arms and sighed. "I can't lose you again."

I started crying softly. When had things gotten so screwed up? "I'm scared."

"I'll be scared with you," Nixon murmured, repeating what I'd told him when I was six. "I'll be scared until you aren't scared anymore, okay?"

"Okay."

"And I'll save you from all of it, Trace. I promise."

"That's stupid." I laughed into his chest. "Boys can't save girls."

"You're right." He kissed my temple. "It's the other way around, because you saved me, Trace. You saved me when you were six and you're saving me now."

"By doing what?"

"Staying alive...and allowing me to rescue you."

"Stupid girls. We always need rescuing."

"Stupid boys, we always jump at the chance to do it."

"I love you." I kissed his lips softly.

"I love you too," he said, kissing me back. "Now, let's pack. It looks like we'll have plenty of time to slumber party in the next few months."

"Yay." I rolled my eyes.

"And..." Nixon grinned shamelessly. "Maybe we'll find some time to work on that whole goal you have before you die."

"What goal?"

"The goal." He eyed me up and down. "You know, about not dying a virgin."

"Ass." I threw a pillow at him and laughed.

"Hey, I'm just offering to help with the bucket list!"

Monroe burst into the room. "Is it true?" She looked between me and Nixon and back at Nixon again.

He nodded.

She closed her eyes and let out a heavy sigh. "They're going to come for all of us."

"I know." Nixon walked over to her and pulled her into a hug. "But we'll be ready."

"Promise?"

"I promise." He held her hand and reached out to me. We hugged together and began packing the rest of our room up. It was going to be a long night, but not nearly as long as the rest of the school year was going to be. Whoever said life was boring clearly didn't go to Eagle Elite.

Would you die for the
one you love?

See the next page for
a preview of

ELECT.

Prologue

I hid in the shadows hoping he wouldn't see me as he hit Ma again. He'd promised Ma he'd stop drinking. He'd promised he wouldn't be mean anymore, but he never kept his promises—not anymore.

"You stupid bitch! I know you were looking at him tonight! You think I can't tell?"

"I wasn't!" My mom wiped her eyes and tried to reach for my father's hands, but he pushed her to the ground and kicked her stomach with his foot.

Afraid, I looked around the room for help. Chase was right next to me; I could see his knuckles turn white as he clenched his hand into a fist. He was just as helpless as me. I swallowed as my eyes fell to Uncle Tony; slowly he shook his head at me. He stood motionless in the corner, his gaze without emotion. Did he want me to sit there and watch? Watch while my father killed my ma? Weren't men supposed to protect those they loved? I felt my nostrils flare in silent outrage. Someone had to do something.

I heard another shriek and then the sound of glass hitting the floor. I turned just in time to see my mom hit the ground, blood spewing from the side of her face.

"Ma!" I ran toward her, pushing my father out of the way. I had to save her, I had to protect her. "Ma!"

"Nixon." A hand reached out to stop me. "Don't."

I looked up into Chase's sad eyes. "I have to save her."

"You can't."

"But I can! I have to—"

"Nixon, you're my best friend in the whole world, but Dad said if you make your father angry again he's just going to turn on you. The way I see it, he's gonna pass out soon anyway."

"But..." I looked over at my mother. She gave me one terrified silent nod before my dad landed a final blow to her face. Her eyes fluttered closed as her head hit the ground. I watched for her lips to move so I could tell she was still breathing.

Her chest rose and fell.

Alive. She was alive—this time. Paralyzed with fear, I kept watching, counting the seconds between each weak breath, hoping, praying, that it wouldn't be her last.

"Nixon, come on." Chase tugged on my arm and led me outdoors. The minute my feet touched the grass I took off running.

I pumped my legs until they hurt, finally stopping at the tree on the farthest edge of our property.

"Nixon." Chase was behind me, out of breath, but still behind me. "I'm sorry, Nixon. I'm so sorry."

I nodded. I knew it was the right thing to say, that he was sorry; I was sorry, too. Sorry that I wouldn't listen to Chase and that one day, I would kill my father for what he was doing to my ma. I would kill him and I would go to Hell for it—but I didn't care. Dad said I was going there anyway.

"Let's make a pact." Chase put his hand on my shoulder.

"A pact?" I sniffled and turned to him. "What kind of pact?"

"One that's forever. One that protects people rather than hurts them."

"How do we do that?" I was suddenly interested. What if I could make all the hurt go away? What if I could save everyone!

"We do this." Chase pulled out his pocketknife and cut open his hand, then nodded to me to do the same thing. Without pausing I cut open my hand and handed back the knife. "Blood brothers. We're never gonna hurt each other and we're gonna save those like your ma, Nixon. Ones who can't save themselves. We're going to protect them."

"How?" I watched as the blood dripped from my open palm.

"Rules." Chase shrugged. "They keep people safe, right? At least that's what my mom says." He smiled. "We make rules and we start our own club. That way, we don't have to listen to anyone but us."

I liked it. I chewed on my lower lip. "What do we call ourselves?"

"The chosen?" Chase offered.

"No, that sounds lame. We have to sound... more powerful than that."

My eyes flickered to the road, and a sign poked into the ground. It said ELECTION. "Elect." I pointed. "Let's call ourselves The Elect." It made sense; after all, the president was elected, wasn't he? We weren't exactly chosen, but we were making the choice, we were electing ourselves protectors. That's what we were.

"Who else can join?" Chase asked.

"Tex and Phoenix. They'll want to." A weight suddenly felt like it was being lifted off my twelve-year-old shoulders. "Should we shake on it?"

"Yeah." Chase smashed his hand against mine as our blood mixed. "No going back, Nixon."

"No." I shook my head. "No going back."

*   *   *

I pressed my fingers to my temples and watched, replaying that moment over and over again in my head as the outline of Chase and Tracey flickered in the moonlight. Would he really do this to me? After all the shit we'd been through?

I gauged her reaction, hoping that I would be wrong. Praying to God that Trace would just this once listen to me. Her eyes flickered with interest for a few brief seconds before she looked down at the ground.

"Shit." I waited in the shadows. A part of me knew this would happen. The part that told me to damn my feelings to hell and ignore all the warning signs that I'd been seeing. But now it seemed like it was too late. I stayed, planted where I was, watching, waiting.

"Chase, you can't…" Trace shook her head. "You can't be like this. We can't do this!"

"We aren't doing anything," Chase said in low tones, reaching for Trace's hand. "Don't you?" He looked directly at me, although all he saw was a shadow. I knew I was well hidden. "Don't you feel the same way?"

Trace jerked her hand away from Chase's. "It doesn't matter what I feel. It's not about me, Chase."

"But it is." Chase reached for her again. This time her hand grasped his in such an intimate embrace I thought I was going to vomit all over the ground. The outside air was cold as hell as little pieces of ice tried to find their way into my wool coat.

"It isn't." Trace sighed. "It never was."

Chase jerked her toward him. She fell against his chest and looked up into his eyes. "What are you doing?"

Chase sighed. "What I should have done a long time ago." He grabbed the back of her head and pulled her in for a kiss. Their lips touched.

I had to look away.

The only sound in the night was that of my soft footsteps as I walked away…leaving my heart in broken pieces where I'd last stood. She was lost to me; it wasn't even the Sicilians who had taken her, but my best friend.

A gunshot rang out loud and clear in the night air. I turned back around just in time to see Trace collapse into Chase's arms.